Underneath New Orleans Copyright © 2016 by Peter Laurrell. No part of this book may be reprinted or used without written permission except for short quotations for the purposes of critical articles, essays, or reviews.

Cover designed by Patricia Laurrell (the author's mom.)

For more information, use the internet.

ISBN: 978-1530230181

ISBN – 10: 1530230187

W0007382

Part 1: The Timothy

I survive because the right people like me. I know it. Most of us who work in a brothel know it. Most of us who work in an anything know it.

If you want to go deep, sure, we're all alive because somebody liked us enough to get us to childhood. That's not what I'm talking about though. I'm saying I know how I make my money. And you probably do too. It might upset you to admit it or maybe you're rich and none of this applies to you, but most of us accept how this whole life on Earth thing works. Or we don't make it.

Then there are the people who stand for something. The people who only ever adopt the runt. The people like Letty.

***

Letty had a david who had a kid who killed cats. The david's wife was trying medication on their kid who was a boy named Anders. That didn't seem to be working because Anders still killed cats. Or maybe it had worked, the david would say to his wife. Anders hadn't done anything to a human yet, the david would say. You don't know what he would be without you.

He wouldn't exist without me or you, the wife would say. Especially you.

The wife took her son to therapies physical, psychological, and chakra and eliminated gluten and sometimes she even shared articles on social media that didn't entirely totally trust vaccines. And she felt lonely. Then the husband would get angry because the wife was cold and withdrawn and interested only in their odd offspring. He would ask the wife how she could be like this. How she could make desperate decisions all by herself about their child only to come back to the husband and tell him he didn't care. Why do you exclude me then blame me for not playing a part, he would ask.

OK then, the wife would say. You take him.

"Well…" the david buckled his belt and tied his tie.

"…Letty, you don't have kids yet and you haven't been in a marriage for 30 years, or maybe that doesn't matter and it's just me. But honey, I'm tired of living in this. You can't even understand what it is to love someone and hate what they do to your life until you're in your 30's. Then you start to get older, you get used to it in your 40's, which is so weird to look back on when I think about it now. It's like, what were you doing, man? What were you doing? Then your 50's hit and you see the end. You really do. In a way you cannot now know, Letty, I only have so many good years left. I can't have Anders in the house anymore, I'm sorry but I can't. It's killing my wife, seeing him every day. I love my wife, Letty, but she is so wrapped up in this. She shuts down then she lashes out. Shuts down, lashes out. Shuts down, lashes out. She spits at me the absolute worst poison she can draw up in her brain. Has nothing to do with anything, all she's trying to do is hurt me."

Hurt you like she hurts, Letty thought.

"So we drug him, me oh my do we drug that kid. Still find animals everywhere. And that's bad. Finding animals your kid killed is bad. But you know what's worse, Letty? You know what's worse than finding them? Not finding them. Because in those rare weeks we don't come a carcass, my wife gets the beginning of herself back. She'll open a great bottle of wine for us and cuddle up. And every last debt I know she owes me is paid. Every awful thing she's said, every lie she's told her sisters about me, it's forgiven. Like that."

The david snapped his fingers.

"I mean, I'm wanting to tell her 'Which of these scenarios is more likely: do you think the kid didn't do it or do you think we haven't found what's left of it yet?' But I don't. I don't say what is logical because my wife is back. Then we find a leg or a head and I let her say the worst things she can think of to say because that's what a husband does."

Letty leaned back against the headboard and nestled enough of herself underneath the sheets to splay her legs without being sleazy. Akimbo but covered, lovely Letty listened.

"They're torn apart, Letty. The animals, cats mostly. Slaughtered. I don't know what happened or why but this is not a cry for help, this is slaughter. I... Letty, he's putting up these videos on YouTube all about how he doesn't understand how women can hate him but bang those frat bro douchebags. He's talking about guns and rampages. My son is talking about killing people. My baby boy. And he doesn't even have to talk about suicide, please, that one's been on the table since before pubic hairs. He's in college now, still lives at home but he's in college because she won't let him go. And he's mad and he's scared and he thinks he's thinking, but really he's feeling and he doesn't know what to do about it. He's smart, Letty, he really is. And deep, and troubled, and creative. Not like me..."

The david's job was to manage film production teams.

"...I know how to operate a creative machine, I'm not creative myself. I know that. But he is. I'll tell you, Letty – my wife and I are good people. We're not perfect but we're in it together, at least I am."

The david stopped short of all the way looking at Letty. Instead he deflated at the toe of the bed, head slumped and swaying. Letty stayed laid where she'd come back to after peeing.

"Jesus, I'd like my wife to like me again."

The david sighed his second sigh of the party. Letty gently rubbed his back and said what she knew how to mean.

"I can help."

Then she said that it would be all right and that young men go crazy if they don't have sex. That it was different for girls, and yes sex does important things for us too but no, we don't go crazy without it. Then she frowned because it was sad that animals were dying and the david was in pain and the wife too. The poor wife. Letty felt like she was the wife's partner. Letty felt that she was a partner to many wives.

Then Letty laughed and said welp, she didn't know if it was cultural or biological or so cultural it had become biological, but if Letty knew one thing she knew that young men needed sex. For their sanity young men needed sex. The david agreed and said Confidence. Yes, he said, Letty, you get it. Young men need confidence.

Confidence, he said. Connection, Letty said.

She finished by saying the david was a wonderful father and that she'd take the case. The david braced and said he was all for help and all for health but that he couldn't scrounge much up at the moment. Then he shrugged his shoulders and opened his hands.

Now,

Letty swallowed a great many quirks of her johns and davids. As did and do we all. Pompousness, dishonesty, telling us how beautiful we are then fielding requests (or sometimes not even that courtesy) to ejaculate on the very parts they called most beautiful but a few pumps prior. Most of us learn to wear the face and take the money.

Not Letty. Nope.

Truly, Letty did not judge the sexual depravity of men because the brain is strange and she wanted to help. She could deal with gross. She could deal with dishonest.

Letty could not deal with rich men being greedy.

Rich men being greedy was Letty's trigger. Rich men being cheap with their family. Letty hated rich men being cheap with their family. We don't all have money so it was one thing when a waiter cried poverty, but someone with the money who wouldn't spend the money on their own kid? Letty was a woman who did not begrudge a man his wealth nor his sexuality because we have each been born an animal into an uneven society and we're playing it out. But we are humans. We are all humans. We must be in it together and when you figure that out then you know the truth which is that to help someone else is above all else, to help yourself! It's so obvious. Letty was a woman who was, for whatever reason, born knowing that if you help other people you actually are helping yourself. Not being better than anybody or paying down your ticket to Heaven, you are functionally helping yourself.

On the other hand, Letty was also a woman who was learning how to admit she had learned that someone sucked as a person when she first observed they suck as a person. Especially men. This david had declared himself the sort of person who did not deserve Letty's understanding and sacrifices which was who Letty was, she could not shut that off. She would not shut that off. That david was never going to appreciate Letty because that david was not an all right guy. That david was an Asshole. Yet, a younger Letty would have found a way to justify his behavior to herself without ever asking him the questions that she knew would corner him. A younger Letty would find a way to apologize for him. But this Letty was learning how to share her spirit with people who deserved it. This Letty was learning she was a human being, too.

So that david never came back to the Huxtable. Not because he lost interest in Letty or had any sort of choice in the matter. Letty the Seventh Bed made sure that he was forever barred. We were able to do that at the Huxtable as our revenue stream was secure beyond a single david. It wasn't easy – oh no. It was a monster hassle to deal with blackballing anybody, huge inconvenience it was. But sometimes you scramble to keep up with whatever it is that your top talent cares about.

Likewise, Letty committed to making a timothy of Anders. So she contacted the mother who was all for Anders spending time with Letty. The mother said she could pay with cash or jewelry or whatever was appropriate in this type of situation. Letty said that for people like Anders, like her son, it was Letty's pleasure to do it for free. The mother was so grateful for Letty that she cried for hours and hours and hours after hanging up the phone.

One of the things that I have found most surprises people about sex work is the number of mothers who support our services for their sons. Normal mothers, homemakers and moms with jobs the same. As their sons age untouched, it is often the mothers that find the Huxtable. They do it quietly, through proxies because they know their sons don't want their mothers involved. The mothers have been thinking about it for a long time because love to a mother is spelled W O R R Y so they couldn't go get someone off the street. They wouldn't want a skuzzy first time for their sons. So if the mothers are particularly great at research and get particularly lucky, they find us. Then a fraction of those who find us work up the desperation and the confidence to contact us and then they are shocked at how happy we are to help, how normal we are, and how utterly normal their request is. Then we see the son and receive Christmas cards from the mother every year thereafter, as they would a fine family doctor. The Huxtable had boxes of hand written gratitude squirreled away in its recesses.

So it was that a few weeks on from that david's banishment, Anders's mother knocked on the bathroom door and asked if Anders was all right. His flight to New Orleans left in two hours and he'd been in there for 40 minutes, was he all right?

Anders did not respond. He was watching the shapes his pills made in the swirling, flushing toilet water.

\*\*\*

Because it's disgusting, that's why.

It isn't disgusting.

Yes, it is. These girls are runaways – they've been trafficked and they're in slavery.

Unless they're not.

But they are.

Some are, I think the Asian massage parlor ones are. But not all of everyone is.

YOU'RE PAYING FOR SEX!!!!

I am.

You screw some chick? That's what gets you off?

This is why I don't talk about it with you.

Because you'd rather lie to me and give me HIV?????

Honey, it is in the interest of the establishment to keep both client and provider healthy. Everything is protected and the women are constantly tested. At least at the place I go to that's how they do it.

It's disgusting. DISGUSTING!!!

Why? I love you, I want to spend the rest of my life with you, you're going through something so sex does not interest you right now. That's OK. To be satisfied in my life, I need a sex life. I would rather it be with you but even more than that, I'd rather you be comfortable and not force you to move at my pace. Our partnership is more than our parts as far as I'm concerned.

And you have to pay for it?

I want to pay for it.

No, you want everything to be easy. You're pathetic. YOU'RE DISGUSTING! Oh my God. Oh my God you're the guy who pays for it. That's what it is. You have to pay. I can't believe I'm with the guy who has to pay. I cannot believe it.

Well listen, as far as paying for it goes, think of it like food. Let's say you're a chef. Best chef in the world. You are incredible (and by the way, you are, honey, you are incredible.) Let's say you eat out one day. No one knows you at the restaurant and you pay for a fine meal – you could have cooked something better or maybe not, that isn't what matters. The point is that if you're a chef and you pay for dinner, do you think that all of a sudden means you can't cook for yourself?

***

The front was a dive. It lived alone on the corner of Some Street and Saint Charles in New Orleans, Louisiana. The front had a navy blue awning with white words reading, *Bayou Fried Dough Sto,* although a willow tree hid so much of the sign that you had to know us to find us. Whole front side was a window wall, entrance door said "push" but pulled open as easily, cowbell, old linoleum floor going gingivitis yellow, one counter, two powdered sugar shakers, a dry erase menu board, a parody of a ceiling fan, a refrigerator, and a big cook so stuffed into a small kitchen you figured either the walls or him would have to pop. Five pairs of numbers and three words were written too long ago to get rid of without scraping on the dry erase board:

12:$8 · 10:$7.50 · 8:$6.25 · 5:$5 · 3:$3.50 · *No ones dough*

Most customer visits went like this:

> Cowbell rings.
>
> Jalopy, the giant fry cook, calls out from the kitchen:
>
> Hullo der! How many?
>
> Then there'd be a second or two of hemming and hawing, maybe a moment of squinting and looking at the dry erase board.
>
> Well, uh, how about three, then?
>
> Tree 't is! Dat be tree fitty, leave it on da counta, I cook em up fuh yuh ri' now.
>
> Two minutes later, a ham hock masquerading as an arm would reach out from its service window with a grease spackled brown paper bag.
>
> Shuga on da counta. Thankyuh now.
>
> More cowbell.
>
> Scene.

That is to say, the great majority of patrons to a front are not there for the back. A good front is popular so it can provide the cover the other business needs. There's a myth that fronts are those vacant or always closed liquor stores. Those aren't fronts. Those are failing businesses.

A good front does not feel like a front.

The Huxtable rarely accepted johns, and never did so without a personal voucher from a david. Timothies were a different deal. To be clear, a john is a one-time consumer of retail feminine (or masculine) wiles. The one-time designation refers to the frequency by which the consumer has employed the prostitute in question, not prostitution itself. Alternatively, a david is a repeat consumer of *the same prostitute.* Thus, a man named Dave may be a john of one prostitute because he's a david of another prostitute who is currently out of town. Everyone is a john or a david or in the peculiar case of the Huxtable, a timothy. Timothies are what set us apart, one of the things anyhow. I mean, lots of whouses have freebies, my guess is that they all do. But as far as I know, the Huxtable was the only whouse that had a system in place for people who really needed it, who really deserved it, but who couldn't get it. That's what a timothy is – someone who needs sex, deserves sex, but can't get sex.

So we give it to them.

As much as the protocol seemed reasonable to those of us who worked at the Huxtable, a man with an erection is a different sort of listener. These unknown unintroduced would-be johns would be hanging around for fifteen minutes, staring at Jalopy like they were dogs at dinner time. They would offer him tips, they would drop names, anything to get in and under. They thought Jalopy had a say in the matter. All he had was a computer printout of names and faces and associated passwords. And the best beignets in Louisiana.

Jalopy had played football in college until his feet figured out that they belonged to a human not a bear. Stress fractures started writing their way up from his toes to his knees. When the school recognized their property was in trouble, it was too late. The termites had already eaten out the load bearing beams. The school cut his scholarship.

Jalopy's mother was a prostitute so Daddy had known her for years. In fact, Daddy had watched Jalopy play football in high school. Daddy laughed when he watched Jalopy play high school football. I did too. It tickled to see that dumptruck line up against teenagers. All you had to do was take one look at the set up and you had to laugh because what chance did the puny normal sized human child have against Jalopy? You figured he was about to nuke somebody. But Jalopy only ever moved his competition as much as was absolutely necessary. Everybody needled him, told him he wasn't as strong as he looked. First they called him Just Enough because that's all he seemed capable of – just enough to move someone or stop them. One of his mother's davids was the one who started calling him Jalopy. Same idea as Just Enough only Jalopy sounds better. A Jalopy got you from one place to the other and that was all it did. Sometimes it feels like everybody on earth fails to appreciate the implications of a deliberate pace because everybody ogles impact.

Daddy wasn't a sucker for pop, though.

Between being gigantic and focused on restraint and also abandoned by the school system, Daddy saw a lot of potential for Jalopy in whouse security. So he offered to take Jalopy on as the Huxtable fry cook and elevator man. He offered to pay for culinary school as well. He said that if Jalopy wanted to match his size with cooking skill, well that was fine as time on the beach by Daddy.

Jalopy appreciated the offer but said that he'd grown up fending for himself so was already nifty in the kitchen. Really, Jalopy didn't like the idea of another scholarship getting cut. He knew his mother had been looking forward to going to his graduation more than anything else to which she'd ever looked forward. She had practiced saying, this is my son, the college graduate. Jalopy didn't want to put her through that again.

***

You could see that Anders was teetering. He had shown up at this flop house of a fry shop, in a tie, sidled up to the cashier to order three beignets with

"Ahem, honey but not sugar. I said, honey but not sugar."

And waited. Waited like an unclaimed kid after little league practice. Other people streamed in and out, mostly drunk White tourists and fat Black locals, everybody ordering but nobody saying anything about

"honey but not sugar. I said, honey but not sugar. Ahem."

Anders was in the top floor, The Bayou Fried Dough Sto. There were a few floors at the Huxtable but the top one is the one everyone saw.

Fronts are necessary in the illegal whouse industry and are most often massage parlors or strip clubs (because what thunder god of genius could ever guess that a strip club would employ prostitutes.) Occasionally they will also be motels. There is only one that is a beignet shack.

*** 

Twenty-three minutes in and Anders hadn't even had anything to eat much less what he was supposed to get which he wasn't sure he wanted. Jalopy never told him to wait or hold on or that yes, you will have sexual intercourse shortly but please allow me tend to these beignets first.

So when the last customer received her order, a chunky middle aged lady wearing a navy blue skirt and a nametag with wings on it, Anders tried to ride her wake to freedom. She grabbed her bag of swampsnacks and tottered back out into sumptuous New Orleans. Anders waited for Jalopy to turn back to clean his station then started to slink away himself.

As ginger the footfall of 117 teenage pounds be, no one came in or out without the cowbell telling the cook.

The bell rang.

"Where you gon?"

Anders froze, his foot an inch off the ground and his back hunched. He looked like he had discovered himself to be stepping on a snail. The wiry young man and the hugely humongous man were the only two people in the Bayou Fried now. Jalopy shook his head because he always got a kick out of the timothies that Letty brought in.

"Git you in here."

Anders let the door close under its own weight and puddled a centimeter beside the threshold.

Jalopy smiled. Anders did not.

Then Jalopy shook his head again but this time also pushed a button on the underside of a tabletop. The front door latched.

And locked.

Anders pressed against the door that had been a flimsy flap when he'd walked through it a half hour ago but was suddenly strong as a bank vault. The handrail imprinted into his hip.

Jalopy breathed a deep breath, this was going to be choppy waters for a while but so it goes. Jalopy took another breath, this one not so deep, then pressed another button and a new door, a refrigerator door, flung wide open. The refrigerator belched out a paragraph of icy air. Anders started to hyperventilate.

"You good," Jalopy said.

Anders gasped and gawked at Jalopy like he was pleading for a mercy kill. *Mother Murder make an end of this which I have lived within.*

"Them's bags on da counta. You breathe you in'n'out. You good, you good." Jalopy'd preset the bags on the counter knowing that a not insignificant number of Letty's timothies hyperventilated.

Anders darted to the counter and snatched a paper bag. He smushed it to his mouth. The paper bag crinkled and uncrinkled.

Jalopy didn't like pushing the buttons on Anders like that, freaking the kid out like that, but it was either push the button or let him run off. And it was not a good thing to answer for jobs gone wrong, especially not Letty's timothies. Every other Bed would get on him if a david got delayed or too few johns with money got under – Letty was the only Bed he'd ever met who got on him about timothies.

So Jalopy trapped Anders then gave him the space to freak out while Jalopy did what he did when someone was losing it. Jalopy cooked.

First, he took to dusting his cutting board. The flour puffed up and settled an even grey film on the big black tarp covering Jalopy's muscles and blood. Then he separated squares of dough on the butcher block and also monitored Anders. A titanic teddy bear cooking for a whippersnapper cat killer breathing into a brown paper beignet bag because he was scared of sex which was change in his brain but just sex in life, it was nothing but sex, and it's the quirky cute you can only find in the spaces society shuns that always appealed to Letty.

It didn't take but a couple of cycles of inflating and deflating the paper bag for the timothy's lungs to unhummingbird.

Anders took the bag from his mouth. He tried to be as quiet as he could while he folded it back up to look as close to an unused bag as he could manage. Then he set it as close to corner to corner square on the stack that he could manage and shuffled back to stand next to the exit, equal parts dread and etiquette upon him. Anders folded his hands over his belt buckle over his crotch. Jalopy nodded.

Then Jalopy took his butcher block over to a fryer where he dropped the cut up dough into the oil. It crackled which startled Anders but didn't send him back into a tailspin. What scared the kid got all over the cook. Spatter jumped up all over Jalopy who didn't react. Not to the kid, not to the oil. Jalopy was a long way gone from wincing.

\*\*\*

Eat vegetables for health but not morality

because the carrot

did not survive

the salad

either

\*\*\*

Beignets cook quick so just about as soon as he'd finished dropping them, Jalopy was pulling them back out. He banged the basket to get rid of the cottonseed froth because real beignets are categorically cooked in cottonseed oil. Then he dumped them out onto a plate, dribbled on some honey and made a powdered sugar snowstorm. Then he set the beignets on the sill between the kitchen and the main area.

"Welcome to em if you want."

Jalopy plucked one, unfurled his teeth, and took a satisfying like that first suck of cigarette kind of bite. Anders watched the cook eat first because he wanted to be sure his mother wasn't trying to murder him. This whole sudden trip to see an uncle he didn't know in Louisiana thing reeked of problem solving to Anders.

Jalopy didn't die. Anders took a beignet.

It was like someone fried a cloud. The skin was almost crunchy to the tooth but then it was fluffy and airy inside. Experiencing those beignets made Anders close his eyes and be cozy.

Jalopy loved smoothing Anders out like that. Jalopy wasn't a prideful thing but he loved that he could make a human do that. Whether for timothy, john, or david, Jalopy loved that he could make a man melt. Especially in our business, you have to remember that these guys were coming in a snort short of being rodeo horses. They knew what was waiting for them a couple floors down. To make a man savor in spite of his boner or terror was Jalopy's favorite part of the day.

The fryman waited for Anders to open his eyes from beignet loving then motioned to the refrigerator. It was still open.

"Dat'll take yuh where yuh wanna go. And believe yew me, yew wanna git where yew wanna go."

Anders didn't understand all of the words but got the gist, he was supposed to get into the refrigerator.

"Will you get in trouble if I don't?"

"Don't what?"

"Don't get in."

"I be good."

"I don't want you to get in trouble. It's not your fault."

"Not my fault what?"

"That I'm not getting in."

"Ah."

Jalopy turned to mix more dough. A metallic bowl made metallic sounds.

"Does yuh want more bin yays?"

"I don't want you to have to help me."

"I make some mo bin yays."

"Please don't make any more for me."

"Yuh ain't liking them?"

"…I hate them."

"Ooooo now yuh gonna lie tuh me and get me in trouble with Letty!"

Anders covered his eyes then he uncovered them then he started pacing. Anders moaned too.

"You said you wouldn't be in trouble!"

"Well, you know how it is. E'erbody get in trouble when a job ain't go right."

"But isn't your job to cook? …I liked the beignets…"

"My job tuh cook when people come here to eat."

"Can I leave? Can I just leave?"

"Course yuh can! What kinda question is that? Can you leave? Course yuh can leave."

Jalopy went back to whisking.

"Lemme finish this firs then you go right on out the way yuh came," Jalopy said.

"Thank you." Anders said and let untense his shoulders.

"Ain't no problem."

"I don't like that I'm like this," Anders said and stretched his neck.

"Good you know so young in life."

"It's not so young. I'm in college," Anders said and stretched his arms up towards the ceiling. Then he dropped them.

"Whatchewe studyin?"

"Not sure."

"What do yuh like?"

"…unno…"

"Ain't yuh got stuff yuh like?"

"No."

"Better not to like nothing no how."

Anders was unwound. Maybe he trusted Jalopy, maybe he liked the beignets, but Anders was no longer cracking glass.

Anders surveyed the Bayou Fried. He checked out the old menu board. He checked out the ceiling fan which spun so slow you could see each blade. Anders checked out at the refrigerator which was still open.

Anders stared at the refrigerator which was still open.

His eyes relaxed and if you were really paying attention, watching the hints human beings can't stop themselves from giving, you could see that Anders's lips piqued for a split second while he stared at the refrigerator. Which was still open.

"Say no this time," Anders said.

"I tole yuh I ain't makin these bin yays fo yuh."

"No, I'm going to ask you if I can leave again. Say no this time."

"Oh."

"OK?"

"Do you understand?"

"Yup."

"Can I leave?"

"Nope."

"OK pleeeeease? OK. Oh God. OK. OK!"

Anders dove into the refrigerator. It was an elevator. Jalopy stopped cooking. He pressed another button.

***

Pornography! They cry.

Pornography is our holocaust! It's teaching ten year olds what vaginas look like and they are fake vaginas as if labia are editable. Celebrities are famous for being famous for having sex tapes. Our youth are warping. Every middle schooler has had or provided a blow job.

It's a catastrophe, they cry. People are having too much sex too young.

Look at the data, I say.

Yes, there's a lot of porn. Yes, everyone has seen it.

And you know what happened to the younger generation? You know how much sex the people younger than the internet are having?

None.

Go look at the data for yourself. There are gaggles of studies on sex because reproduction is a sort of important thing to track. People who grew up with broadband hardcore pornography have less sex than the rest of us by huge margins. The over-porned are the under-sexed. Some researchers have said it's because younger people have been trained to be more discriminating because more than being raised in a world with the internet, they have been raised in a world with AIDS. Other researchers suggest that porn actually approximates sex to the tune of not needing sex like Stevia ends sugar. I don't much care but I like to say that the internet ended sex like the internet ended wealth. There's a fixed amount of wealth on Earth. Maybe there's a fixed amount of sex.

All technology did was consolidate it.

***

The timothy made his way down. Or rather, the refrigerator elevator went down and Anders had no choice because he was inside of it. He'd gone into the box, indeed it wasn't so cold because the frost was nothing but crushed chalk, and a wall panel flipped up to expose two buttons. One reading "no," another reading "yes" and there was also a sensor for scanning keycards. The sensor was the only new thing at the Bayou Fried Dough Sto so seemed to Anders to throb with technology. Then Jalopy waved his keycard, something beeped, the button reading "yes" lit up, and the door closed.

You could watch all of that on the security cams. You could watch all of everything on the security cams. That's what I did. I watched.

But Letty preferred to fantasize.

Letty would imagine that moment when her timothies would drain from the elevator into the sticky, lush reds and fantastic oak bar and women – not girls, but women – sashaying like fed pumas from place to place yes speakeasy sexy is the sexiest sexy that there ever was or will be.

Of course, I was actually watching the actual Anders. You had to love that he had forced himself into the fridge but the kid was unraveling. He would go still then he'd spasm and slam himself against the wall, throw his whole weight into it. Then back to statue. Anders was locked in a small space and he didn't know where he was going other than down, literally down. You could see him promising to any god who would listen that he would never do this to himself again no matter what he thought was possible in some stupid instant because it was not possible because he was Anders and Anders was a weak, stupid person.

The boy had lost control. He may have been the one to give up that control but you don't remember that once you're in it. All you can do is panic once you're panicking. Watching Anders thrash, I flashed on what those animal bodies must've looked like.

I'd told Letty that we needed extra security with Kid Felinicide in the building and she'd said I was being ridiculous. He was only a hurt little boy, she said. I said OK Letty. You're right, I told her. Then I went and got the extra security worked out on my own.

\*\*\*

Three Haikus about a Subterranean Super Brothel

Let's start with the bar
Old real oak because so is
Sexuality

No drink minimum
Generous because so is
Sexuality

And Ronnie Camptown
Working the bottles because
Sexuality

\*\*\*

Buttoned up vest, flat brim cap, pocket watch, altogether as close to an old timey trolley operator costume as Daddy could get, Ronnie Camptown was the star of one side of the business. Ronnie knew everything about whiskey, wine, bitters, stouts, and sours and the rest wasn't worth serving so we didn't. Some employees knew that Ronnie was the stablehorse too, but that revenue stream best remains quiet because very straight men can't handle the thought of squiggly sex, even in a whouse. His official gig was to be the bartender. But from time to time, the right client would appear and Ronnie'd get himself a bigger cashout in the sunrise.

Mama, a moving cocoon of scarves also named Mrs. Hildengarder, greeted Anders at the refrigerator. He stared at her like a snake charmer trying to mesmerize her so she wouldn't see his wild pressing of the button. Any button.

"It don't work without a card," Mama said and turned away from Anders.

Let me tell you, 40 years in any business and you start doing the smart thing without having to think it first. Mama knew the way to stabilize someone like Anders is to present your back or throat. 99 times out of 100 they don't pounce, but some men don't get comfortable until they see something upon which to prey. Since women of a certain age hate nothing more than what age does to the human neck, Mama chose to expose her back.

"Come in for a minute a'least. You can leave if y'hate it," she said and walked in like it didn't matter to her either way. She did not look back to Anders, didn't say anything else to him, nor offer him a handkerchief or means to dry himself. Mama knew the kid needed to be a pair of eyeballs for a while. The timothy tiptoed in behind her.

Hildengarder was small and round under all of those layers. Exactly how rotund was a mystery due to the role her gargantuan breasts played in rendering any blouse borne a mumu. Two rouge wastelands plunked down in the middle thirds of either side of her face were flyover country between the loud stencils outlining her eyes and the purple applied so liberally to her lips that it clumped. Lipstick liked her right front tooth and her head was bound in medium length layers of dry black kink.

I remember Hildengarder showing up for her first day of work at the Huxtable. I remember seeing someone who had not yet accepted her deterioration. Someone who had spent a lot of years as the hot one, the one who made the other whouse girls gossip. But egos bend to bank accounts. The woman couldn't make a david anymore. Couldn't do it. Couldn't keep the ones she'd had either. Cut her rates which had bought her an extra couple of years. Although a discount rate life is not a pleasant existence.

You could see that she loathed the idea that twats who were a quarter the queen she'd been would now be the ones looking at her like she was the worthless one, like she was the sad old woman. But you have to make a living. So Hildengarder, who knew it took a special woman to be a Bed and a not dead one to be a mama, took the refrigerator elevator down.

This is what it's like to walk into the Huxtable:

It's dark like a jazz club. You hear the clip clop of high heels on slate floor before you see anybody's face. Olive walls with splattered paint paintings in black frames. A few bundles of blooms, one area for lounging with a sofa and two chairs and another high top table with a pair of chairs as well. Then the bar, the beautiful beautiful bar. Mama walked to the bar and Anders stood behind a stool behind her.

"Ronnie, this is our guest, Anders."

A chestnut complexion ten years older than you'd peg it for stopped polishing glasses.

"Hello son. Interest you in a sit?"

Ronnie smiled genuinely, neighborly. Like he was not being paid to be there. This is a specialty of career service people. Anders gulped and oozed up onto the stool.

\*\*\*

It was 4 PM and no one else would be allowed entry to the Huxtable until nine that night. Timothies were usually daytime deals.

"Letty said she'd be ready in a few minutes, but you know girls," Mama said. "So I will say good day to you, sir and leave you in the capable hands of Mr. Camptown. If I can be of any service to you, go head and let anyone here know to get me. And I'll get got for you."

Then Hildengarder left to attend a Mama's many responsibilities.

Anders sat at the bar, a bottle of shaken champagne if I'd ever seen it. He watched the Beds come across the Stage, each preparing for their night's david. Generally, the goal was a david a night a Bed but that was only a starting point. Between periods and premium clients, not every single one of us had to take a party every single night.

First he saw The Big Redhead. She was probably on the South side of fat, depending on your tastes. Lusty, breasts that'd buttress her jaw in a push up bra, and a bramble of the kind of strawberry, Irish frizz that called out to the Renaissance Fair deep down in all of us. She was a bellowing personality, big and bold and most of the time laughing. Unless she was drinking. Or fighting.

Then he saw The Smart One who had a great affinity for statistics and Vicodin. Porcelain skin and thin whispery hair, sometimes she would wrap herself in sundresses and leggings and Kentucky Derby hats, and other times it'd be neon orange bikinis. Bony, she was known to prowl in a way that made her appear a fly away drifting from town to town. She'd wander into a room, dazed, a waif with a purse that was a maraca when shaken, and she'd attract the type of man who instructs strangers how to invest better. They'd stand together, him a bluster of advice, her asleep on her feet and still 50 IQ up on him, and you couldn't help but want to save this poor woman from whatever was coming. But she was a wolf in rape victim's clothing. In fact, she was the second highest paid Bed with an average annual net of $295,000.

The Mistress made the most money because she was the best fetishist and in the end, anyone who all the way doesn't judge makes the most money which is the moral of the story. A tiny Nicaraguan with hips and cobalt blue eyes, her mother had been a concubine to a crew of Central American guerillas. We didn't hear too much from The Mistress because her role at the Huxtable kept her in the kinkier corners where she excelled with very wealthy men, primarily. After a three-month seasonal stretch where her cut alone was nearly $200,000, Daddy signed her to a Bed and constructed her a velvet dungeon where The Mistress kept to herself. And very wealthy men.

Most johns figured The Blonde made the most money because she was perfect in Texas. 5'5", green eyes, 36-24-36, a honey haired princess born for a quarterback's arm or a senator's trophy case. She was less than liked by the rest of the Beds on account of her being 4-6 years from having the same religion and politics as the richest guy with whom she could procreate. She was a wedding away from forever forgetting the first person:

"We're having the neighbors over this weekend, care to join?"

"We're headed to Mother's."

"We're pregnant!"

The Blonde did terrific with White guys who wore big wristwatches.

Then there was The Black who was a Clydesdale. She was the most spectacular woman any of us had ever seen in person. From deep Africa. The Black was so Black she was Blue, a true specimen. The plague of African Americans preferring light skin to dark would have been cured had she been a public figure. Rich and juicy, The Black was ripe like a perfect plum and her hair was buzzed to her skull. She was tall, about six foot and a lesser whouse would've discouraged high heels. But the Huxtable understood the beauty of full bloom. She would gust through a room. Six inch heels and bang bang bang her steps were ferocious. The meat of her quadriceps would jiggle on stride. You couldn't help but respect any john who selected The Black.

Then Letty and February made seven.

The Seven Beds of the Huxtable. Beds, not ladies, not partiers, not girls, not any word that starts with a huh sound because there are hookers and then there are the Beds. Beds because the Huxtable provided room and board and a salary. Good salary too. In that last year Letty's numbers were $150,000 untaxed per annum with tips and bonuses paid on ad-hoc bases which worked out to $238,000 net and sex with 302 men, 16 women, and 24 timothies. And room and board and medical.

\*\*\*

Anders stared at us like he was waiting for one of us to peel off.

No one said anything to him some because we were put off by his helpless, hungry eyes but mostly because he was Letty's timothy. We all knew better than to mess up Letty's timothy. It wasn't that she didn't want to include us all, she loved the idea of a whole whouse party. It was that only a few of us were into it. And those of us who were into it were not into it for the timothy, we were into it for the Letty. Timothies for Letty were her chance to help humanity and there's something satisfying about helping someone who believes in something. For the rest of us, timothies were soldiers plucked from a pile twice a month because Daddy said we had to.

I say soldiers because most of our timothies were soldiers. Since we live in a time where you randomly thank snipers and sergeants not teachers and baristas, the Beds went with military members for their timothies. Often maimed, sometimes amputated, and always shellshocked, most people who didn't pay at the Huxtable were war veterans. Only Letty took other kinds of timothies. It wasn't that she hadn't blown a bomb tech for free before, but it was the person not the people to Letty.

Anders was Letty's type of timothy. A soul born into a situation who was misbehaving, sure, but not yet gone. Someone who would be so much better off with a little help.

So she helped them.

***

An Older Man Who Draws a Gun

And A Younger One

Who Doesn't

"Can you drink?"

"I'm 18."

"Son -"

"- Anders."

"Son, you are in an underground cathouse in the only state in the US where prostitutes gotta register as sex offenders. It ain't legality I'm asking 'bout. You on any meds or anything like that? Anything that alcohol could screw up?"

"…I don't want a drink."

"You gonna keep answering questions I didn't ask?"

"I have a gun."

"Like this one?"

Pause.

"…bigger."

"Son, that elevator you came down on x-ray scanned you down to the bone. Daddy got the whole thing rigged. Daddy know how to run a business so you might as well stop thinking you're out ahead of anybody in here right now. The only arms you got got fingers. Now can you drink?"

"Will you tell my father?"

"I don't even know who your father is."

"He's rich."

"Then why you here for free?"

"…I could pay."

"Well your money ain't no good now."

"I don't take my medicine anymore. I'm going to kill as many people as I can and myself soon."

"Do you have a list?"

"Sort of."

"Am I on it?"

"Not yet."

"You're not saying that because I got my own gun out here?"

"No."

"Then I guess I can holster her. Provided we share a drink."

"Perhaps."

Have you ever mocked a wine snob? Wafted a swirl of alcohol, fancy or cheap, and spoke through your nose a sort of "Mmmhmmm, yes, brilliant year!" I'm sure you have, we all have. And for good reason too. They do these blind taste tests where they pour nine wines, eight of them are eighty dollars apiece at least and then they throw in a glass of glog. They collect a dozen experts. They say to the experts "OK, pick the best one" and those sommeliers swirl, they roll it all over their tongue, they make rude precise noises, and eleven experts crown the two buck chuck.

Ronnie Camptown was the twelfth.

Ronnie loved something and that something was alcohol. He wasn't an alcoholic because he didn't depend on alcohol to solve other emotional issues, though he did live a split life as I mentioned.

Ronnie pulled seven bottles from his wall and set them in a row on that old oak slab of handsome.

"Anders, this is scotch. Scotch is a specific type of whiskey. The Huxtable serves whiskey, wine, bitters, stouts and sours because the rest ain't worth serving so we don't. Stouts and sours are beers and too complicated to teach you about in the fifteen minutes you got before Letty takes you from me, wine nobody knows but for the labels, and you ain't hungover so bitters won't make sense. Whiskey is the best of the lot anyhow. I'm going to teach you about scotch now, which is usually thought to be the highest kind of whiskey, though bourbons are up and coming. You ain't gonna learn everything, I learn something new every single sip myself. My goal is to give you a bit of a vocabulary and to expose you to at least one scotch that you like. That way, if and when you go to another bar and there a girl there you trying to impress, you know how to order something actually impressive."

He uncorked two bottles, the farmost left two.

"Either of your parents drunks?"

"Yes."

"Which one?"

"I don't ever see my father."

"Whatchya mama drink?"

"Wine."

"OK great, so same with wine there are two types of scotches, blended and single malt. Think of it like wine. Now, you strike me as a learner. Yes?"

"I'm in college."

"Course you're in college, you're White. What I'm asking is are you good at learning. Bout as much to do with being a learner and a student as being a farmer and a cook."

"I learn."

"That's what I figured, good young troubled fella like yourself – troubled fellas are always learners. Learning is a big part o what's troubling yuh, I bet. Let's see then how much you learned from watching your parents –"

"– Mother."

"Mother drink. What kind of grape is in a chardonnay?"

"White."

"No, now – "

Ronnie shook his head and Anders smiled in his eyes.

"Hold up, was that a joke, Anders? Were you being funny?"

Anders didn't blink.

"Ha!"

Ronnie clucked at the blind spot his wisdom had created. Then he continued with a blush more humble upon him.

"Well, as you apparently know my little learner, the grape which is in chardonnay wine is the chardonnay grape."

This time, Anders didn't only blink, he all the way closed his eyes.

"Ahhhhh," he said.

"So," Ronnie leaned in, "What do you think is in a merlot, then? What kind of grape?"

Anders kept his eyes shut. He seemed cradled in the way he had when he ate one of Jalopy's beignets.

"Red."

***

For the next hour, Ronnie showed Anders what it is to love something. He showed Anders single malts and blends, cask strengths, and how a scotch served with ice is perverting the purity but sometimes you find yourself in the business of perversion. Speysides and highlands, what peat was, and how if Anders were to fall in love with scotch himself and also to avoid a heavy sentence from the murders to which he was committed that the most practical path was to begin drinking the Japanese because they cost so much less because they weren't actually scotch even though they were actually scotch. Which is what mattered. They went from one aged 15 years to a 40, Anders had no favorite. He was too happy to care.

Then a bare lightbulb above the doorway to the party rooms lit up green. Some davids called it the mistletoe, the bulb that lit up green. Other davids didn't call it anything because not everything needs a name. Johns that got to the Stage never noticed the bulb because they were never called into the back. They were walked back. Johns didn't have dates.

The mistletoe or green light that didn't need a name meant Anders's liquor lesson was over.

He wilted.

"Listen," Ronnie sat on a stool beside Anders. "I want you to think of the last time you saw a girl who was so beautiful she made you nervous. Kinda girl make the world shrinkwrap around her. People going quiet in conversations follow her through a room like slime behind a snail. You see that hot thing in your head, do you?"

Anders didn't have to think because he felt that way about most women.

"Son, you're gonna go back now and meet Letty who is so pretty that same girl in your head wouldn't want to be in the same room with her. And if the mood strikes you, you're gonna have sex with Letty. You're gonna see what her face looks like when you inside of her, if you want that. And if you don't, then you gonna hang out with her and get comfortable with this lady so beautiful she make the beautiful lady in your head ugly. Then the next time you come across that piece in your head, you'll have the memory of Letty, this thing way hotter than the one you talking with and who picked you. You wait and see who intimidated by who when you got Letty who picked you in your head."

The mistletoe flashed again. Anders gulped.

"Ronnie?"

"Yessuh?"

Anders scratched his left hand with his right one. He slouched and looked back at the refrigerator elevator he came in on.

"…what if she doesn't like me?"

"Then you put her on your list."

Anders shook his head.

"But that wouldn't be her fault."

Ronnie grinned.

"Anders, go in there an-"

"-that'd be Daddy's fault."

"What?" Ronnie's grin waxed. "What was that, son?"

Anders continued the factual explanation of how culpability worked in a business.

"That'd be Daddy's fault, not Letty's. Daddy's the boss."

Everything kindly quit Ronnie's face. His smile, his wisdom, it was as if the last hour had never happened.

"How do you know that name?!" Ronnie asked.

He scorched at Anders who hunched and didn't answer and stiffened again. Anders knew he'd done something wrong but he honestly had no idea what. Ronnie slammed his hands on the bar between them.

"GODDAMNIT, HOW DO YOU KNOW THAT NAME?!"

\*\*\*

It wasn't that we were scared of Daddy, it's that we assumed he'd kill us if we messed up.

Genuine guy, by then he was somewhere in his later middle years and thick like he'd been an athlete earlier in his life, which he had. A few liver spots and old thick black hair gone to salt and bowling alleys. Slow, congenial eyes.

It's a simpler life when you have a good boss. And Daddy was a great boss: he'd back us in disputes with customers, he'd let us take time off, listened to our suggestions, and he gave it to us when we deserved it. We weren't expected to be perfect but we knew which lines were drawn on the edge of a cliff. Daddy was a great boss.

I mentioned that the refrigerator elevator offered two floor button options: yes and no. I also mentioned that neither could be selected without an access card. Find a way to get Yes lit up and you'd end up where Anders was, the area most commonly called the Huxtable (although we called it the Stage.) This was the third floor down.

No aglow would get you to the second floor, the sleeping quarters (occasionally known as the Hive but in practice most people would say that they were going to their or someone else's room.) The rooms were chain hotel for business traveler style, good lighting, every bathroom had a tub. The Hive shared one single kitchen which was the only incident upon which staff reliably referred to the second floor as the Hive.

I'll meet you in the Hive's Kitchen, we'd say.

This was to avoid confusion with Daddy's kitchen which anyone equipped with any of the five major senses was compelled to call The Kitchen.

Beds would have a one on one with Daddy every two or three weeks, Mama saw him most days.

Sometimes he'd have sex with his visitors, but it wasn't more than once every few months at most if you were a Bed. Some of us hadn't seen him naked in years. And he wasn't doing the big bad pimp skim thing when he did sleep with someone. Don't forget that intercourse was a practical part of his livelihood. It was more like the owner of a major potato chip corporation coming down to the factory floor and trying their latest flavor than a silverback reminding his harem.

He talked about money more than he thought about money. The timothy, for example, made sense to people if he called it charity. Sex cost money other than when it didn't and he was blessed to be able to give back, he'd say.

But Daddy didn't institute the timothy to make more people happy. I mean, I'm sure he enjoyed that byproduct because it's a happy thing to be around happy people. No, that man made the timothy because everyone has a tally of reasons for why they're the last good person on Earth. Daddy had the money to make his reasons realer.

One should look good for Daddy but not over the top – $65 dinner kind of outfit. Date night dress. The clock would strike the hour and we'd wiggle over to the elevators, a few ladies jealous behind, but most indifferent. Waiting at the fridge would be Ronnie, Jalopy, or Mama. Along with Daddy, they had the three keys that would get you down. We might chitchat, especially if it were Mama playing gateguard. Some women would be twittering with a head of steam forty-five minutes late already. But this didn't bother Daddy. Late didn't much matter underground.

Eventually, they'd get in. Always alone, Ronnie or whoever would reach in and activate the fourth floor. They'd wave the extra special key card and both Yes and No would light up. You had about 75 seconds between the door closing on the Stage and opening again below, two minutes if you picked it up in the Hive.

Elevator didn't ding when you hit the fourth floor or any other. It stopped without a rumble, and the doors slid apart.

Then you were there.

### Daddy's

Deep below a whouse below a shanty was a commander's palace. Letty had slung math at her feelings once or twice:

We were usually at seven ladies averaging somewhere around $5,500 - $9,000 a day, six days a week (Sundays were dark.) Plus, Ronnie pulling a few grand, then whatever the beignets and bar were. All in, it wasn't hard to see The Huxtable doing $10 million annually. Subtract staff cost and laundering, bribes, fixing this or that and you had no less than three million left over. And the whole thing was untaxed.

The Fourth Floor did not disappoint the accountant inside of Letty.

First thing she saw were the willow tree's roots. That kraken looming up on the front lawn's tentacles somehow rerouted around the Hive and Stage only to reappear as pillars in Daddy's. Two big ones wrapped around each other like DNA.

Fifteen foot ceilings.

Open floor plan although each of the eight areas I will describe to you felt like its own. Good decorating will do that.

There was a trio of wrought iron patio tables and chairs like a bistro built for cigarettes and fancy ham sandwiches.

There was a library. This scrawl of bound books stuffed from floor to ceiling.

There was a parlor with riveted red leather furniture and candelabras. It was the kind of place where you wanted to sit with a leather bound book and soak in the silk of Cavendish pipe puffs.

There was a sauna which had a Jacuzzi, a standing shower with ten heads, and an arrangement of Russian foliage that was supposedly healthy if somebody thwacked you with it.

An entertainment space with stadium seating and a ludicrously huge TV screen that hid in the ceiling until it was called upon to display a movie, Netflix, or its own majesty.

There was a Madison Avenue men's wardrobe too. Racks of shoes and inlets built for outfits.

There was a dining room on a lifted platform with a table built of the same wood as The Stage's bar.

And finally, of course, was The Kitchen. Craftsman and spacious, wood burning oven so he could make his pizzas, hanging pots and pans, and lots of space to chop. The Kitchen was on the far side of the raised dining room so wasn't as accessible as the other areas. But you could find it if you knew to try.

***

"*I asked you how you knew that name?!*"

Normally, Anders loved knowing something that upset other people. And he especially loved provoking them with that information. But that was because he felt like he was the one with the power.

"I…I…"

"*Goddamnit boy, tell me!*

Warmongering, Ronnie stalked around the bar. He circled a famished hyena to a foot from Anders's face. The timothy was stutters. Drunk, nervous, murderous – it was all gone now. Nothing remained in the kid other than the kind of fear comes from the kind of trust you put into your favorite grown-ups.

Ronnie was an edged weapon.

"I asked you. A question. Now. How? Do you know. The name. Daddy. Down here."

"I told him."

The voice came from the hallway behind them. The hallway led back to the rooms people paid to enter and the voice belonged to a woman.

Letty.

"Now are you gonna pull a pistol on me? Or do I get whisky 101 too?" she asked.

Letty didn't flinch nor did Anders but that was because he was paralyzed. Ronnie looked Letty over, searching for a chink in her confidence. But Letty was calm as the quicker gunslinger. So Ronnie retreated to his side of the bar, picked up a rag and started cleaning clean things. He muttered.

"Boy knows things he ain't supposed to down here. I'm ole Captain Hook cause I try to get to the bottom of it all. Boy says he gon kill people and I show him what's what. And I'm the bad guy!"

Not to spoil the St George and the Dragon dynamic here, but

Ronnie was not some villain closing in on poor Anders the Catmangler. He was acting.

Letty had approached Ronnie the day before and told him all about Anders. So they worked out a scene, the bartender and the Bed. They hadn't lined out the name Daddy to be the word that set Ronnie off persay, or any specific word at all. Ronnie was waiting for the mistletoe which meant Letty was ready, then he was supposed to find a way to attack Anders then Letty would swoop in to save him. Because that's what Letty said Anders needed. To be saved.

Back to Letty and Anders and Ronnie who is performing a bartender's busy work: wiping down an already clean bar, polishing crystalline glasswear, etc. Ronnie starts to get into it. He takes on an additional patois because the New Orleans accent is an emotional accent as much as it is geographical.

"It don't even matter, soon's he pay's bill he ain't nothing but nothing far's I's concerned."

(Letty had paid Ronnie $2,000 for the whisky and his manhours the day before. Ronnie told her not to bother, that Daddy would cover it all. Letty insisted. "It's me wanting to do more," she'd told Ronnie, "I should pay.")

"But I - !"

Anders surges forward to exclaim that he had no idea he was being charged for this and that he didn't even want a drink in the first place and that he could leave. He would leave. Drip on out like oatmeal.

Letty lays her hand across her timothy's tiny chest.

"Let's why not call this one even, what do you say Ronnie?"

Ronnie snaps his rag like a whip. It clips an arrangement of glasses and sends a stemmed one spinning off. It shatters on contact with the ground which is an incredible bit of luck so far as the scene goes. It's getting harder for him not to smile so he screams instead.

"IT WAS $1700 OF TOP SHELF! DADDY HAVE MY ASS I GO GIVING THAT AWAY!"

Anders's head pinballs back and forth between Letty and Ronnie, Letty and Ronnie.

"You let me deal with Daddy," she says.

Ronnie scoffs loudly. This last part of the exchange was the only dialogue that they had actually scripted out the day before. They'd laughed and laughed to arrive at it.

"Oh, so he gonna get $1700 for free?" he says and looks away from Letty because he knows he won't be able to hold it together.

Somehow, she does not smile.

"That isn't all he's getting for free."

Ronnie who cannot look at Letty looks at Anders whose eyes are harvested of their lids. Seeing Ronnie looking at him, Anders gets embarrassed and drops his gobsmack where it happens upon Letty's butt.

Whoa.

Her butt is perfect, he thinks. Her hips give enough of a frame that it could bubble but no one would ever call Letty wide. This is...

...His?

Whoa.

I guess it distresses some people when they hear about Letty's timothy scenes. They think that makes her manipulative or a try hard. Like what Letty needed to do was either accept that it was nothing but a gig or approach those poor broken souls straight on. Let me set aside the try hard thing because anyone who accuses people of trying hard is a teenager and teenagers are useless creatures. Now onto the manipulative front:

We're all manipulative. Whether through seduction, brute force, white lies, honesty, tonality, diction, fashion – we're living things, we're manipulative. We have figured out what has worked before in our someday-ending crusade to get what we want and need. So we keep doing that. I don't do this often but I'm going to defend Letty. Timothies were special to her. She thought about them, planned for them, and used her resources to be of service. Letty believed in sex. She believed sex helped humanity because sex helps human beings. A laid person is a better person and we laugh about it but it's more true than most anything because sex is life. It is literally life. So if you're going to be a teenager or a prude, then let's part ways here. Because this is a story about something you haven't begun to understand yet. This is a story about business.

***

I'm happy to stop.

No you're not.

You get it now, though?

I got it before. It's not complicated.

It is though.

It isn't. I have a need that you don't. Not complicated.

You think I don't have a need to have sex with my husband?

Look. Let's not talk about this. I don't want to keep having the same fight.

Then don't ask me a question if you don't want to hear the answer.

I don't mean that I don't want to listen to you.

Uh, yes you do. That's what you just said.

That isn't what I said.

That's exactly what you said.

Then that isn't what I meant to say.

Ah.

So OK. Tell me then. What is bothering you? Tell me, I want to listen to you.

No you don't, you want me to tell you that it's hunky dory if you go to brothels and then you want me to sleep with you.

I mean, that'd be nice…

You think that's funny?

Jesus Christ, it's a joke.

How can you make a joke?

Because I want to live a fun life. I want to joke. I want to have sex.

That you can even possibly think of a joke right now makes me see how much you think of this. And me. You think I'm the one who doesn't have a need but it's you. I have the need for sex, oh you bet I do. I also happen to have the need to connect with my husband.

Why do you do this?

Do what? Talk when you say you want to listen?

Always make it miserable. Bait me into getting angry and yelling. All that ends up happening is you feel insulted and I feel pathetic.

Oh no, I feel pathetic too.

See? I don't want to keep having the same fight.

You don't want to keep having the same fight? You don't want to talk through something that is crushing the woman you say you love every day? Then you don't want to have a marriage.

***

That Baffled Sourpuss

Anders had never held a woman's hand other than his mother's hand which he hadn't held since his mother found what was almost a kitten in the egg drawer. He figured his lady days were also an abortion.

But here he was.

Him.

Anders.

Anders the Freak, Anders the Geek not even Smart enough to be Smart, Anders who had plotted the quickest path between sororities if pursued by police.

That guy.

He had a woman too beautiful to be as heroic as she was guiding him by the hand back into a room to have sex with her.

By choice.

By her choice.

"I'd have a drink with you but after that crap at the bar, I need to relax like now. Like right this instant. Ahhh!" she shivered, "I'm so tense!"

Anders computed the inferences of her statement. This either meant she wanted him to make sex to her or take a bath. Anders's hand secreted its concerns into the ludicrously appealing chick's hand holding it. Letty continued.

"Do you play League of Legends?"

"The, uh, computer game?"

"The, uh, number two Korean sport?" she said. "The, uh, second biggest source of online data in the world? Yes, the uh, video game."

Maybe it was that he knew what she was talking about, maybe it was that she had spoken to him in the mocking manner he most often used to speak to himself, but for the first time in the springtime of their relationship, Anders did not hesitate before responding to Letty.

"Yeah. I LoL."

"Great," they stopped at a door to the room Letty had designed for him, "Because I'm trying to get through Bronze."

Then Letty opened the door.

***

Walking into that room made Anders forget all about sex and cat killing and the way his parents never said what they meant when he was with them. Six stations set up with sleek leather chairs, jet engine sized computers whirling lagless, a full buffet with sternos blue flamed and lapping hotel trays brimming with breakfast burritos. A portable bowl of fake baked cheese snacks. We'd eat the leftovers for dinner the next few nights.

It's a funny setup to an adult, an altar for video games and cheap fingerfoods. Made me laugh to see Letty setting it up with Petunia, the whouse girl, anyhow. But it was what an isolated eighteen-year old wanted which is what made Letty the best. That and what she did next.

Letty kicked her slippers into the space. They ricocheted off of a lamp towards the back so she snorted in laughter and bent at the waist and looked up at Anders with a face so full of joy, so full of vivid living spirit that a knot buried too deeply inside of him to feel during the day but choked him to sleep every night gave way.

Letty grazed the back of Anders's hand with her fingertips then bounded to one of the computers. The little whiffs of I-want-you.

Anders unlaced his dress up shoes and left them symmetrical by the door.

\*\*\*

Anders didn't know sex. Anders didn't know scotch. He didn't know how to wear a button up shirt without looking like a spelling bee contestant. But Anders did know what a mother who didn't want you to die but wished you would disappear looked like. And he knew the video game called League of Legends.

Letty had taken a seat at one of the computers and asked Anders for his help in getting better at this game. Anders walked over to Letty and his hand unclammed because he knew he knew how to be of value to her. Her legs were crossed then she uncrossed them and Letty kissed Anders when Anders was close enough to be kissed.

Letty played tour guide. Here's what a butt feels like, you're allowed to squeeze it and even smack it sometimes. Here's what a bra looks like and how to unhook it, you'll never get it right, so accept appearing a klutz. A flaw is lovable if accepted. Here's how a woman looks at you when she lays on her back and lifts her legs while you take off her bottoms. Don't be creepy. Here's a condom and why they're funny. Here's what a blow job feels like, touch her hair and encourage but don't be creepy. Don't. Be. Creepy. Here's the sound a woman makes when you enter her. This is what wet is and you don't want to start until she's this. Take your time.

Women need time. This is where it feels good to her. This is a loving pace. This is a hard pace. This is what it looks like when a woman is on top of you. This is what it looks like when you are behind her. This is an orgasm.

Now we go again because the trick to sex with a virgin is immediately doing it again. He was more attentive the sequel through, not as tentative, had no idea what he was doing which was precious but the timothy was so aware of Letty. So conscious. He held the back of her head and laid it on a pillow like she were Fabergé. He cupped her breast and nibbled her nipple and she twitched.

He stopped immediately.

"Are you OK, Letty?"

Anders didn't know what pleasure in a woman looked like and Letty would love him for always for being so sweet as to stop to check on her. How many men wouldn't stop? The psychopathy, the awkwardness, the apathy, underneath it all was a young man who wanted a woman to be with him and to be well. That's the person Letty knew had always been in there, he needed only to be nurtured.

Letty laid her fingers across Anders's jawline and purled into his mouth. Her right hand wrapped around his bare back and pulled his chest to hers. They were naked and feeling her skin on his made his hands wrap around her. He felt strong like he never had before. Strong like he didn't have to be anything other than what he was and he knew what to do and wasn't stupid and secretly being laughed at or pitied by everyone. Letty lifted her hips off of the bed and his fingers made divots in her buttocks. They were squeezing and breathing. Sweat and belly skin on belly skin and forehead to forehead, she stretched her tongue to lick anything she could reach. He slid inside of her and she was wetter now. She was cooing and panting and as she watched his face change to that baffled sourpuss, Letty loved without judgment and wrung his testicles to make him feel it that much more.

*\*\*\**

A Signpost in the Swamp

New Orleans isn't big or easy. Every other street is a one way and, being a football town, drivers do not wait for walkers.

It's sticky and it's mystical. Haberdashers have commerce in New Orleans.

It's segregated like a fantasy novel – villages of hobbits, villages of ogres. Occasionally a quest will call for fellowship but for the most part, New Orleans is an alternation of the races.

Yearbooks are family albums, big Southern broods, reunions with Grammies and great grandchildren. Housing is cheap so the ghettos are filled with more Mercedes than they are elsewhere in America. Mansions, real mansions, with columns and brass doorknobs.

A lot of folk are heavy although the mystery is why everyone isn't fat. Beignets, gumbo, po boys, in any other tourist town, tourist food is a thing for tourists. But Louisianans feast the same as visitors.

Most people seem to be running for judge. And the names! Beau Higginbottom for Judge. Treat Grumblewarble for Judge. Grant Scattles for Judge. Campaign banners, flags, and porch furniture – that's how you appointed your property.

Sorcery is disregarded but not laughed at because everybody knows somebody who knows not to trifle with voodoo. The Bible is The Beginning and to-go drinks from bars are real things. Marijuana is neither legal nor a cultural norm. The Quarter is brass bands and bums and barf, some from the bums but most from the trumpeters. Some bars have Video Poker machines, some are Laundromats.

Brunches last until the Saints play. Crime is uncontrolled. Storms sweep in and out in an hour. Old men wear class rings.

Come you down to New Orleans.

Come you to drink sazeracs with her and share a stroll along a shaded stretch of Saint Charles. Come and let her cook for you, and lick you your plate. Take you a bath with New Orleans in a clawfoot tub and read poems to each other. Love her in the thunder and stop answering texts.

Yes, come you to New Orleans and join the dream she's been dreaming for three hundred years.

Because it is a nicer life spent dreaming, my child.

It is a nicer life.

\*\*\*

You had to love the way Anders walked out of the Huxtable that day. So much lighter in step but firmer in stride. He said hello to us on his way out, chipper like the bank manager saying good morning to his tellers. That saunter upon him. Oh the saunter that comes upon a sexed fella! He even went to Ronnie to say that there were no hard feelings then offered to take care of the bar bill. Ronnie asked Anders how he planned on doing that. He said he would wash their dishes or sell his guns. Something, he said, again possessed of the air of a confident supervisor problem-solving with his employee. They could work something out he was sure. Then Ronnie said that what's done is done and it's only money in the end, what mattered is if Anders had enjoyed his visit.

They're people, Anders said. Women are people.

Oh yeah? Ronnie said.

Yeah. We're all. I don't know. People.

There was a letter for Anders at the bar. That was what he had in his hands when he graduated from Professor Letty's course at Huxtable U. That was what all of Letty's timothies had in their hands as they walked off campus back into the same world they had forgotten about for a few hours. Anders opened the letter on his ride up in the refrigerator elevator. It read:

> To Anders
>
> You don't know me but you should take your medicine. Mean people think sick people don't deserve to be better

because mean people suck. You know they suck and they probably know they suck too. But you're sick and you should listen to me. I'm sick too. Mean people make us think that we're the ones who have a problem but we can take medicine to be better and they have to be different people to not suck.

I love you,

February

PS We're all lucky to have met Letty.

Ronnie called Letty to the bar once Jalopy had confirmed that Anders had left the building. They laughed together and talked about February's letter and Ronnie's performance.

"I told you I can get intense," Ronnie said.

Letty finished her drink and said it was about as hard to be intense giving it to a kid as it was to be memorable to a virgin. Then she dimmed herself to ask about February. Ronnie said he didn't know. Ronnie said that the letter had arrived without a mailman he'd seen, as had all of the others. That every time Letty finished with a Timothy for the past six months, Ronnie had showed up for work and there was a letter waiting for him. Letty nodded and did not ask if February was all right. Sometimes she did but that time she didn't. I don't think there was any particular reason for Letty's not asking about February other than you stop asking about things that don't change.

"And when is the big meeting with Daddy, then?" Ronnie asked.

"Tomorrow night," Letty blinked to rid herself of the things she didn't like thinking about in February. "I need to get a dress."

\*\*\*

Daddy had made a mistake. He'd been busy with a million other things and he'd happened to cross paths with Letty for a moment who asked him if she could be in charge of the Timothy Program at the Huxtable. The Timothy Program? Daddy laughed.

Yes, The Timothy Program, Letty said.

Daddy said all right and that they'd talk about it if she kept up being the best Bed Mama or he could ever imagine. Letty told him he could count on it.

This was the mistake Daddy had made. A promise made without metrics is the boss's cardinal sin.

So Letty, of course, goes and takes more davids and johns than every other Bed for weeks on end all the while going further and further over the top with timothies. At first, Daddy was good with it like he'd found twenty bucks he'd forgotten about it in his pants. The woman was a worker. Then came the complaints. Other Beds couldn't believe how extravagant Letty's timothy parties were and they'd ask Daddy why they couldn't they have that kind of budget for parties that actually made money. He would tell them that she was paying for them out of her pocket and that Jalopy, Ronnie, they were all helping Letty because they wanted to help Letty.

Didn't matter.

Not all of them, not even most of them, but a couple of the Beds had decided that Letty was getting special treatment and deserving of their scorn because there is balance in the universe and if no one else is going to do it then you have to be that balance yourself.

All of that said, jealousy in a whouse is regular weather so Daddy, Mama, most of the Beds, me – we didn't care. Daddy did watch the video of Ronnie and Letty stringing Anders up at the bar though – that was unusual. It had been a good while since Daddy had taken the time to watch a full video of a party, much less a timothy.

At first, Daddy laughed because the kid was terrified by Ronnie who Daddy knew to be a soft-palmed demon at worst. Daddy also laughed because the whole set up was clever, he had to give her that. Then his laugh reduced like soup on a stovetop because Holy Moly was Letty good. When you see someone that good at anything - sports, art, business - when you see someone that good at a thing and you know what goes into being that good then you sit and you simmer and you watch. Greatness makes you let go and Daddy's eyes went wistful watching Letty. He watched the video all the way through and for a few seconds even after it was over. Then he shook his head. Then he set up the meeting.

***

Then why do we even do this?

Because I want to make you happy.

Don't make this about me.

But it is about you!

This is not about me.

Then what is it about?

Stop already! It's plenty that you duck my face, you don't have to duck my questions too.

I told you that I didn't feel like it.

Then why would we have sex?

…Because I want to make you happy.

I'D BE HAPPY TO KISS MY WIFE

Be happy she let you screw her.

Oh for crying out loud!

You want understanding, I give you understanding. You want sex, I give you sex. What do you want from me?!

Again, this is not about me. I don't have to know what I want al –

– That's the problem –

– I DON'T HAVE TO KNOW what I want ALL of the time. But I'll tell you what. I know what I never want and I never want a wife who won't kiss me when I'm inside of her for the first time in six months.

Make me want you then.

That's bullshit!

You think I'm bullshit, OK. Then why do you want bullshit?

You think you're making me happy?

I'm doing the best that I can.

Well, you know, I'm not going to keep competing with you for you. That's what I'll say.

Please. Please be happy. Please. I can't do this if you're not happy. I know you don't believe me but it's true. I can't do anything if you're not happy, I can't kiss you, I can't talk with you, I can't look at you. So you say you want sex and it takes everything I have to do it for you. For you. And then you say that I'm not trying because I don't kiss you! Do you so not see me?

Now you're trying but you weren't before.

I am!

Yes, you are, that's what I'm saying. We agree. But you weren't before or you would have kissed me, that's what I'm saying. You have to admit that.

Oh my God.

Look, you're screaming at me right now, that's trying. You laid down and didn't flex for thirty seconds before – you think that's trying?

OK.

All I'm saying is that you have to admit that it is different effort levels.

Yup.

I'm not saying that you're not suffering or that I'm perfect, what I'm saying is that the words you are using with me to convey your feelings are incorrect. Do you agree?

Yup.

Oh come on. I'm trying too. I can't be right about anything?

Oh no, you're dead on right about plenty. You should keep going to your prostitutes.

Don't do that, come on.

No no, you're right. You need sex. You should go get soooo much sex.

I'm sorry I told you about that.

You're sorry you told me about that?! You're sorry you told me?

I don't know. I'm sorry, that's what I have to say. I'm sorry.

Don't touch me. You want to know why I didn't kiss you? I'll tell you, do you want to know?

I'm sorry, honey.

I didn't kiss you because it's disgusting. It's disgusting, that's why.

\*\*\*

A Special Penguin

Letty and Ronnie shopped Magazine Street for something to wear for the big talk with Daddy. Most of us who lived and worked underground and at night had a crush on New Orleans during the day. We loved that everyone had a party they were planning and another they were recovering from. Elaborate masquerades, bluesy fish fries, parades and parades and parades. New Orleans entertains 9 to 5. Stores are open, more or less. A few will even sell you stuff. But the cashiers have conversations you are interrupting.

Letty and Ronnie found a blue-grey dress that fit her but did not flaunt her. It went from her knee to her neck which made the face the focus not the boobs. But the boobs weren't smushed either. Ronnie told her it was professional and personable all at once. Ronnie told her this because Letty liked it and wanted to buy it but it cost more than she'd said she'd wanted to spend which was something like fifty dollars. Sometimes women will try to contain their excitement by containing the cost of their dress.

You like the dress, Ronnie said. Buy the dress.

Letty took a breath and pulled the dress closer to her and scrunched up her body and face. She closed one eye and looked at Ronnie through the other. He smiled and she let everything go and she laughed and she bought the dress and brought it back to the Bayou Fried.

Jalopy delayed activating the refrigerator elevator by asking her to wait for a special celebration beignet. Jalopy knew how much this meant to her and Jalopy was excited to have company that wasn't customers.

Letty gazed out the window wall while Jalopy fried. Between the drapes of willow droop she could make out pedestrians crisscrossing on the sidewalk. Letty always expected to see tourists when she looked out that wall waiting for the regular special beignets Jalopy used to bribe us of our company. Green visors, sixteen-fold graveyard map fiascos. But it never was the quaint bumbling she imagined.

It was poverty. Skittering poverty.

White shirts, black hats, and pants sagged or that didn't fit. Everyone walking much too fast or much too slow. People pushing laundry down the street.

The beignet was cinnamon and delicious and she went down with her dress after eating it. Ronnie stayed up top to talk with Jalopy.

A few hours after admitting this meant more than her than a fifty-dollar dress, Daddy greeted Letty at the refrigerator elevator in his penthouse basement. He took her hands and smooched in the direction of her cheeks.

"Look at that face!" he said.

She thanked him for having her and he said that the pleasure was his. He said that this was a long time coming. Her heart thumped.

Daddy palmed the small of Letty's back and pointed her towards the dinner table. It was stocked with small plates on bigger ones. Daddy was wearing a polo shirt with a crest on its breast tucked into a pair of pressed khaki slacks, brown leather belt and brown leather wingtips with flaps of greened gator hide.

He lifted his hands and clapped twice to call Petunia, the whouse girl, who was playing waitress that night. Then he winked to acknowledge how campy it was to summon someone like this. Letty smiled without laughing because she knew how much Petunia loved having a job and also because Letty had conflicting thoughts about how loud she was supposed to laugh.

Out came Petunia in a tuxedo jacket with a tail. Pink and white and pasty faced, her hair was freed from its usual ponytail which made her forehead seem more normal. Only one eye was bruised.

Daddy's little helper dawdled to them. She was thrilled. We'd seen it in her face earlier that day when Hildengarder made a pageant for those of us not included in the dinner. Not that Petunia ever made eye contact with anyone. She fixed her vision a foot or so off the ground and slightly to the left, about where most wall sockets are. But you could see how stoked Petunia was to have an extra special job ahead of her.

"Petunia," Daddy grinned, "Now where are the drinks, Petunia? Remember the drinks?"

Petunia's tongue rolled out of her mouth and onto her cheek.

"Remember the pop?"

She didn't move. He bent at the waist.

"…and the fizz?"

She gasped and fisted her hands and they shook. Daddy stood straight up again.

"Go on then, Petunia."

She exited electrocuted. Daddy called after her.

"Walk now, baby! Remember to walk."

Petunia glued her arms to her sides and shortened her stride like a good girl caught galloping by the lifeguard. Daddy offered his elbow to Letty. She took it and they wafted together to the table. Petunia returned with her tongue already deployed. She was [sort of] balancing two flutes of champagne streaming with effervescence on a silver tray. Daddy leapt to get the drinks before the floor claimed them.

"Excellent job, Petunia! Wouldn't you say so, Letty?"

"Beautiful. And I love your jacket, you look very official."

Petunia was bright with pride. Letty was her favorite Bed. Letty was pretty and nice.

"Now what do you say to Ms. Letty?" Daddy asked.

Letty looked softly upon Petunia. Petunia scratched her pants at the spot where her hands hung on their own. Her face was red where it wasn't blue.

"Go on then, honey," Daddy said.

Petunia balled her hands again.

"Thank you, Ms Letty."

\*\*\*

His is a Folksiness

Letty and Daddy ate purple potatoes fried in duck fat and shrimp a la jalapeno jelly.

They ate ribeye served rare and cheeses smooth,

Cheeses sharp,

Cheeses smelly.

And they talked about nights gone right and others gone wrong. And he laughed more loudly than her and she asked more penetrating questions than he. They both complimented the food. Daddy'd had a chef from up the road cook them dinner.

"Get it? Up the road?"

She did. She groaned. "I do."

"Careful who you go saying I do to, young lady." She laughed, he didn't. "Oh, if only I knew when I was you, that as our brains age and rot, all that's left are rhymes and things we think we remember our parents saying."

He wadded his napkin then threw it a foot in front of him onto the table. Daddy kept talking.

"You've lived so damned long people figure you're an interesting person. You get old and you get interesting, Letty, my love. Say, you don't have an Instagram do you?"

"Mama said that we're not supposed t-"

Daddy sneered.

"I know what she says – Courthouse says you ain't supposed to do what you do but you here now too, ain't you?"

He pulled out his phone. Letty didn't answer.

"Well even if you do, that's all right. I do anyhow. And I tell you, these girls on Instagram take these pictures, yeow! Young things too, 13, 14, pushing it out and making faces, coochie shots! I tell you, that's the world now. It's all internet. Whouses ain't nothing but for fun now."

He scrolled through social media and called out for Petunia. He didn't clap this time, instead Daddy used his words. Petunia zoomed in then screeched to a halt. Her speediness delighted him so he made a joke he made often.

"Whoa now! I tell you, why would they call it Downs when they so up!"

Petunia purred to herself, glad in the way a pet can be.

"Honey girl, could you call up to Jalopy and say that I'd like a coffee, plenty o cream and sugar. Tell ole boy it's for Daddy. Mademoiselle?"

He turned to Letty.

"Black coffee please," Letty leaned towards Daddy. "Do you want me to call?"

"Why ever for?" he asked.

Letty looked at Daddy like well-what-do-you-want-me-to-say. Daddy looked back at her with then-say-it on his face. Letty bent away from Daddy, back towards Petunia.

"Black coffee, please," Letty said.

Daddy nodded then Petunia scurried off.

"You gotta let people play their role, honey," Daddy said. "That's what being the boss is. You give a role, and you let the person themselves rise or fail."

"I understand that, Daddy," Letty said. "It's only that I've been here almost two years and I've only ever heard Petunia say three different things. The third of which was telling me thank you not an hour ago."

"See that! Growth!"

He slapped the table and shoved his phone further from his place setting like it were more dessert he was declining.

"Now Letty, tell me what's bugging you."

Letty said nothing was bugging her. Daddy said something was bugging her.

"This a hard way to make an easy living, Letty. Most times when a body wants to change something like you're about to tell me you want to, they got something bugging them."

Letty said that nothing was bugging her. Honestly, nothing. Daddy picked some persnickety steak from his teeth.

"So tell me what you would do with the timothies then," he said.

Letty said she loved the timothies. Daddy said he could see that. Letty said the Timothy was an awesome, unique, wonderful thing. That to work in any business where a portion of profit is dedicated towards making the world better is what life is actually about, she said. Daddy agreed. Letty said if anything, what she wanted was to make the other Beds approach timothies like she did. Daddy asked her to be specific. She told him to take Anders for example. Letty said that Anders had felt powerless and sort of like an orphan because his Dad was greedy and his Mom was checked out. So Letty manufactured a moment to make Anders feel strong and normal and protected too like someone in the world liked this misfit little boy. Then they slept together twice so he could be good at it once.

"Well not good," Letty said. "But at least not bad. Or not as bad."

"So do you want to be the boss of timothies?" Daddy asked.

"I mean, I want what's best," Letty said.

"Who you want what's best for? Army men? Them kids like the one you told me about? The women you live with? Who you want to have what's best? Yourself?"

"Definitely not me."

"Definitely not you?"

"Well yes, me. But this isn't about me, Daddy. I want what's best for everybody."

"Everybody then!"

"Everybody."

Petunia came back with a steaming white cardboard cup in each hand, one for Daddy, one for Letty. He took a drink of his.

"Perfect," he exaggerated his response to compliment his whouse girl. "Lots of cream and sugar, just perfect. Letty?"

Letty could see her coffee was tan because someone had put creamer in it. Letty said it was fine. Daddy giraffed towards the drink.

"Let me see that."

He saw that Letty had not received what she had ordered. Daddy turned to Petunia.

"Petunia, baby, Ms. Letty said black. Now I am disappointed in you. You go on back up there –"

"It's fine, really. It's only coffee."

"No, you asked for black."

"Really, it's fine."

"Now Letty, you gotta let a body fix a problem when they make it too."

Letty said she understood but that she'd just as soon get on with it. Daddy said all right then widened his eyes at Petunia like a teacher at a Kindergartener who wouldn't share. Her face dropped.

"You listen better next time Petunia, go on now."

Tears welled in Petunia's eyes, both of them, although she only wiped one because the other was still too tender to the touch. She trudged away.

"Now Letty, where were we?"

"We were talking about how –"

"Yes yes, everybody. Well, you are an absolute star. And I want to be real honest with you, that's my concern."

Letty moved back from the table so she could cross her legs.

"What do you mean?"

Letty crossed her legs.

"You don't know if you want to be a star or a boss yet, honey. All you know is you like doing something and all I know is you're good at doing it."

Letty crossed her legs the other way.

"OK."

Daddy sipped then swallowed and waved the whole conversation to a halt.

"Let me say that I'm promoting you."

"You are?!"

"You backed me into it. You're in charge of timothies. If you want to be that is."

"AHHHH!"

She shot up out of her chair and threw her arms around him.

"Daddy, we are going to help so many people!"

"Everybody, I know. But hold on, there's more. And I want to say something to you too."

Letty let go of his neck and sat back down without crossing her legs. Daddy continued.

"First off we gonna start with a pilot. I want you to pick one Bed to start with and then we'll go from there."

Letty was shining. He kept on.

"Letty, what you did with that boy and all the others was something to be proud of. You done so well you cornered your Daddy. So I don't have a lot of options here but to promote you or let you spin your wheels. So I'm promoting you. But running the business isn't doing the business, Letty. My concern is that what you think is strategy, this whole staging the timothy's issues then resolving them and canoodling, my concern is that all that other stuff didn't matter as much as you think it did. That you are a gorgeous woman and that you are blue ribbon in the sack and that that's that. That you have invented strategy to explain away something unfair."

Daddy paused so Letty crossed her legs.

"Letty, I learned this having been alive as long as I have. When you're really talented at something, like one of the best on earth talented, truly. And you are Letty, you are that talented. Well, it isn't fair, honey. You know it. It isn't fair that you you and Petunia Petunia. But we got us a business, Letty. You remember that people is different. Here's one my Daddy used to say to me growing up – he said the special ones prove themselves so by trying to be more of the same and failing."

"I'm going to be a good boss, Daddy. You know I will."

"I know we're all rooting for you. That include Mama, y'know."

"I know."

"She don't think like you do, Letty. She don't come from a place where a whouse did a thing like timothies. A whouse to Mama just a way to make money."

"I know."

"It don't mean she don't like you and it don't mean we ain't got a real business too. I love the timothy, and I love you love it even more. But you remember that when it come to it, everybody either wanna be rich or the pretty thing a rich person purchase."

"It's fine, Daddy."

"We all like yo-"

"- I get it –"

"Hold on, woman. Damn."

"Sorry."

"I know you're excited honey, but slow down. I wish I could go back to tell myself the same thing when I was your age. Slow. Down. Every swing ain't your last chance to get a hit. You cannot believe how long a life is, Letty. What I was saying is that we all like you but you gotta be a leader now. People ain't gotta like the leader."

"They have to follow the leader."

"Correct."

"Daddy, I'd like to work with February."

"Oh Letty…not February."

"Yes February. You know what, Daddy – yes February. I'm tired of being the only person here who thinks of her."

"I haven't seen the woman in weeks."

"Well, Daddy, the woman works here. And you know what, she believes in me. Did you know she has written a letter to every timothy I've had. Every single one."

"I imagine she has."

"So, yes February. She's a part of this whouse too. Isn't she?"

"She is," Daddy said.

"I can do this," Letty said.

He stood up.

"Who would dare doubt Letty?" he said.

Letty stood up too. They walked back to the refrigerator elevator.

"Also, Daddy, I'd like to observe a few timothies, see what the other Beds are doing already. I have an idea but I'd like to see it for myself."

"I'll arrange it."

"Thank you, Daddy," Letty said. "Thank you for the opportunity. And dinner too, what a treat!"

"Yes indeed," he said and watched her think fifty things at once. "Letty," Daddy said.

"What?"

"Letty."

"Daddy."

"Honey, I want you to hear me."

"I always hear you, Daddy."

"Don't go serving every dinner on the fine china."

"OK."

"Did you hear me?"

"It's paper plates and being a boss for me, Daddy."

"Oh Letty."

"Oh Daddy."

Then she got into the refrigerator elevator and went back to her room like she had a prayer of getting to sleep like it was any other night.

***

In his younger and more vulnerable years, Ronnie'd had a david who would lay with him for hours. The david was old enough to have grey chest hairs but still spry enough to bend without shattering. About the age Ronnie had found himself arrived at when he was helping scare timothies straight with Letty. He was such a man, that david was. That's how Ronnie remembered experiencing him.

Such a man.

Masculine in proportions of body, not a muscle bound caricature or even an especially fit specimen. Slight gut, carpeted on the chest and arm and crotch. Dark too. Is every real man dark? Ronnie being impressed and young would ask the guy questions about life. Ridiculous gigantic questions about purpose and happiness – the type that campers ask their counselors. The David of davids would clear his throat, shake off the cobwebs gathered after enjoying someone young and say:

*Ashes to ashes,*
*dust to dust.*
*We live when can*
*And die when we must.*

Ronnie used to love that. It used to quench him. Ronnie would wish to end up as that david had – fleshy and poignant. Now, arrived at his age, all Ronnie could see when he remembered those days was himself. A kid prone to singsong and tiger lilies so long as the speaker delivered it with aloof conviction. The david was cumming and rhyming and saying nothing. Hooey well worded is well-worded hooey and good god are young people young.

Ronnie saw the same Letty that Daddy did. A fantastic young woman so talented and so trusting that you had an urge to slap her down yourself so no one actually awful would do it first.

***

Letty observed three different Beds fulfill their timothy quotas. She'd set up shop in what looked to be the control room – this dingy domain of chairs on wheels and keyboards and fans and screens and screens and screens.

The Blonde, The Smart One, and The Big Redhead. This is what Letty saw:

### The Big Redhead

Ensign Steve only wanted to talk. Not uncommon for men to want to only talk, at first anyhow. He told The Big Redhead all about the three street treats of Thailand – street food, street performers, and street walkers. Two of the three will get you sick he'd said and The Big Redhead laughed that glorious massive laugh of hers.

Being on a boat with men for months, Ensign Steve was no stranger to navigating the line between homosexuality and relief. But now that he was home for at least a few months, he was in need of behavioral retractions.

His wife wouldn't like it if he told her to jam anything up his ass.

But that was how he was used to cumming.

So that's how he came.

And he needed to be cumming correctly for his wife because his wife was a good wife so didn't prioritize her orgasm but if her man stayed corked, she felt it an indictment of her value on Earth.

The Big Redhead said it sounded like Ensign Steve's wife really loved him.

He said "I know" and stared through the wall.

The Big Redhead conveyed her concern for Ensign Steve's situation and said she'd be happy to use a strap on or dildo. He appreciated the gesture but said that wasn't what he was looking for. He was looking for an onramp to normalcy. He knew he wouldn't get there in a single day but he couldn't think of a better place for a kickstart than the Huxtable. If The Big Redhead could maybe get him going in the right direction, give him some homework even – he'd do it, he would totally do his homework – that's what Ensign Steve needed. Homework.

The Big Redhead suggested Ensign Steve starve himself out.

"Same what happened on the boat only backwards. No contact like that with anybody, no jacking off, nothing but your wife. Try that for a couple weeks."

Ensign Steve thought on the issue then asked to see what kind of toys The Big Redhead had. He spent the next twenty minutes on all fours, simpering with a simulation half a foot inside of him. Ensign Steve eventually came then he asked The Big Redhead if he was weird and she said no. He asked again if he was weird and added that she could tell him, honestly, he could take it. The Big Redhead said of all the things she knew about Ensign Steve, that he could take it was on the top of the list. He laughed and went home.

The Smart One

The miracle of the penis is never better demonstrated than on badly burned boys. Which is not to say that it's fit for a dip in magma, no, the male member is a dainty instrument. But in Hildengarder's lengthy history with people on the surviving side of fires, the number of dangles maintaining their sashimi grade on otherwise tepenyaki bodies was memorable as recurring lotto numbers. At least until she brought it up to The Smart One.

"94% covered. According to records, he 94%. But there it is like nothing ever went wrong before. Ain't it something that God spare soldiers' dicks?"

Mama handed the dossier to The Smart One who leafed through paperclipped pictures.

"He spares the bottom of feet too," The Smart One said.

Mama smiled the smile of a cat with a caught tweety bird.

"Do my ears deceiveth me? Did the heathen say that God spareth the sole?"

Getting one over on any Atheist feels good, but to nail The Smart One was special treasure in the Huxtable. The woman was sharp. Unless she'd taken too many pills. Then she was less sharp.

The Smart One, who considered the miracle of penis placement level with the miracle of homophones, withdrew one of the pictures of Sergeant Jorge Perez from his file. The photograph showed the middle of his thigh to a few inches above where his belly button used to be. His skin looked like what happens when you let a swirl of ketchup and mustard dry on a paper plate. Like when you let a five-year old serve themselves at a barbecue.

The Smart One pointed to the oasis amidst the meat loaf.

"It's where something is. No one is protecting the bottom of a foot, it evolved to be in a place where it's unlikely to burn. Armpits too. See?"

Mama was an olive branch once she'd felt she'd won.

"Sounds to me, honey, like one of us saying Spanish and da other saying Espanol. Man's dick is his purpose. You gonna take him?"

The Smart One said she would. So they slotted Perez into a weekday window.

Wednesday would be a sunny stormy day in New Orleans, Louisiana. Perez the crispy timothy arrived in sunglasses and a sweater and a beanie and a compression suit.

"Are you Oxy or Vicodin?" The Smart One asked.

She held a bottle in each hand while Perez loitered by the threshold. She could see Perez was still uncomfortable, both in the Huxtable and his new brittle body. A different burned person had described it to her as if he had been rendered a raw nerve covered by fingernail clippings.

"Zohydro."

She tossed the bottles over her shoulder.

"Zozo?! Yowzers! 'Oxy or Vicodin' like I'm hardcore! I must've seemed like a real tool talking about all this kiddy stuff with Zozo in your pocket."

Perez didn't smile because he couldn't. On the other hand, he kept his sunglasses and doo-rag on because he wanted to. The Smart One turned on a lamp above the bed. Between the pills she'd thrown and kit she'd laid out, she had a few things to clean up. The room was simple – a bed, two chairs, and a conjoined bathroom. She'd learned to take major burn victims in boring environments. The Smart One was the go-to Bed when it came to trauma patients.

"I've only done Zozo once," she said. "Knocked me on my ass!!"

The Smart One paused before returning the razor blade and mirror to the sock drawer.

"I shouldn't do a line of Zozo, right?" she asked. "That'd be nuts, right?"

The face remaining on Perez rasped.

"I wouldn't know," it said.

"Why not?"

"Are you a moron?" the face asked.

"So…"

The Smart One parked on the bed.

"…no. This is not how we do this. If I ask a question, you answer directly. Especially while we're sober. When we get high, then we can loosen the rules up. Anyhow, if the answer to 'why not?' is 'because I've never done it so I'm uncomfortable' that's acceptable. Say that. Do you want a blow job?"

He stayed at the door. She asked him again if he wanted a blow job. He said he didn't.

"Why not?" she asked.

"Because I don't."

"Give me a Zozo. Will you let me suck your dick then?"

"You'll pass out."

"I'll take half. You can have the other half."

"I won't be able to get hard."

"So you do want a blow job, then?"

"No."

"Why not?"

"Have you ever done this before?"

"Answer my question."

"Because I'm disgusting, moron."

"To whom, genius?"

"You."

"Incorrect."

"Well I'm disgusting."

"Not to me."

"Then me."

"And what does that have to do with me?"

"Have you ever done thi –"

"Ah ah ah – answer my question."

"Nothing. It has nothing to do with you."

"Continue."

"Have you ever done this before?"

"Have I ever done what before?"

"Been with a piece of bacon."

"Yes."

"Sexually?"

"Yes."

"Do you still want a Zohydro?"

The Smart One took the pill then had careful sex with Perez. The Tetris of their copulation was less complicated then Perez had expected – he lied on his side and she did all the work. But the call to expend energy is strong in any nineteen-year old, much less the only living debris of an exploded armored vehicle. Perez experienced a stabbing in his kit kat ribcage when he tried to surprise The Smart One by spanking her. Perez used to spank women because he used to give it real hard because he was an idiot teenager who mistook the slap of flesh and the cries of women as evidence of ecstasy which was evidence of his masculinity/value/you-can't-leave-me-now. The Smart One told him to stop, which he had already done because it hurt like his lungs were on crucifixes. Between his agony and arousal, Perez relented on the issue of oral sex. He finished in her mouth then left. The Smart One zonked out.

### The Blonde

The Blonde's principle concern was fairness. And not having to be treated like everybody else.

"I very much doubt that *every* girl is reaching their quota. You mean to have me believe that *she* is completing two every month? Every month?!" The Blonde tilted her skull towards The Black who was crossing the Stage. Ronnie and The Black shared a glance.

"Daddy run a tight ship," Ronnie said.

The refrigerator elevator coasted in. The timothy had arrived. The Blonde vocalized.

"Bleck."

She kneaded herself on the barstool like she were picking a wedgie. Then she planted her elbow on the oak and hung herself against her hand. The Blonde was wearing a brown velour jump suit and the granniest granny panties she could find. Only foundation on her face. No mascara, no shadow, and obviously no lip gloss. She'd even scrapped chapstick for fear of its glisten.

"Howdy!"

His name was George Dithers. He had worn a brown suit himself, though his was pressed cotton rather than fluffed billiards table. He'd buttoned both buttons on his door-to-door-salesman jacket. The dry cleaner's tag peaked up from his collar like a flag for the nation of nincompoop. He sat two stools down from The Blonde at the bar, minding the Bed as if she were nothing but a fellow visitor. George ordered a drink.

"A beer, please. Whatever's cheapest. Oh I'm sorry, are you open yet?"

Ronnie set a napkin on the bartop in front of George.

"Sure am. You prefer something light or dark?"

George squared his shoulders to talk with Ronnie and Ronnie squared his shoulders to talk with George. This boxed The Blonde out.

"Whatever's cheapest," George said.

You could see that The Blonde was allergic to the phrase 'whatever's cheapest.'

Ronnie took his leave to get the timothy's drink. George shifted his weight and happened upon The Blonde glaring at him. He nodded.

"Ma'am."

*...whatever's cheapest...*

Ronnie arrived with the beer, a foamy golden Belgian. George licked his chops.

"How much I owe yuh?"

"No charge, Mr. Dithers."

"Saaaaaaaay."

George grabbed the drink with all of the sophistication of an oil rigger. He saluted to Ronnie who bowed a bit. Then George Dithers took a mighty slug of his beer. His neck bent backwards to provide for a more direct dump. The Blonde was aghast.

*WHATEVER'S CHEAPEST???!!!*

"Ah!"

He wiped off the suds moustache with the sleeve of his jacket and slapped his stomach.

"Ma'am." George nodded at the Blonde whose chin quivered and nostrils flared. Ronnie was tempted to let the situation play itself out but as satisfying as it was to watch The Blonde meltdown, the fallout lasted weeks. Ronnie stepped in.

"Perhaps champagne for your date, Mr. Dithers?"

"Who dat?"

"Your date, Mr. Dithers, would you care to order her champagne."

George Dithers looked down the bar. The Blonde glared. George looked back to Ronnie.

"Her?"

"Yes Mr Dithers."

"Her? She my date? You sure?"

"Yes Mr Dithers."

George shot from his barstool and hopped to The Blonde. He dried his palms on his pants.

"My God, please excuse me, ma'am. I'm George. George Dithers."

He reached out to shake her hand. She leered. Then, slow like a koala eats eucalyptus, The Blonde extended to pinch the top of his manners. She managed to say she was charmed.

"I'm the charmed one, I tellya,"

George pulled out the stool next to her.

"May I?" he asked.

"Mhm."

George climbed aboard. Then Ronnie delivered The Blonde a glass of frizzing white wine from a French sounding vineyard in California. Ronnie winked and The Blonde sneered to Ronnie like George Dithers wasn't there. Then she blinked loudly and ran her hand through her hair and collected the flute's stem between her thumb and middle digit and fanned out her leftover fingers. The Blonde lifted her wine off of the bartop. George hoisted what was left of his beer. They clinked without toasting.

"Honestly, I think somebody messed up. How come I get someone like you."

George guzzled the last bit of beer. The Blonde did not look at him.

"Figured they'd give me a moose. When I saw you, I thought you were here waiting for a movie star or something. Didn't want to bother you. Thought I'd get drunk."

"Mr Dithers?" Ronnie surrounded the depleted drink.

"Oh, uh, I better not."

"It provokes and unprovokes."

Ronnie retired into the Huxtable, thus rendering The Blonde shipwrecked on the island of timothy. She hated it when there was no one left to see how much better she was than who she was with.

"Never been a bubbles guy myself. Not even much of a drinker. Save my money, that's what I do."

She parroted him.

"What are you saving for, George Dithers?"

George leaned his ear into her ever so slightly. He'd sat on the wrong side because he'd been hurried because he'd been so embarrassed earlier.

"What am I saving for? Oh, uh, nothing much. House maybe. Family. Rainy day. Might have to take care of my pop."

"Is he ill?"

"What's that?" He ducked a good foot into her. She spoke with disdain for the syllables she'd been forced to repeat.

"Ill. Is he ill? Ill. Is your father ill?"

"Ah, ill!"

George's head sprung back up to talking height.

"No, he's not ill. He's old. You know, getting up there."

"Your mother?"

"Long gone. See this?"

He loosened his shirt collar and The Blonde found herself looking. She followed his neck to his ear. It was stuffed with a contraption. He pulled out a necklace.

"Gold and silver. Gold's 14 carat, the silver is pure though."

"Did she give that to you?"

She lifted the jewelry to inspect it.

"No. I thought I could get you closer if I pulled out something shiny."

Her eyes switched from the necklace to his goofy grill. A demure came upon The Blonde. She laid the braided metal on top of his shirt and tie. She went back to looking at anything that wasn't George Dithers as she had before. Only this time, she wasn't repulsed when she looked away.

"George the Saver has an impressive necklace," she said to the bar.

"You like it?"

The Blonde flipped her vertebra to take a big swig of classy white wine.

"It's magical," she said.

"You're magical," he said.

After satisfying the letter of the law, The Blonde did not withdraw from George Dithers. This was irregular. The Blonde was an escaped convict after the average timothy. But with George she swathed herself on his bare chest. She giggled at his musings and synced up her breath with his and when he gifted her the necklace, she blushed in embarrassment and surprise and ooey gooey gratitude. But she did not say it was too much. She did not say the necklace was more than she could accept. The Blonde did not say no to George the hard of hearing timothy.

Of course the necklace had been from his Mother.

*** 

The Announcement

Daddy gathered us up to tell us about Letty's promotion.

He huddled us up under the Stage's fluorescent lighting setting and started by thanking us and saying how excited for and proud of Letty he was. He said he was proud of everyone and that it was a powerful moment in a man's life when the people he trained start to pass him by. He gave kudos to Jalopy and to Ronnie for their willingness to play along with Letty. He figured most people had watched the video he had so then he asked if Ronnie would mind telling everyone how exactly Anders

"knew the name Daddy down here!"

The Blonde snorted because Daddy had made the joke. The Blonde had not seen the video. Then she covered her clavicle and made deeply knowing eyes with Daddy. Ronnie stood up and said.

"Because I told it to him."

We all laughed at that. Since we laughed, Petunia checked with Hildengarder who smiled to say that it was all right to be like us and laugh. Petunia couldn't go too hard though because her rib had been cracked the night before.

We laughed it out then Daddy told us that Letty would be taking a bigger role as far as timothies went. He said a pilot program was under development. He said that the pilot would be with February as per Letty's request. February who was not there in the meeting. February who hadn't been at any meeting in a long time. Then he asked if Letty wanted to say anything. She did.

Letty thanked Daddy then said that she understood she was a maniac and that not everyone was going to take timothies like she did. We chuckled about that. She said that was fine but that having a job where you help people was the best kind of life to have. She mentioned The Big Redhead and how flexible she was to doing the things her timothies wanted rather than what she thought they needed. Letty said she could learn a lot from that. Letty said that instead of looking at it as though timothies were chores we had to do, that timothies were our chance to experiment during free fares in order to grow our offerings. To do better by the world, sure, but to do better by our johns and davids. Timothies were the path to more money. This was what Letty said she learned watching The Big Redhead

Letty said that doing better with timothies didn't mean the work itself had to be boring. She pointed out finding shared interests with them as The Smart One had. Why not have a good time with timothies? This was what Letty said she learned watching The Smart One.

Then Letty mentioned how excellent The Blonde was with giving timothies the chance to be generous. And how awesome generosity for a timothy must feel. Timothies wish they could pay, she said. That's an important thing to remember. No one wants to be a timothy and giving them a way to pay makes them feel more like men. Giving men a chance to be of value to you, that's what Letty said she learned from the Blonde.

Nobody chooses to be a timothy, Letty said. And what mattered, what really mattered, she said, was that when it came to timothies or johns or davids or each other, whatever, what matters is that we know in our souls that we are doing our best. When we know we tried our hardest then we know we did it. Letty said she didn't want to be so presumptuous as to think she'd teach that to anyone, but she said she hoped that's what other Beds saw when they saw Letty with timothies.

She finished and most of us clapped, well we all clapped but The Blonde also rolled her eyes and Letty noticed but that was all right – sometimes you've got to hold true and let bitches be bitches. Besides, Letty was in front of an earnest applause, not a standing ovation or anything, but an earnest applause for a good woman. We'd heard her and we were happy for her, or at least those of us who weren't in the process of balancing how happy for and threatened by someone we should be were happy for Letty. But I do have to imagine that all of us, with or without screaming egos were all thinking the same thing:

Oh Letty... not February.

\*\*\*

To Randy F.

You don't know me but you should go back to playing music. I bet you know you were better than you say you were, now, too. I say I used to be bad but I know I wasn't. I say that to have an excuse when I don't want to do things that I like to do but I think make me look stupid. I think you are also doing that. I think it is probably also about that you don't make money doing it so you think you look stupid again.

I love you,

February

PS We're all lucky to have met Letty.


To Mr. Smith

You don't know me but you should tell your son that you have cancer. I know you say that you are trying to not burden him and his family (which is also your family) but what you are really doing is trying not to feel sad. I also do not tell people I love how I feel so that they won't feel bad and I won't have to feel worse than I already do. But this is your last chance and you should let yourself feel sad because then you'll feel his love too.

I love you,

February

PS We're all lucky to have met Letty.

To Bill

You don't know me and I'm sorry I don't know any more about you but I know that you're with Letty so you want your life to get better and it will too.

I love you,

February

PS We're all lucky to have met Letty.

\*\*\*

To no one's surprise, Letty was unable to make contact with February. Letty called and Letty texted, Letty knocked on February's door. Letty would spend the daylight between davids telling the door that never opened that she would be back again in an hour and a half, then she'd say Actually let's call it two hours to be safe. Then she'd come back in an hour and a half and she'd chirp that she was checking in. Letty would stand there in the hallway hearing nothing but the kind of quiet where you know someone is right there, not saying anything back.

Letty thought she couldn't tell Daddy that she was unable to get in contact with February because that would be all the proof Daddy would need to tell Letty that she wasn't a leader. But she thought she could tell me.

I listened to Letty then I told her to go tell Daddy. She deflated and said noooooooo like a balloon loses its helium. Letty, I said, if anything, you abandoning February would be proof to Daddy that you have a better chance as a leader than he'd thought before. And you're giving the old man a way to be right. Not only right, right while you're being wrong and young and cute and gosh Daddy thank you for the advice – I'll listen better next time. Then he gets to say, no, if you weren't such a plucky beauty that you wouldn't be you. Then you say thank you, he says no thank YOU and you do the whole deal without having to deal with February.

Letty said she knew and that I was funny and right too. She said she'd give it a week. She had those addict liar eyes on her when she another week and I wanted to scold the stupid out of her. Instead I said, Good luck Letty and she said thank you and left and I popped online to get the one thing I knew would get that door open for her. Letty hadn't been around as long as I had so she didn't know how to get February to do things yet.

\*\*\*

Three days after we talked, Petunia came to Letty and presented her a shoe box.

"What's this, Petunia?"

Petunia blushed and didn't say anything because it was intimidating to be all alone with Letty. I'd written her a note and put it on the box that said

Letty, since it's too late to stop you now, try giving this to February. Might take her a minute, but she'll come around for this. She always does.

Letty removed the lid and saw a puppy dog. It was tan with black ear flaps and bug eyes. It was a bulldog pug mix. The puppy shook not his tail but his entire hind quarters. Letty melted.

"Oh my God I'm supposed to give you away but I'm going to steal you and keep you instead!"

Letty set down the box and held up the pug who was a boy. Folds of skin gathered like a necklace of brains where Letty gripped him. His tongue dangled happily, dopily.

Letty asked Petunia if she wanted to pet him. Petunia's tongue came out too and she bunched her hands by her mouth. Letty said it was all right and Petunia reached her miniature fingers without much moving her hands from her face. The dog wheezed and Petunia touched its back. She made a murmur in her throat because the doggy was very sweet and didn't mind that Petunia was rubbing him.

They did that for a little then Letty said she had to get the puppy to her new mommy. So Letty said good bye and spun the dog around to face Petunia and said "Good bye Petunia" on his behalf and waved his paw. Petunia thrummed again then waved and limped off because she'd sprained her ankle flinching the night before. She knew she wasn't supposed to flinch, she was trained not to flinch, but sometimes you flinch.

Letty headed down the hall. She stopped at the door no one could seem to open. Letty knocked then said

"February, I have someone here who wants to meet you."

Letty stood outside of February's barricade, holding the puppy in her arms. He was happy to be where he was so the little guy didn't move other than when he licked his face or Letty's. When he did lick Letty's face, she gasped and laughed like you do when a dog goes straight for your mouth. Then she pulled away and scratched his head and held him high and tight and safe. The puppy googled his eyes about the hall, taking in wherever it was that life had taken him to now. He didn't breathe so much as he snored.

Letty and her buddy stayed like that for a few minutes. Didn't knock but the once, didn't say anything else either. He would scope out the new digs and then he'd remember how awesome it was to lick Letty's face and he'd do that. Letty would laugh and his tag would make little clink sounds.

Then came a voice came behind the door that didn't open.

Not a voice from deep inside the room, oh no, a voice from directly behind the door like it had been there waiting.

Waiting.

"Dogs aren't people, Letty."

The voice was casual and a little annoyed and keep in mind that Letty hadn't so much as seen February in about three months by that point. Letty looked at the door to figure out a response. Since she was focusing on forging ahead with the relationship that stood between her and the next evolution of her life, Letty stopped managing the distance between the puppy's head and hers. He took the opportunity to pounce and he lovelicked her to the physical limits of lovelicking. But Letty didn't laugh this time, the licking didn't make her feel loved or happy or cute gross, it annoyed her. So this time Letty didn't cuddle the puppy away from her face, instead, she yanked him a little from her head and shifted her weight to hold him off to the side. The puppy yipped and like a spark, the door ripped open.

***

Be advised that you don't love me.

Thank you for saying that you do love me, it's very kind of you.

You don't actually love me though, which is fine by me, don't feel like I'm asking you to leave or anything because I'm not. I'm telling you this because you're too sweet to even know what it is to love someone yet and I'd like it to hurt less for you later on when you stop confusing hope with love and finally see me. Also I'd like to feel less trapped which I know you don't mean to be making me feel but you are.

We can have sex but it's only sex OK?

OK.

***

The door could only crack an inch open because it was held in place by the interior chain lock. An eyeball wide strip of face looked out.

"Is the dog OK?!" February said and saw Letty and the puppy see her. February darted away from the opening. Then the door slammed close.

"February," Letty said

"Yeah?"

"Hello, February."

"Hello Letty."

"Do you think we could come in?"

"Dogs aren't people, Letty. So you lied to me when you said someone wanted to meet me and again right now when you said we. It's you. It's you and it."

Then February's body betrayed her by making noises when she slid it down the back of the door and plopped it onto the floor. Letty grinned and the puppy was well-mannered.

"I apologize for that February. I didn't mean to lie to you."

"You can't come in."

Letty didn't move and neither February hidden by the door and cloaked in the quiet. Letty didn't respond this time. She had never been like that before; Letty had always been the one to ease the pressure of silence. How many more people would get what they want if they'd learned how to shut up, stand up, and obviously want something?

"I won't be able to take care of it if I leave, Letty and I won't let it stay here either. You can't do that either. Promise. It can't live here without me."

"I promise."

"Good.

"Where are you going, February?"

"If I leave. I said if. If. If."

"Oh. Well are you leaving?"

"Is it a boy?"

"It is. He is."

"It sounds like it's dying."

"He's fine. He's part bulldog so he sounds like this. He's all right though."

"It's all right, not him. It."

"It's all right."

"It has fleas."

Letty turned to the puppy which had been all over her room and licked her face too. She continued to hold him, loving still and actively trying to filter what February had said through the February filter, but Letty was ever so slightly aware of fleas too.

"I don't think it has fleas, February."

"What's its name?"

"It doesn't have one yet. I thought his new mommy would want to do that."

Then the voice said hmf and February's body made lots of noises because February was standing it up. Then the doorknob did a slow somersault. The door opened again but leaked all the way in this time, dragged by its own gravity. This exposed both February and her room in their entireties.

"Then he's Oscar. And he's not a person so I'm not a mommy. Come in, he needs to eat."

\*\*\*

February's Lair

February lived inside the child of a ransom note and the hyper media consumer culture. Her walls were filled with scraps of magazine ads arranged into unintended sentences that [sort of] said things in between images of components of women. A nose, a neck, bunches of eyes. Quarter completed crafts projects all over the place too.

February herself was in her chic gypsy uniform: well-fitting blue jeans on her well-shaped legs and tattered, multi-colored blouses covering what she had always wished were bigger breasts. How February had longed for breasts. But February was flat chested which bothered her but not men. Long dirty blond hair sometimes straight and sometimes braided Sacagawea style. She had a thin pretty face with a crooked nose that was either detracting or spectacular depending on your position on asymmetry in thin pretty faces.

Letty came into the room and February zoomed from Papier Mache station to jewelry assembly kit to Letty who was holding the puppy. Then February hammered Oscar with an intense inspection. Letty noted that the door was still open.

Then February flicked her wrist.

"Crap," she said and she buzzed into her bathroom. Letty heard February rummaging in drawers or cabinets in the bathroom.

"February?"

Then there was a clang and February said "Ah ha!" Next Letty heard her moving some sort of newspaper or big cardboard thing. Then a faucet turned on and off.

"February?"

February returned with two silver dog bowls, one full of water and the other of kibble. Oscar, the puppy, kicked his legs and swam his arms. So Letty let him down while February put the bowls on the ground. Oscar dove straight for the water. His rump wiggled. February grimaced and said Crap then she knelt down to pick up a piece of kibble.

"Here you go, Oscar, you dum dum. You eat this, see. Eat."

The puppy stopped drinking water to watch February. See Oscar, eat. She exaggerated the chewing motion. Letty looked at February.

And then Oscar the puppy went to the food bowl. He behaved as if he'd been presented with options, he'd thought it through and made the call. Letty stopped looking at February and laughed. Between the puppy being ugly lovable in that way bullpugs are, February being a zigzag, and the whole thing working, all Letty could say is laugh like you do when you see two druggie convicts kiss and you have to admit they make a cute couple.

"Wow," Letty said.

"What do you do when it is your fault but you're not doing it on purpose?"

"I'm sorry?"

"I'm nervous, I love you."

"That's fi —"

"I know you're the only one who likes me. And Oscar but he doesn't count."

"I think he counts, February."

"You're the only one, Letty."

"No I'm not, February."

Oscar kept eating the dog food February had waiting in her bathroom. Letty and February kept talking.

"Yes you are Letty. You're the only one who likes me and you only like me because everyone else doesn't and you don't think that's very nice of them because it isn't and you're awesome. The other girls hate me. They say I'm racist because I don't do African Americans. But I'm not racist. I would do African Americans if I could do African Americans. But I can't do African Americans because I'm too little. I'm too little so they can't fit, Letty. They cannot get in. Other girls always hate me without asking me anything about myself – they see something that I can't change and they get mean because most everybody thinks if they can see it that they can change it but they never see themselves, Letty. Not really. Most everybody is waiting to gang up on someone and it's usually someone who seems weird but is really just little. You care, Letty. I know you do and so telling you feels sad and good. That's why I'm February. It's the littlest. I'll take care of Oscar."

Then Letty said that Beds can be tough and asked February about the Timothy Project. What did she know and would she do it? February said she didn't know anything and that yes she would do it. They talked it over while Oscar ate and Letty said she had to go because of a david but maybe they could keep eating over dinner? February said she'd already had dinner but they could talk later. It was 2:30 in the afternoon. Letty left.

As Letty was leaving, she noticed a word etched long ago on the dog bowls February had brought out.

They each read "Oscar."

\*\*\*

A lot of people don't think pretty women are workers. Those people will use words to describe pretty women with their friends that mean sex appeal or sexuality in the dictionary but mean women are poopy in those people's sentences. And the kicker is that a ton of the people who are like that are the ones who pay us money to make them feel better about themselves through the very faculties they hurl at us as insults during their regular lives as upstanding citizens.

Have you ever slept with a hypocrite? Someone who you know will cry out for you and need you then use your reputation like a rag to rub out any stain on their sport coat? Live a while, honey, you will. And you'll probably find out that you'd been doing that for a whole mess more years than you'd ever imagined. Then you'll promise not to be so naïve next time.

It wasn't that Letty failed to see the distasteful inconsistencies between human beings having sex and human humans playing society, she wasn't Pollyanna. It was that Letty saw the cause. She saw the pain of assholes. And you can only know something and not doing anything about it for so long until you are no longer yourself.

So Letty spent the next few days and nights putting every free minute she had toward moving her project forward with February. Letty would dip out between davids, hustle over to February's and work. A half hour, an afternoon, it didn't matter, if Letty's day had airspace then it went to the project.

February would answer the door because February always answered the door for Letty now, Oscar curled up on the bottom corner of her bed.

Finally, a plan emerged. Here I am this barnacle of a sex worker, and I was so happy for Letty that I smiled for a month. Because it is an incredible thing when you get to watch someone you like turn their passion into a plan.

And it was a good plan too!

It was empowering. It gave everyone a role to play. Letty, February, The Black, The Smart One, The Big Redhead, The Blonde, The Mistress, all of us.

Although, you could see which parts of the plan had come from February. For instance, they were going with a lady timothy which was 100% February.

This might not mean anything to you but there is a particular type of woman who works in the sex business who only ever has sex with other women. No, not a lesbian. Oh please, you're long past being straight or queer by your second second in the sex business. But women who require their customers be women are a funny lot. Ever met a loner who you can see hates to be alone? Sort of like that. I don't know. Hard to describe girls who only go with girls. But ask anyone who is in the sex business and they'll know what I'm talking about.

Anyhow, a lady timothy meant more work and less sex. Ladies demand pageantry of the evening in a different way than do men. Men want a ballgame and a blow job, women want opera and conversations in spots with ambience and foreplay and a touch of penetration. I'm exaggerating. There are obviously men who want more and women who want less, but when you look at the population as a whole, men don't like excess until they get into bed. Then they don't trust you unless it's yoga poses and showgasms, like if they haven't so riddled with you desire to move you to uncomfortable positions that it hasn't been real. Women are inverted, they'll savor a cheesy musical but they want verisimilitude in the sack.

So Letty and February finalized this plan. They distributed it to all of us and there was some pushback, as you'd expect. Some of us didn't want to spend the time and energy on it and some resented being told what to do by another Bed. In the end, we all agreed to do it because Daddy had said so. But there was chirping in the recesses. So it goes to work with people.

When the day did come, there was juice in the Huxtable. Even the most venomous Beds were twittering and practicing lines under their breath in the morning. We'd cleaned off the schedule for a whole hour, no one would be in or out but the lady timothy who had come back from Iraq or Afghanistan or one of those sandy warry countries.

Jalopy called to tell Letty that the timothy was a'comin round the mountain. So she signaled to February who nodded to The Black, The Big Redhead, The Blonde, The Mistress, and The Smart One who scampered to their places and giggled and groaned and hugged each one last time because that's what happens when the audience is let in. That is always what happens when the audience is let in.

OK Letty, I thought. You got your way. Now let's see what you can do.

***

Letty Wins

No Petunia, no Mama. No Daddy either. No john or david would be in or out of the Huxtable. The piano was tuned and the stage was set. Ronnie was cleaning a glass with a rag and shaking his head to himself.

Letty was set to be the first thing that the lady timothy saw when she got out of the refrigerator elevator. Letty's curves had been corrected by an emerald green three-piece suit and black top hat and a painted moustache like an eye black equator splitting the uprights of her girl boy face. Her look screamed community theater, or, as the script had said:

A bankrupt burlesque production of the Wizard of Oz.

The doors slid apart and revealed a dark featured young woman, 25 or so. She had short black hair and wore a plain black t-shirt, tight, which demonstrated her muscular arms and upper back. She had a pull-up push-up kind of body. Jeans on the bottom, also black, also tight, but not in a way that said sex as much as it said roadie.

"Welcome!"

Letty's arms rose like a ringmaster greeting the crowd. The lady timothy chuckled because people in bad costumes trying their hardest has a kind of charm.

"We have been waiting for you. Please, allow me to guide you to your seat as the act is about to begin. The first act, that is."

Letty led the lady timothy to a small wooden scaffold which had been placed where a sofa normally was. It was quite the setup. There were curtains that were bedsheets with quilt patches crafted to create that turn of the century train hopper hobo vibe. An old piano was clinging to life too. Letty seated the lady timothy in the single chair which made up the audience. Letty delivered her a bottle of cheap Mexican lager and continued the routine. Ronnie was less than thrilled to serve crap but went along with it.

> "A beer, my dear. We fear you'll peer too clearly at our production.

> "To veer from jeers, we've engineered a musicalcoholic seduction."

The lady timothy toasted her drink with a lift and a tilt. Letty nodded then acquitted herself to the piano where she positioned herself to sit. Letty clapped twice.

Nothing happened.

A beat.

The lady timothy smiled.

Letty cleared her throat, smiled an apology then clapped again.

Nothing.

Beat.

The lady timothy chuckled.

Perturbed, Letty apologized once again, this time in the fashion of raising her finger to the audience. She cleared her throat once again, then removed a shoe and flung it at Ronnie who was behind the bar reading a pre-World War II nudey magazine called "Dames." The shoe bounced off a wall near the bartender.

"Oh, now?" he asked.

Letty nodded and smiled professionally but also in such a way as to broadcast her dissatisfaction with her minion. Ronnie loped to the light fixtures on the wall, the picture of poor henchmanship. He stopped at the switch and stared at Letty who once again, commanded the stage with a flourish of presence. She proceeded to clap twice.

This time, obviously, the lights dimmed and a spotlight rose on the piano.

Letty bowed.

The lady timothy laughed. Outright laughed.

Letty flipped up the tail of her terrible green suit and took to the piano bench, a shabby pew. She flipped up the cover and rested her fingers with great élan upon the exposed, ramshackle piano keys.

Letty closed her eyes.

Letty inhaled the mise en scene.

The lady timothy snorted.

And with the pomp of the consummate artist, Letty began to play the piano. At this juncture, it would be worthwhile to note that Letty had neither received training nor natural talent in playing said piano. None of us is good at everything, right?

Immediately, there came the ruckus of someone banging on a piano. Letty stopped and the lady timothy laughed her loudest laugh yet. Letty paused. Letty was in it, God that was great to watch. She was totally plugged into what her audience was waiting for. Letty like Charlie Chaplin thought to herself for a moment after failing at the piano. You were waiting to be delighted by her.

Eureka!

She uncrowned her tophat and reached in, Felix into his magical bag. She searched for a moment, tongue stuck out like Petunia paying attention. Letty discarded various objects, a piece of wire, a hardboiled egg, a rubber chicken, then discovered what it was she had been looking for. She turned again to the lady timothy. Letty winked in self-smug.

Another toast of beer from the lady timothy.

Letty took a small stereo system out of her hat then held it next to her face like a game show model demonstrating a prize. Then Letty placed the system on the top of the piano and, with the same maestro with which she approached her previous attempt at making music herself, Letty pressed play.

Saloon music rattled from the speakers and the lady timothy spat out beer she was laughing so hard. Letty acknowledged the applause with great diplomacy (tis about the work not the recognition after all) and sat. She also handed a handkerchief to the lady timothy who wiped her face.

Next the curtains parted and out came The Blonde with a grey wig on her head and a libretto in her hand. She read robotically and with a dreadful accent.

"Now what has that niece oh mine and her dog. [Turns page.] Done this time."

For the ensuing fifteen minutes, the Seven Beds played a parlor show. The Smart One was the Scarecrow, The Mistress was the Lion, The Black was the Tin Man, The Big Redhead was the Wicked Witch of the West, Letty was the Wizard who was also sort of the narrator, The Blonde played Auntie Em as well as a number of other bit parts, and February dedicated herself to Dorothy. Oscar was Toto. Yes, he was adorable.

None of it was any good. Not in the slightest. That was the point. It was more karaoke than concert, it was designed to feel small and welcoming which was the opposite of February's interpretation of the military experience which was that it was big and challenging. You had to rise up for the military.

You pretty much had to take a nosedive to get into the Huxtable's Wizard of Oz.

Of course, it was also designed to tell a story, one quite contrary to the discovering of the value of home with which the source

material is renowned. This is how the Huxtable's Wizard of Oz
went:

Everyone but February read their lines from a script they held
onstage. They often broke character, if you called what they were
doing characters. As the rest of the actresses laughed and acted
with escalating amateurishness, February stuck to playing it
straight. She spoke her lines loudly as if she were inviting her
fellow performers to pick up their cues, their goddamned cues. She
repositioned actresses onstage and attempted to follow the
choreography, even when Toto peed on the magical hourglass. She
seemed to be trying so hard to make something good for the lady
timothy.

And the audience could see that.

What began as something funny became something sad. It became
the story of being too small to make the show go well. It became
the story of trying as hard as you possibly can, caring as much as
you possibly can,

And failing.

Whereas the lady timothy laughed at the hijinks at the beginning
of the show, the veteran came to make no noise. Finally came the
crescendo, the "and you were there and you were there and you
were there" scene. The Blonde had reentered in her flying monkey
outfit rather than Auntie Em's apron and wig while The Mistress
and The Big Redhead were getting naked with each other. The
Black was so bored it hurt to look at her and Letty had taken to
fisticuffs with Ronnie. The Smart One had slipped into the

Overmind, granted entry by loads of pharmaceuticals. And February,

February wanted only for her show to go well.

She began to cry.

No one but the lady timothy noticed. Not even Oscar.

February dropped the act and wept.

So it came to pass that with a passed out waif and a monkey clad princess, with a pissing pug and a pissed off transvestite, with a lame light tech and a bored beauty painted grey, with a small central American eating out a big Ginger, a soldier tread her way to an actress weeping on a stage onstage.

"You're February, aren't you?"

"Yes, I uh, I'm so sorry, I tried so hard and I'm so-o-o-orry."

Tears, disconsolate tears were rivers on February's face. She was even blowing her nose on the sleeve of her costume.

"I like your voice," the lady timothy said.

"You...you do?"

A glimmer of hope arrived on February's face. But she didn't allow joy take hold, not yet. Oh no, the master awoken, February held her sadness out like a loose tooth to the lady timothy. I hadn't watched her pluck a customer's violin in so long that I'd forgotten what February was, what she was capable of when she wanted to be. I guess The Huxtable had lost track of what inspired February.

You want to blame her but the truth was that we weren't managing her well. Daddy knew it. He knew it wasn't money that lit up February, not any more it wasn't. It wasn't stimulation and it wasn't survival. In that room in that moment you knew exactly what February had left in her heart.

It was Letty.

All at once, I remembered that as inconsistent her attendance at meetings, as half done her room and madcap her theories on the African American penis, February was still a Bed. The First Bed.

"...no you don't, I suck!" February said. "You're only being sweet."

The lady timothy turned from February.

"You can ask anyone I know, I'm not sweet. I'm not a sweet person, February."

February reached for the lady timothy's hand.

"Yes you are. You're the sweetest person here. Everyone else is stoned or fighting or..."

They turned to The Mistress and The Big Redhead who slobbered and made suckling sounds. The soldier disgraced and the Dorothy deposed laughed a sanctuary of each other inside the insanity of realizing you are in a world gone amuck.

"February, would it be all right if we went somewhere?"

February sniffled then she looked up a woman almost come undone but held together by the kindness of a stranger. February was a clinic in sex work that day.

She nodded then the lady timothy helped her to her feet. They held hands and stepped down from the stage. Oscar scuttled behind them, hurrying to keep up with his human and her new friend.

*\*\*\**

Purged of its audience, the show ended without applause. Letty and Ronnie stopped fighting as The Big Redhead and The Mistress stopped their melodramatic cunnilingus. No bows. The Black walked off to wherever it was that The Black walked off. The Blonde rolled her eyes and waited for someone to remove the ludicrous monkey wings from her back because she sure wasn't going to do it. The Smart One was high but no more than usual. Letty thanked everyone. Then Hildengarder stamped out like she'd watched the whole thing which maybe she had, who knows. She told the ladies to

"Gussy up! All y'all got work now!"

Then she signaled to Petunia who had two black eyes that day and who was behind Mama. Petunia went about cleaning up.

Letty thanked the stragglers and moved to help Petunia. Mama told Letty that Letty was the one who did plays, so it was Letty who should know to let everyone play their part. Petunia's part was to clean up other people's messes. Letty's part was to make money.

So go make some money, Mama said.

\*\*\*

Daddy used to say that men want women to want them. And women like to live the story. Women are environmental creatures. Costumes count in a woman's carriage. Give a woman a location, Daddy would say, a costume, give a woman a story then she will be everything a man could ever want. All a man wants is a job, and to be good at it.

That was the stuff Daddy would say. He'd round us up and deliver pimp scripture from the mountaintop. You could see that Letty couldn't quite put her finger on it because Daddy sounded so smart. He'd say these things and you'd want to think, This man is a genius. I am in the company of a genius.

Then you'd live with him a bit and his behavior wouldn't jive with what he said. It wasn't complicated if you were confident to know what you saw but young women so seldom are. Yes, Daddy was rich. Yes, he had been with thousands of women and yes, he controlled your livelihood.

No, he did not know how to feel emotions as he felt them. Couldn't do it.

That's why Daddy could never see in you the things you were obviously feeling. This baffled so many Beds because understanding seemed to be the knifepoint of the things he'd say that you'd have an urge to think him a genius for saying.

Sometimes, when a Bed who wanted to believe tied him down and vomited upon him what they were feeling because they didn't know how many more fake things they could manage to say before cracking in half, Daddy could trick them into thinking they weren't feeling something at all. That they were a part of whatever great grand truth he was about to spin. And he would talk and talk and they'd listen and listen until they were feeling safe and confused but safe in his arms.

Do you get it now? He would say.

Then they would cry and sometimes say they did, but that part was unnecessary, the kind of crying these women would be doing is answer enough for men who cannot feel as they feel.

More than a few Beds ended up terminally hornswoggled because Daddy may have been unable to feel but that man's tongue was the poem maker. You'd be talking with one of the lost Beds and they'd be ready to spread the gospel of Daddy to you but they just couldn't quite say it right. They'd get frustrated, or they wouldn't, but they would always make sure you knew that Daddy could explain it and all you had to do was ask him. Then you'd start counting to yourself because Beds don't last once they're gone like that. Mama would not tolerate the fortifications that their zealotry would require.

See, when you first met Daddy you'd figure him an impossibly confident man. Perfect in that way. The man you knew had to exist somewhere out there even before you met him. You know how much you doubt yourself sometimes so it has to follow that somewhere there is your exact opposite. But as you got to know him, and more to the point, got to know yourself, you came to understand that Daddy was someone who did not know how to be honest.

That was it. Daddy could not be honest.

Not that he was lying, no. There's a gap between being honest and not lying. Big things he could say, truths of the universe that sounded the way that good butter on good bread tastes. And he could make the shape of someone listening.

But Daddy had given up honesty many years before.

\*\*\*

It's Not About Fault, It's About Fit.

It had been two days and Letty was up early for the weekly staff meeting. This would be the first time the Huxtable got together to talk since the big scene. February and Oscar the Puppy had come to Letty's room the night before to make sure that Letty was going to be at the meeting the next day. Letty had said Of course. Then February had said Good, I'm going to bring Oscar and I don't care if anyone gets angry. Then Letty had swallowed her smile and said she didn't either.

The clock ticked up enough for Letty to call it morning so she flung off her covers and went topside to put on some coffee at the Bayou Fried. She put on two pots because she knew the rest of us would all want some. She also put on two pots because she was so excited to talk about the big scene that doing anything once would not expend sufficient energy. Letty ground the beans and poured in the water and flicked the red switch fourteen times back and forth because the light was broken so she didn't know which way was on. Then she told herself Enough already, picked a flick and stuck with it. In half a minute, the coffee was percolating and Letty was looking through the window wall out at 5:18 AM New Orleans.

The Sun was coming but not there yet so the big black night was bending blue. Street lamps were off and the moon was hanging out. The drunks were asleep and the junkies hadn't yet become fiends. Go-getters stuck to optimized vectors on their walks to work.

A few joggers.

A chubby runner who kept grabbing at the bottom of her sweat shirt. Letty loved chubby runners. She always wanted to cheer behind them and hoot and scream "you keep on going, gurl! You got this!"

Then that sputter of air when the brewing's finished called Letty back from the window wall. She poured herself a good morning then Letty sipped that first sip of hot coffee. That sacred sip where you suck the skim of the mug, where you're careful because you know it's going to be hot but you know you can't say no to it. What are you going to do? Let it cool? Please. You and I both know that you are gonna burn your mouth and savor the roast and watch the steam spin off into calligraphy then the air itself. Me oh my, fresh coffee and a place to sit and watch the world wake up around you? That right there is the working woman's church.

I'd love to start waking up early again. I used to be a morning person, but the Huxtable is such a third shift. Which is about as upside down as it gets because who is good at sex at 2:30 in the morning? Letty loved to talk about that, about how categorically better day sex was than too-tired-or-drunk-to-drive sex. Then that would lead into those well-trod rants about how backwards we are about sex in America, how advertisers can't show nipples but a movie without a murder is an unfunded script. The sideboobing of our souls. Then Letty would get rolling on why it was so important to do timothy work. I'd listen to her and I'd nod and then I'd be agreeing to be part of another one of her cockamamey scenes. Then she'd leave and I'd laugh because, once again, I'd agreed to go on a quest with Letty. We were off to see the Wizard about all of the horrible people who are too stupid, too lonely, or too fat to feel how horny they are. As if the crooked spine of society could be corrected one cum at a time.

Then I'd laugh because she'd done it again. That was my experience of knowing Letty. She'd get going on how she was going to do something and are you with me?

Sure Letty. I'm with you.

Of course, I was never so silly as to confuse my sense of satisfaction with progress. I wanted to make the woman happy. That was it. I couldn't tell you why I was like that with Letty. God knows I have made a life of ignoring other people's feelings save the ones for which I have been compensated care. Prettier that Letty, smarter than Letty, sweeter, meaner, richer, bitchier, more like me than Letty – I have lived and I know my life is my responsibility.

Then there was Letty.

Letty Letty Letty.

"There you are."

Letty turned to find Daddy behind her.

"Hey there Daddy! Fresh coffee on the stovetop."

"Oh, my sweet baby…" he said.

Daddy's eyes were swollen with bags looked like rolli polies.

"…I've never done this before. Funny too, yuh'd think I'd have done it all by now. 43 years. I mean, I done it before but never someone like you. It's like I'm putting down my best sheep dog."

He sat beside her and looked out at New Orleans. It was more awake now. Chunky joggers had transformed into recently retired friends power walking. One bum wobbled.

"I gotta let you go, Letty," he said.

"What?!"

He shook his head and twisted his mouth.

"This is the hardest moment of my working life, Letty. Might be the worst day I ever had. But we're letting you go. You've done… you've…"

Daddy paused to pass tears through his brain rather than his eyes. Letty's first urge after hearing she'd been fire was to help the man who was firing her deal with his emotions.

"You're one of my highest performers," Daddy said. "And I thought about other options. I truly did. But the truth is, you outgrew our family. You and February, I'm letting both of you go. Not that she's got nothing to do with this and - "

He dabbed her shoulder then he couldn't hold his hand up so it dropped.

"I let you down, Letty. Knew I was doing it as I did too. And you're going to do so well, we both know you will. Maybe you don't but I do. February I worry about, but you, you'll be so much better off without us, honey. I've got to let you soar."

He searched her for activity. Any sign of thought or feeling.

"Letty?"

Nothing.

"Letty?"

"Why would you fire me?"

Hildengarder's voice materialized behind her. She seemed in the vicinity of sad too, although she did not have to search for words like Daddy had.

"No, Letty. This's it for yuh here. That car out there waitin' for you, it'll take you to a hotel in Baton Rouge. You got a week there all paid up then yuh on yer own. Don't worry none bout February, we dealing with her. Yo stuff'll come later tonight along with your last pay."

"Why would you ever fire me?"

Daddy said Oh Letty then Mama put her arm around him. She shouldered him towards the refrigerator elevator.

"Jalopy'll be here in 10 minutes, Letty," Mama said. "… But none of us want that."

Then they weren't in the room any more.

Letty looked out again. More professionals but mostly homeless men by then, more light and it was hard white daylight, a couple of addicts or stroke victims or both. A towncar at the curb. None of them looked at her. No one going about the beginning of their day looked back at her as she had at them. No one wondered or ached to urge her on as she had them.

New Orleans did not notice Letty.

***

## <u>Let's Check Facebook!</u>

What a morning, they write for you to like.

What a miraculous life is yours to hold and dance don't walk, DANCE BECAUSE THE UNIVERSE IS MUSIC, they tic tac type in quaint typeface for friends and friends of friends to see and like and share.

Love life and love work and love and like this post.

Just love, they say by way of Wi-Fi.

Just love.

Part 2: The David

Letty woke up whacking back and forth between the same two thoughts she'd passed out thinking. One of the thoughts was a question. The question she kept asking was:

Why would he fire me?

Letty hadn't been able to stop asking that since the morning before when Daddy had fired her. She'd asked it so many times that she didn't know when she was saying it out loud or only in her mind any more.

The other thing she kept thinking was not a question. That thing was a thought that had come to her an hour before she'd finally fallen asleep that first night. The thought was:

I will crush him.

Letty had been deposited in a hotel room with a small bed and a television in a cabinet with drawers. Her clothes were already there when she arrived. Every time Letty came across a new component of her termination that must have required orchestration while she had been doing exactly what he had told her to do, Letty would think:

I will crush him.

Every time Letty interacted with the hotel staff who were inane and unthinking and who were being paid to perform a function, she would think

Why would he fire me?

Letty would think of The Blonde, libido like a jelly fish. The Blonde had a job. The idiot at the front desk who could not for the substance of his existence in the miraculous eternal universe figure out how to adjust Letty's room's thermostat outside the parameters of Arctic tundra and arid hellscape - that gem had a job.

Letty did not have a job.

She would ask herself Why would he fire me? And she'd spiral down that staircase for a while. Then, after numbering the injustices yet again, the pinball would stop bouncing in her brain, and she would think one thing with more resolve than she had ever thought any thought before. Letty would think:

I will crush him.

***

It Did Not Slake the Carolinian

Letty may have believed in sex in the way vegans believed in almond milk, but The Blonde was not so hippy a humper. The Blonde knew things.

The Blonde, born in North Carolina in a refurbished servants quarters, had come to The Huxtable after it hadn't worked with Thurston, whose father found him with a man. Discovering her fiancé was gay hadn't bothered The Blonde, as if discovering were the right word for a man who properly employed soup spoons and salad forks and found football distasteful and used words like distasteful. You fall into things, The Blonde's grandmother told her, geckos end up newts in the bog. You can't help but to trade sports shaped gapes for the company of men in North Carolina.

Thurston's father considered his son's choices a mark against The Blonde. Nana agreed with Thurston's father, in part, at least, she agreed. True, her granddaughter did not seem capable of making due with her native resources, but what sixteen-year old can be held accountable for wrangling a nancy? Course you can take that complaint right to the President, Nana told The Blonde.

A wakeup call is a wakeup call no matter when the rooster crows. The Blonde needed to stop the stiff squid act once it came time to solve the man.

Nana was like every Southern grandmother: she wanted her granddaughter to be with the wealth her beauty warranted. But she could not afford a proper positioning for the girl who would become The Blonde. Due to Nana's most recent husband's departure, The Blonde's father being a rapscallion and mother being most likely dead, their social status survived on the triumvirate of welfare, social security, and The Blonde being hot. So they scrambled for invitations and bought gowns on bad checks. I'm sure there were lessons with banana shaped objects too.

Nana's clock struck midnight at a cotillion in Raleigh. Her shoulder seized and she knew a heart attack was imminent, so excused herself for a spell of fresh air and a private expiration. She died on a balcony overlooking a golf course. Her body was discovered by the help. The Blonde went home that night with a man's man with a wife who went by Robert on Sundays, Mr. Dilling during the week, and Bob on Saturdays. What else could Nana have wished for?

The question of rape is such a finicky issue in committed relationships. Particularly in the adultery arena.

This apartment ain't free, you know, Bob would say through one of his secret cell phones. It was not, neither by price of skin nor coin and we call it traditional when those costs are split up neatly by gender. As the path to prostitution is often paved by the confluence of tradition and isolation, The Blonde found herself clicking around for a few hours, creating a fake online dating account and all of a sudden, making her own money.

Daddy found her on a Friday which delivered unto the Blonde that surge of screw-you and you-could-have-had-this-if-only-you'd-listened that gets us hurt. Physically hurt.

The Blonde told Bob about how much men were willing to pay for her the Saturday after talking with Daddy. Bob had thoughts on the matter. The Blonde spent Sunday at the doctor who said it wasn't broken. Daddy skyped with her on Monday and said of course the Bed was still hers and he was amazed at the jungle inside of so many so called gentlemen. The Blonde was on her way to New Orleans that night.

And Jalopy was on his way to North Carolina.

Robert Dilling was discharged from the Hospital two months later. He never walked without the aid of a cane again.

***

Letty sat in her unexceptional hotel room texting rich men. She had some money saved up, enough for a fun year or a thin three. So it wasn't like she was texting for grocery money. No, Letty was finally doing what she had never ever allowed herself to do before. Always The Nice One Letty was. Always The Respectful One, The One Who Sacrificed for Others. And look where that had gotten her.

The Huxtable wanted to play the game? Really? That's what The Huxtable wanted? People always did that with Letty, they would think that because she didn't stoop then that meant she was weak. Eye rolls and snipes, eye rolls and snipes. Letty had always stayed on the fray because you have to play a little but had she been the nasty gossip? Had she lied and made great cases of her every little whim even when she was in the right? Oh, they wanted to play?

Fine.

Letty had more rich men in her phone than any king on earth and in a span of ten texts she had an evening each with four of the richest set up.

They wanted to play? Really?

Fine.

What had Daddy thought was going to happen? Had he really expected Letty to shrivel up? Get desperate and get married? Had he expected davids wouldn't want her if she wasn't at the Huxtable? That they would transition like liquid between cups to another Bed? What a fool. Daddy was so fragile that he must have seen Letty as a threat. That was why he'd fired her. Kind of pathetic actually and Letty felt bad for him.

Then she said no, it was time to stop feeling bad for people doing bad things. No matter the reason, start tending your own garden first, Letty. Besides, if Letty was going to feel bad for Daddy it wouldn't be for the little boy he'd bottled up inside his brain and protected by inflicting his hierarchy on good staff, no. If Letty were going to feel bad for Daddy, it was for what was going to happen next.

Oh yessirree, Daddy had it coming now. Because Letty wasn't going to stop with taking some of her davids with her. You thought she was texting rich men so she could keep her davids?

Oh no.

Beds take davids and Letty was no Bed anymore. Not now not ever again. Letty was through with that noise.

Letty was going to crush him.

Letty was going to build her own damned whouse.

\*\*\*

Another Roadside Attraction

Daddy found The Big Redhead in the way one comes upon off-brand theme parks. He'd decided to take the drive he'd grown up idolizing in celebration of a birthday which left his age evenly divisible by 10. So he rented a Porsche 356 Speedster and took Route 56 from Missouri to New Mexico. Mama asked him why he didn't buy the stupid thing. He slipped on his new white driving gloves and black Zeppelin pilot goggles and said

Guess I'm the renting type.

Daddy never stayed in any place that cost more than $50 a day unless it had a sign out front advertising "Free HBO." Then he'd allow for $60. He observed the speed limit other than when he went a hundred in the areas with windmills and murderers on the lam. The sky and open road made Daddy's head quiet.

One day, Daddy pulled into the kind of diner where his server's name would either be Florence or Flo or Dorothy or Dot. He parked the Porsche a few extra feet from a steel frame Ford truck with a shade under infinity miles on it. Parking wasn't an issue at the Sunny Cafe in Lucky Loo, New Mexico.

Red bar stools that were too rusted to spin and a smattering of desert people inside. Couple of truckers in a corner. No hostess but an aproned lady behind the counter told him to take a seat wherever he wanted. She lived a life 35 minutes on either side of a cigarette. Her apron said Rosie.

Daddy considered the Sunny a sort of spiritual cousin to the Bayou Fried. Beat up joint serving cheap food right. I don't know if anyone ever understood how much it meant to Daddy that the beignets his business served were delicious and his Beds were the best sex in the country and not a bad value when you knew the industry standards.

Daddy ordered a patty melt which is one of three things you can order at a diner in a desert exit, the other two being a slice of pie and a breakfast special. Wouldn't it be something if it was a front, Daddy thought.

He swallowed coffee he hadn't had to ask for and began to eavesdrop out of no particular concern. Four booths out of about 30 had customers, one guy in dusty denim and work boots was sitting at the counter too. Nine men all told in the Sunny Cafe, including Daddy, and only two were talking. They were sitting together.

One of the two guys at the talking table was tanned with a lush, filthy moustache like two paintbrushes had been dipped in tar then glued butt to butt underneath his nose. He might have had a hair lip, Daddy couldn't get a good enough look to tell. The other guy was younger, sweet faced and lean. He was doing his best to slurp beef barley soup between fits of laughter while the moustache told a story. Actually, there are four things you can order at a desert exit diner - soup without seafood is OK, too.

"...she come right up and start in on him. Right there, at the table. She come right up, start jacking him off and says, she says "Roger, you better win this hand because I ain't cheap!"

The one who was listening sprayed soup from his mouth and nose. He dropped his spoon into his bowl and it clanked so the one who was telling the story leaned in to keep up the story but lower the volume. Daddy could still hear.

"So you know how she is and what she can do to a man, but there's this other guy at the table who don't know how she handle it. City guy, thinks he a rounder. Here to take some desert rats' money. Like we ain't grown up with a 52 card deck and balls else to do. Anyhow, he looking at Roger getting all hot and bothered while she work on him. Poker hand still going on, mind you. Roger and the city guy still in a hand. And we all saw her walk into the room after the cards got dealt, so we know she don't know what cards Roger holdin'. She can't. She doing it to him. But the hand still going so she start acting for him. Funniest thing I ever seen."

"Did she check his cards?"

"No! That's the thing, she start acting while she jacking him off. Starts raising too! Wouldn't you know that girl raise it? And Roger is getting close to popping. Rest of us fold. But the city boy is left and like I said, there's money in the pot. Good money. Roger all panting and whatnot and she looking at the city guy like, 'your move, my man' still jacking away. Well, the city guy won't have it so he pushes."

"He did not!"

"Honest to God, man pushed every penny he had in. Has to be a month's mortgage in there now. And Roger is over the moon, I know you know how she do it!"

The one who was listening unplasticked a packet of crackers. The older one put his back against the booth's torn cushions.

"And she don't take a goddamned second, not a lizard lick between that man pushing in and her saying *call.*"

Rosie arrived with Daddy's patty melt.

"Thank you, more coffee would do us right," Daddy said like he wasn't a tourist listening to a stranger's sex story.

Rosie told him it'd be a minute because she had to brew a new pot. Then she left, flicked the old red switch on the haggard gadget, and went outside to smoke. Daddy had a thought that they might have had the same coffee machine back at the Bayou Fried.

"So the city guy show and he holding a couple of queens. Roger is all shaking and blowing up in his pants, and we are dying. So you know what she does?"

"What she does?"

"She waits for Roger to do it, bombs it all out. Pulls her hand out his pants. You know what's next, don't you? Yup. She goes and licks that goop right off her fingers. Then she flips his cards over and wouldn't you know…"

"Aces?"

"A deuce and a five. Roger was bluffing! Whole time, it'd been a bluff."

The two men stood, threw a few leaves of money on the table and strolled out together.

"And Roger could not have cared less. Plus, she gave him a cut of what she took from the city slicker when she did him next. Probably worth more than whatever he lost."

By then, Daddy had been on the road for about a week. A week away lets you decompress from work to be able to think about business again. So Daddy decided to sacrifice his sandwich to serendipity and he stood up. He left too much cash on the table and followed the men out. They were piling into the red truck.

"Say there boys, can I get your ears for a minute?"

They were suspicious of him at first as desert people are wont to be. But Daddy was Daddy and Daddy could melt the moon. They started with cars then it was about his trip and his Porsche then it was the girl from the story was either at the truck stop off of Capitol Road or at Glen's Barbecue Pit. Daddy thanked them kindly and checked the Pit first. He got brisket and she wasn't there.

While parking wasn't a problem at the Sunny Diner, obstacles abounded at the Capitol Road truck stop. Most of which were broken glass or broken human. Rooms were $11 an hour.

As he docked in the closest thing to a safe space he could find, a lady with purple eye shadow, a belly necklace, and a belly trundled over to him.

"Hey babe."

Daddy said hello and asked if she knew where the woman from the story was. She commenced to the lighting of one cigarette with the ember of the one she was finishing and said she didn't but she had the same stuff in her panties. Daddy thanked her then said no thank you and that he'd be inside if she did happen to come across her friend. He said that if she did find her friend, that there was something in it for her too.

Daddy strode through the saloon doors. Flannel and reunion concert tour tee shirts everywhere, open snorting of methamphetamines, and no one in sight who fit the woman's description. He took a seat and asked for a beer and a whiskey and the woman. The drinks cost four bucks combined and the bartender didn't know who he was talking about. Men camped out at the bar close enough to overhear who Daddy was looking for couldn't help but to share a chuckle with their own beer and whiskey. Daddy nodded to the man beside him. The man beside Daddy nodded back.

After fifteen minutes or so, the starlet who had greeted Daddy came up to him at the bar, this time with a dose more dainty on her canter and carriage. She waved and winked to a few of the other patrons and said Howdy Boys. They growled. Then she went belly up beside Daddy at the bar. She told him she was hungry after all. He said of course she was what with her wasting away like that, and he gave her a hundred-dollar bill. She said someone wanted to meet him back at his car. So Daddy chugged his beer, nodded again to his neighbor who nodded back, and he left the bar.

Daddy heard the laugh first. You always heard The Big Redhead's laugh first.

That magnificent whooping like a coyote in a full moon. A mangy faced trucker was performing oral sex on The Big Redhead who was on Daddy's car hood, one breast out, the other banging around in her black wife beater like a big grapefruit in a loose tube sock.

Daddy liked her straight off. Bawdy kind of lady – looked exactly like her laugh which is what you look for out of your redhead. That hunch of chewing tobacky and dirty beard was working on her crotch and she had a clutch of his mullet in her one hand, making a pillar of his mug so she could get her grind on. In the other hand, The Big Redhead had a flask and she lifted it a few inches above her head when she saw Daddy.

In an hour, they had come to an agreement. Daddy made her The Big Redhead by giving her two thousand dollars cash on the spot and offering her a plane ticket to New Orleans. She took the money but not the ticket. She preferred to go by train, she said, see the country before cooping up in a whouse. Daddy nodded and said he understood.

\*\*\*

Letty had dates scheduled with four rich men so into Letty that they hadn't asked the price. Their only questions had been when and where.

Letty left the cheap hotel and checked into the penthouse suite at the most exquisite hotel in Baton Rouge. She made appointments with the most spectacular stylist and the most sought after make-up artist.

Even though she was telling herself that it was all right to unleash her spending, it did make Letty uncomfortable to be burning her stash like that. Not that she'd been cheap before but Letty didn't make a fuss about having to have the newest this or that. They were sweat pants for God's sake, why would she spend $300 on sweat pants? Letty was fine if her pants fit and her phone worked. She had other dresses that cost plenty that she could whip out when the occasion called for it. Letty was a lady who had some nice things, who had some less nice things, and who took care of it all because that's what you do. So watching her wealth evaporate like that felt scary and uncomfortable and Yowzers! is it a moment when your bank account has one fewer digit in it.

But there was something clarifying about it all, too, spending like that. It felt like she had nothing to hide behind now. Like it was time to do it, it was finally time to do it for real. Plus, it is the teensiest bit of fun to live the extravagant life every so often and the dates were set so she'd have more money at the end of the week than she had coming into it. Not much more, but some more.

You can do this, Letty would think. You know what to do, what's been missing in all of the places you've worked all along and what's been right too – don't be so butt hurt as to throw out the good stuff you've seen. You can do this. You're going to do this. You are going to build the best whouse ever.

\*\*\*

The First Bed

"Who gonna give a trick a salary?"

Face flushed and cleavage more prime meridian than evidence of breasts, this was a conversation from back when Hildengarder still disagreed with Daddy on matters of consequence. Back when she'd wear shorts.

"Now now, you got a salary."

"I ain't no trick. I graduated."

He wasn't so different: hair not all the way gray yet, maybe more aggressive than he'd be in the decade and change later, but essentially the same animal.

The brand new bartop shifted when Hildengarder leaned against it. We'd end up redoing it with a david's construction team a few years later. Although I have to say that the bar never felt so homey once everything was stable. There's something wonderful about the barely held together.

"I hear you. And I know this is a very different arrangement. But look around you, this is a very different whouse too. You want to give your employees clearly defined jobs as explained by clearly defined goals, then you want to give them as much peace of mind as possible to get them achieved. Or why are they your employees at all?"

Hildengarder looked around. The Huxtable, or what would become The Huxtable, was a hodgepodge of shipped containers, translucent plastic sheets speckled with paint, blue tape peeling up from the edges of things.

"And Ronnie?"

"Ronnie got going what Ronnie got going. He's him and you're you."

She kicked the bar and it coughed up sawdust.

"Listen," Daddy said. "You gotta trust your horses. 9 times out of 10, the whip is for the jockey to feel like he's doing something. But the horse gonna win if it's slept well, if it's in good shape, eating good, got good breeding, if it was born a runner or not. The horse that wins ain't the whipped one, it's the one that's been taken care of. Nobody does salary because all them Daddies ain't nothing but pimps, they ain't smart businessmen. If it were dumb to pay salary, then how come every smart business pays salary? Huh? Tell me why bankers and CEOs get salary if it ain't smarter? People don't want to worry about their money all the time – they want to think about work."

She picked a labeling sticker off of a chair.

"Well it don't matter how you pay these tricks, yo ass need to get some dang men in here awready."

"That's fair, that's fair. You right. Now what did you tell me they're called again? I know john, but what is the other one again?"

He knew the names. He also knew that men get women to stay in formation by making them think they're needed. Careful with that ladies, be careful confusing the times you feel needed with the times you're actually needed.

"Davids. Goddang you ain't remember nothing! Davids."

"Right right, david. Johns and davids, johns and davids. Important to call things as they are, iddn't it?" He cricked his neck and continued. "You know, I been thinking…"

"…oh lawd help me."

"Now now, bear with me, Mrs Hildengarder. We got johns, we got davids, don't you think we ought to have one more? You got to have three of a thing, right?"

"Dear God in Heaven, you are gonna be the end of me, Oscar."

"I'm Daddy now, Mama. It's important to call things what they are."

"Daddy, Oscar – you are something, all right."

The space had been excavated and the general blueprint fulfilled. They'd decorated the Stage, or what would come to be called the Stage, and although Ronnie brought clients with him to amuse the coffers, The Huxtable needed its bell cow.

They'd whittled the list of applicants down to three.

First there was Sarah who went by Anna in Boston, Bambi in Los Angeles, and Chevy in the Netherlands. This was Mama's pick – 28 years old, 5'3" Blonde, classic look. Tiny arms, slight shoulders, had been in the business for a while, the kind of chest that could only be referred to as big fake tits.

Then there was Jilleeza who was a local legend. Mama was indifferent when it came to Jilleeza who was already 37 (though Mama suspected her on the northern border of 40) but came with a deck of davids.

"Hire a bunch, we got a whole whouse to fill. Why you wasting time getting but the one?" Mama asked.

"Man hiring for the long term only ever hire one at a time. Hire a thousand if you don't care if they stick. But if you want years out of someone, then you spend the time to get the one. When you hire more than one person, you're hiring all them people sure, but you're really pinning on hopes they work well together. Then they don't because they're human and either you stuck with a situation or you fire down to the one you should have started with."

"Or they work out."

"Worse yet! They do work and you ain't all built up to handle a team like they become so quick. You think you ready to have a clique develop while you building out this on top of taking care of everything else, Mama? Well I have no desire to end up with a company no one can control inside my own whouse. We hire one at a time. That's what we do."

Third candidate was the girl Hildengarder called Problems. Seventeen years old, I guess not technically a runaway but she hadn't seen her parents in more than half her life. Problems had grown up in the Forest, as we say. Thin, definitely a pretty young thing, and scattered as a dragonfly. She was all over the place but even Mama had to admit that she looked great getting there.

"Don't do it, Daddy. Don't you dare do it. Get you Sarah, she's a safe pick."

"Well, here's the thing, Mama…"

She knew what that look meant. She threw her head up and did a Hail Mary towards St Charles Street.

"There ain't a cheddar chunk's chance in a rat cage that Problems star in a whouse like this! You need a girl with jugs. Damn girl got zits for a chest. Men like jugs, ain't you knowing that, Daddy?"

"Listen Mama, I know that Anna looks like a porn star –"

"Sarah."

"Bambi, Anna –"

"–SARAH! You the one who just said it important to call things what they is! She ain't no Bambi or Chevy to the whouse she working at. She Sarah. I'm Mama and she Sarah. That's why I should get a salary and she should get a cut."

"Well we're not going to do that but Sarah if you prefer Sarah. Sarah looks like the lady in videos. The lady that guys smack it off to because that's who's onscreen when it's time to smack it off. But there's a million of them."

"Ain't no million blondes with jugs out there."

"She's a type, Mama. That's what I'm saying. She's a type. Nobody got to come down here to get them a Sarah."

"And the auditions?"

"Jugs noted how big I was on a good thirty-five occasions, which was the peanut butter to the thirty-five spoonfuls of jelly she took to tell me she was cumming. And the surgeons must have gone in through her nipples cause they look like a Rottweiler chewed them up. Good ride, too much bump than grind for my taste, but we could work on that. Give her a B. For Boobs and Blonde. A B for Bambi."

"And an F for February?"

"Oh that young woman. Sharp, sharper than you might think anyhow. Got a lot of thoughts in her, passions, she's interesting company at the least, I know we agree there. Does she go overboard? Of course but she's young. Falls right asleep when you rub her feet. Why don't you draw her up a contract, Mama?"

"I know you ain't asking for no contract for no trick for no salary, ho man you are a whackadoodle."

"Listen, Mama. We've talked about this. It has come upon us to do things correct now. Make something great. I want us to be clear with our ladies. So yes, I'd like for you to put together a contract for the young woman. I want her to be clear. Clarity in role, goal, and compensation – that's what we stand for."

"That so, Oscar?"

"Yes Mama it is. Clarity in role, goal, and compensation – that's good management. Now let's go build us the best whouse ever was."

***

The first david of the rest of Letty's life was a Wall Street guy who always wanted anal. Luckily he wasn't big so lube before and Tylenol after undid the trick. Letty almost didn't text him at first because he was the kind of man who undoubtedly had less money than he presented. But he still had a lot of money. So Letty texted.

It's a weird thing how many rich men lie about how much money they actually have. Because they still have money. They're still rich.

Really, Letty texted Wall Street rich guy because she knew he worked in finance and investment so he'd be a good one to ask about financial stuff. Plus, guys who fixate on particular acts are easy to please. First you get them all excited and they ask Tonight? and you apologize and say No, not tonight. Then they say of course, of course, your call. Then you switch gears and have suuuuuuch a good time that you can't help yourself but to give it a try and they get to think they've won because now it's not them being grotesque, it's you being hungry. Then you take the Tylenol and you ask your questions.

Wall Street rich guy didn't know the first thing about whouse finances but he did say it was a good bet that you'd want a top laundering team. So he set Letty up with a top launderer. Expensive, he said, but not a mob member. Also Wall Street rich guy said a good piece of general advices was that real estate was usually a terrible investment but rates had gotten so low and rents were so high that he had to admit real estate made a lot more sense than it ever had before. Then he got up to leave and said he'd figured he'd pay what he'd paid at The Huxtable and left Letty more money than she'd made in a week back when she made money for Daddy. Wall Street left.

Wow, Letty thought and looked at the money and laughed. What a dope she'd been, she thought.

Davids three and four were both entrepreneurs with extremely public companies so Letty had scheduled them for the end of the week. She had figured those would be the most important so she wanted to gear up for them, especially date four who was number 72 on the list of richest men in the world.

Date two was kind of her way of taking a break – retired railroad man named Gus. Old money. Old guy too. On more than one occasion in the past, Letty and Gus had lovely evenings without so much as a kiss. Letty had mostly texted Gus because she was worried he would be lonely without her because he was old and why could she not stop doing that? Why could she not get it through her head to stop taking care of everyone else? She was literally cast off in a hotel room and she was still worried about some old man.

It really is this shallow, Letty forced herself to think. Either you can learn to play or you can get fired and there ain't no points for being a good girl.

Gus showed up to the suite with yellow daisies. He wasn't geezerly yet but his back was starting to curl at the top and he had a cute smile because his eyes twinkled. Letty answered the door in what her expensive stylist said was going to be her new power look for her new power self. She had on extra dark eye shadow and extra tight clothes. Heels like spikes.

She said hello to Gus. He said hello back.

Ohh! Letty said. Daisies. Ursosweet!

Gus looked at Letty. He did not enter the penthouse nor did he extend his person for a hug or hello. Letty waved him on and said, Come in, silly.

Gus squinted then asked if the evening was his.

What was that, honey? Letty asked.

Is the evening mine?

Of course! I don't understand, are you asking if I have other things to do, silly?

All right then, he said. Now you go back there and you get all that shmutz off your face. You take a shower and you go put on some clothes you can breathe in. I'm going to leave now. You, I don't want to see again tonight. I don't ever want to see you again. I'm going to go across the street to the po boy place. You go find Letty and tell her I'll be waiting for her there. I don't want you. I want Letty.

Then Gus left. He took the daisies with him.

***

Hard Pretty Women

Everyone wanted to be The Mistress. Made the most money, cared the least about rumors. Everyone wanted to be The Mistress. And no one wanted to be The Mistress.

Slinky like the shadows in old gumshoe movies, The Mistress's mother was what Americans would call a sex mystic cook storyteller nurse. But in Nicaragua, they didn't give her a word beyond her own.

Leila.

Leila read the weather.

Leila used the jungle to make the men well.

Leila organized the stars into constellations and allowed you to worship her.

The girl who would become The Mistress never asked her mother who her father was. Maybe Leila knew, likely not, though she would never have told either way. Between the complementary threats of incest and a campmate rattling what could be a campmate's daughter, most guerillas laid off raping The Mistress. Those that that did not, died in ways designed to harden the killers.

As a child, The Mistress was the Rebellion's mascot. They protected her, taught her about Russian guns and following orders. Eventually, she came of age to assume a formal apprenticeship to her mother. So she huddled up in the tent marked with the grey flag which meant that it was off limits to marauders. The Mistress thought it was ridiculous to expect any marauder to respect an enemy structure but for a flag – she sure wouldn't. Leila told her daughter that sometimes we create safe spaces in dangerous places so that we may be justified in our anger after they are inevitably invaded. The Mistress said that was stupid. The Mistress did not have the patience for riddles and shamanism. Leila shook her head and said That wasn't a riddle, girl.

The Mistress became a passable soothsayer but a legendary lover. Leila became more partner than parent as is the course of things. She concentrated on plants and being a minstrel while her daughter made the men more sane. This did not bother Leila. It was the course of things.

Likewise, The Mistress did not weep when Leila's head exploded in front of her. She stared at the daylight coming laserlike through the hole the bullet had made in the burlap wall and observed the gurgles her mother's body made. And as the righteous anger came upon the men who had declared the grey flag special, as they routed the marauders who had outnumbered them and outgunned them, The Mistress escaped into a part of the jungle so old and overgrown it stayed dark during the day. The place where spiders hunted birds. Sometime later she found society again and earned renown applying her trade. Then Daddy found her because he kept his eye lidless in search of sex. Daddy brought her out for an audition where The Mistress made more money in less time than either of us had seen in our decades in this business.

So the Second Bed went to Leila's daughter.

This story did not surprise anyone who had met The Mistress. You could see her as a refugee warrior witch. On the other hand, it shocked people to discover that The Mistress was married. And not a forgotten matter of logistics either, not an appendix husband of a life long ago discarded.

Actively partnered. The Mistress was married.

Every year she left for two months to go home to the jungle to fill a role she never tried to explain in the Huxtable.

Once, while the wealthiest Bed was away on her annual break, I stumbled across a picture of her husband. This was when pictures were rarer candy than they are now because you had to have a camera and have the film developed. I had always imagined The Mistress's man a hard man, a bearded man.

Instead I saw a softie. Light green eyes and sketches of scruff across his thin, unblemished face. The Mistress was a ray of light next to him, happy and smiling in the way you hope you do in photographs with your partner. They were the picture of such a happy couple that you almost missed the rifle hanging over his shoulder.

Yes, everyone wanted to be The Mistress.

And no one wanted to be The Mistress.

\*\*\*

"Look who it is!"

Across the street from the fancy hotel Letty had decided to call headquarters was a counter and a cash register in a suspiciously greasy room. You could buy po boys there and you could sit at the public bench outside to eat them. That's what Gus was doing when Letty arrived wearing sweatpants, an LSU hoodie, and house slippers. She'd been crying for the past twenty minutes so her makeup had been removed the natural way. Gus was chewing a tremendous mouthful of po boy.

"Hey Gus. Look…"

Letty slunk up and started to apologize. He said it was fine and that she should sit down because it was an eating time not a talking time. Gus was contending with a sandwich so full of fried shrimp and oysters and mayonnaise and shredded lettuce that you either welcomed the mess and loved it or you are likely wound too tightly.

Go eat a sloppy sandwich, you only get the one life.

Letty said it wasn't fine and sat down. She said she was really sorry. He said it was fine and motioned to the other half of his sandwich that he'd had wrapped up either for himself for lunch the next day or for Letty right then if she showed up.

A spurt of mayo squoze out of Gus's sandwich and splattered a little onto Letty's foot. He apologized. She said it was OK.

They stopped talking. They sat on the bench, two people eating a po boy. People walked by.

*** 

## The Only Way Out Is Through

If only their parents had made less money she wouldn't have been a prostitute. Or more, obviously. So thought The Smart One's sister, Hanna, as they went through the spreadsheet.

Hanna had traveled from her home in New England to New Orleans because their mother was distraught. She'd sic'd sister on sister.

"Hanna!"

"Mom? It's 2:15 in the morning. Dan and I are asleep."

"Your sister, she, she, I can't! Talk with your father – Ted! Ted come here, it's Hanna. HANNA, your Hanna, yes."

Mother had discovered that one of her daughters, one of her angels, was working as a woman of ill repute in New Orleans.

This had shattered her. This had also surprised Hanna but knowing her sister, she expected it was under control. Way more control than anything anyone else in the family was doing.

It didn't matter - Mother was a catastrophe. Fix this, she keened. This was an elder sister's responsibility.

Please, Hanna's father had said, the phone forced upon him. Please do as your mother asks.

So Hanna went south to sit with her sister at a dainty place for tea.

"Hanna, the numbers are simple."

"You gave her a heart attack."

"No, she gave you a heart attack."

"Well, she does that."

"Did she even pay for the ticket?"

"No but I had some frequent flier miles."

"Well, I'll give you the money."

"No, come on."

The skinnier of the skinny sisters drinking tea deployed a laptop on the tabletop. They waited for it to turn on.

"How's Dan?" The Smart One asked.

"Meh."

"Yeah?"

"Yeah."

"It's nice to see you."

"Yup."

"Nice to get away from Boston?"

"Nice to get away from the winter, definitely."

The Smart One repositioned her sunglasses. Hanna sipped her tea. They were sitting outside.

"Here we go."

The screen flashed so they moved their chairs closer to the screen which was also closer together.

"Can you see, Hanna?"

"Yes."

"OK, so I did this a couple of weeks into senior year. Right when everybody was applying to colleges."

Hanna leaned in. She didn't mind spreadsheets, but this one was a lot to take in. Hundreds and hundreds of entries, mostly numbers but a few words too. The Smart One continued.

"This is a monetized risk analysis, which means I looked at a number of potential ways to make money, applied some risk factors, then let the numbers decide for me."

"This is how you ended up... here?"

"That and good luck. Or lack of bad luck, I should say. Lack of bad luck is the best luck. Bus accidents and blood viruses are real."

Hanna scanned the columns, some colored red, some green. The whole thing was interlocking too, change one number in D8 and a hundred other ones changed too.

"You're going to have to help me out here," Hanna said.

"Right right. OK, so first off, big picture. I want to retire at 45 at an annualized income 10% above the mean household income of a family of three living in San Francisco, California, assuming a 3% return on principal. This is the actual definition of making it. I thought about using median income, which is a much better gauge of economic reality, but if I'm retired, I want to be safe. So I went with the mean. With me?"

"You don't want to work and you want to be rich...?"

"Not rich. 83% of people with wealth exceeding 200% of the mean in their environment, the actual rich, experience an over-flexibility that leads to bankruptcy, either moral or fiscal."

"...but not too rich."

The Smart One clanked down her tea.

"Listen, you want to know? You want to report to Mom? Then you better pay attention to the numbers. It's the numbers that matter. The numbers. So like, enough with the attitude."

Hanna patted her sister's hand.

"I'm sorry. I'll stop being cute."

"Well..." The Smart One lifted her drink, "...you could never stop being cute."

They smiled beside each other and sipped their chamomile tea like synchronized swimmers.

"So I need about $4.9 million if I assume a 3% return and draw principle to offset occasionally. That keeps me at $147k. I could do more than 3% but again, playing it safe."

"Good money."

"But not crazy in San Francisco."

"You're moving to San Francisco?"

"No, I'm using that as the baseline."

"Why San Francisco?"

"I'm not much of a farmer, Hanna."

"OK, keep going."

"So I started listing income ranges for various professions, the likelihood of my gaining them, and the cost of attaining them. So here, you can see pharmacist. $61,000 – $162,000 range, 100% likelihood and $88,000 minimum cost of entry."

"All right, let me see if I follow. So I get the salary range, that's easy. You're saying that you have a 100% chance of getting that job if you went after it, right?"

"Correct."

"100%? You really think there's a 100% chance of anything in life?"

"Obviously not, Hanna. I was the one talking about lack of bad luck. It's algebra. 100% is the highest likelihood modifier I gave any career. I could have used 42% or a hundred quintillion percent. True, there are basic issues, again the bus and the blood virus. But those variables are independent of profession."

This was how it went for a few hours other than when The Smart One went to the bathroom to swallow six pills and also pee. In explaining her spreadsheet, a great number of other explanations became necessary: the nature of algebra, accuracy in measurement vs. the law of diminishing returns, what constituted addiction and what constituted medication, how she learned to use Excel so well. Eventually Hanna acclimated to her younger sister's systems. These were the answers to the questions everybody is asking at that age, she said. Not really, The Smart One said, they are the questions phrased correctly. If you ever really ask the question, most answers are automatic. Yes, she could make better money as a brain surgeon than a teacher, but the start-up cost was so much greater in brain surgery that it didn't make sense without a scholarship or a rich family. Also, brain surgeon carried with it a 31% likelihood factor, some of which was understanding if she could stomach splitting someone's skull.

Hanna said 85% likely sounds easy but if that 15% gets you then the whole thing is nil. The Smart One said yes sister, that is indeed how numbers work. Same deal with 2% possible, Hanna said, because somebody has to win the lottery. So math is only math too, Hanna said.

Then The Smart One said the worst part of the brain is it can know the numbers or at least basic factors but think that somehow, the percentages do not apply to it.

"Emotions win. It's why I'm high," The Smart One said. Hanna said that didn't matter to her and that she didn't have to say that. Hanna said how her sister lived her life was her business and that she loved her no matter what. That's why she was here, Hanna said, because I love you. The Smart One didn't have to explain herself to anybody, especially not her own sister.

"Yeah but I do for me not for you, Hanna. I'm in hibernation. I turn off the feelings so the numbers can play out. And now I have to say that because I think you're thinking about that I spent too long in the bathroom and my eyes are dilated but you're not saying it because you're sparing me."

Hanna started to say that wasn't what she was doing but The Smart One didn't let her finish.

"Whether or not you are, doesn't matter. *I am.* I am thinking that's what you're doing because I'm feeling like I let Mom and you down since you have to come out here to check on me. Then that lights a fuse back to me being a kid and stuff there."

"I don't think that at all. Oh my God, is that really what you think?"

"Hanna, just because I try to be logical doesn't mean I'm not emotional. I'm a person. It's not what I think, it's what I feel. Then you feel and your brain reacts with thoughts. I'm a human – my feelings always win. I am high because humans cannot feel numbers but the numbers are right. It's why we cannot create the world we obviously should. People have seen Jaws and Sandy Hook and those images take over. They don't feel the numbers. Humans cannot feel numbers. Think about how many loner young men there are right now? Millions. Billions. And maybe two or three every year go ratatat tat on an elementary school? Even if it's 20 of them, it's a 0% chance that you know or have even come across the next Columbine. But I bet you know a couple creepers who you could see picking up a rifle and spraying a class. How about this: Women suffering from postpartum depression murder sixteen times the number of children unkempt men do. Fun fact, huh? And that doesn't count suicide, again, a mostly female phenomenon. At least, until men get older. Retirement kills men and the end of pregnancy does us in. Now, do we get nervous for the unborn children of pregnant women? Do we think – oh Lord, the likelihood of that baby suffering through a depressed mother who kills herself or even them is almost a thousand times higher than them being in the wrong room of the wrong elementary school on the wrong day? You're not going to be attacked by a shark, is what I'm saying. But your feelings don't think that. They feel the turban your brain remembers seeing in a grainy beheading video or the Mainstream Media and the trenchcoat and the great big ocean below you and then you feel something that actually controls your thoughts until you talk it through. We know feelings lie. We all know that for a fact. Other than for right now, of course, because this time it's different. This time we're due. If you don't talk about feelings once you have them then they take over. Which is why I have to talk now because I am high because I love you and I'll need you for my whole life which is different than why I have to stay stoned for another few years. I'm telling you Hanna, it's different. Drugs blunt the inputs and I've got a few more years on auto-pilot until I have what I'll need for the rest of my life and I can help you too."

Hanna looked at The Smart One who sipped her tea without agitation.

Then Hanna looked away and recrossed her legs. Then she grinned and looked back at her sister.

"Do you want to keep going?" Hanna asked.

"With the spreadsheet or me? Because I'm good on me unless you're not."

"I'm good on you."

"The spreadsheet then?"

"The spreadsheet."

The sisters went down the list of professions together. They looked at tech start-up which carried with it the highest possible payout but also the lowest probability. Functionally, it made more sense to work minimum wage than to try and pollenate a product into a business. Investment banker. IP lawyer. Novelist, Nurse. The list was alphabetized.

Until it wasn't.

After Proctologist but before Quality Assurance Inspector was an entry reading "candymaker."

"Wow, Hanna I haven't looked at this in so long I forgot I called it candymaker."

Hanna looked at the entries for candymaker. $70,000 – $500,000 salary range, 95% likelihood, and a negative $280,000 start-up cost.

"Did you mean to put a minus in front of the start-up cost for candymaker?"

"Yes."

"Why is that?"

"Because I could start right away. Wouldn't have to go to college."

"But isn't that $0 then?"

"$0 isn't the baseline for cost. Time is the baseline. Anything you can do right away, it's an asset, or in this format, a negative cost. So let's say the cost of college would've been a minimum $150k but also it would have taken four years, again minimum."

Hanna shook her head.

"Took me five and we still have 110 in loans," Hanna stared at whatever was in front of her. "It comes between me and Dan."

"Does it?"

"Oh," she smiled. "Yes."

If you let the numbers decide then candymaker was the winner.

"It's so weird. I called it that in case Mom ever found the spreadsheet. I didn't want her to flip. And now, here we are. She flipped. Never did find the sheet though."

Hanna crossed her legs.

"Did you not recognize him?"

"I didn't even know him in school and I'm 2000 miles away literally working underground, Hanna. How was I supposed to recognize Freddy Templeton from Gunner Hill High in the Huxtable? And how did he recognize me?!"

"What a slimeball."

The Smart One tilted her head one way then the other.

"Oh I don't know. If you found out that your ex classmate was working where I work, you'd tell people back home too. It's interesting what happens to people. You end up talking about it. Apparently he remembered me."

"I don't think Mom would be as scared if she knew you were making 500 grand. Also, Jesus Christ, you're making 500 grand?! You can pay for the plane ticket. I will allow that."

"Well thank you. I mean I am and I'm not making that much. I make around 300, but I bring it all home. And I get room and board. So it's really more the equivalent of 580 or so. I don't have a car, health is all taken care of too. I'm ahead of schedule actually, but that has to do with the stock market more than anything. I've harvested my gains so unless inflation kills me, which I doubt it will, and I keep making about what I'm making, then I should be able to retire at 34 or 35. But there are different risk factors in candymaking. Ongoing risk factors."

Hanna cringed.

"Is it horrible?"

"It's a job."

"Yeah, but…"

"Well, you know, is it horrible with Dan sometimes? Do you have a glass of wine and watch stupid murder investigation shows instead of constantly plumbing the depths of your relationship and situation? The Huxtable is about as good a whouse as I could hope for. It came down to it was either that or become a surgeon. But you can see the start-up cost was huge. I'm broke for a decade to become a surgeon and then I HAVE to like the work or I'm dead meat. You know surgeons have the highest frequency of sociopathy of any profession? It's a prison, Hanna. You get hundreds of thousands of dollars in debt, you work 80, 90 hour weeks as a resident and the whole time, the WHOLE TIME, you know that if you don't like what you're doing that it doesn't matter. You're in it or you're dead. The only way you pay it all off is if you complete the gauntlet."

Hanna finished her tea.

"Mom and Dad made too much money for you to qualify for a good scholarship. But not enough to pay for school."

"It's not quite that simple. I'd need the same emotional support I had growing up which is statistically unlikely in the financial situations behind most of the scholarships and grants you're thinking about."

"Because poor girls don't do what you do?"

They stood and gathered their bags.

"The type of candymaker you're thinking of has as much to do with what I do as a douchebag at an open mic does with John Lennon."

"Can I see it?"

"What?"

"Where you work, the place."

"Of course! And you can meet Jalopy too."

"Who?"

"He's this guy and everybody loves him. It's the strangest thing."

"That has to bug you."

"Why would you say that?"

"Because you don't know what to do with yourself when you can't figure something out. You've always been like that. It's precious other than when I want to strangle you."

"Well OK then," The Smart One closed her laptop and almost put it away but then she stopped and said. "Of course I do know why everyone loves Jalopy."

"I'm sure you do."

Hanna continued gathering her things to leave.

"Everyone loves Jalopy because Jalopy makes the world's best beignets and normally he's relaxed and kind but he has to hurt people sometimes for his job."

"Oh my God, do you have a crush on this guy?"

"Hey listen, girl's gotta have a crush. Girl's gotta have a plan and girl's gotta have a crush."

\*\*\*

Letty and Gus licked the bits from their fingers and decided to take a stroll through Baton Rouge. At first, Letty said she couldn't because she looked like a disaster and was wearing house slippers. Gus asked if Letty felt comfortable. Letty said no and Gus told her to stop confusing the words comfortable and desirable. Gus said there was nobody left to impress but him and street signs. Letty said whatever.

They walked around Baton Rouge, enjoying the evening. They had consistent conversation interrupted by pops of excitement or pleasant disagreement played up. He was wearing a simple suit that didn't quite fit anymore because none of his clothes quite fit anymore because you shrink as you get older. Gus looked like a ne'er do well uncle walking his niece around the racetracks. And Letty looked like a young woman who needed a night off.

They started off by talking about what had happened at The Huxtable and she described the firing and she said she didn't get why everyone always talked about doing the right thing which she had always done and been punished for it. She'd never been the nasty gossip or the greedy liar. Why do the right thing? Gus asked if she needed any money. She said no.

"You don't need money, Letty?"

"No, no – thank you, but no."

"So this was supposed to be a complimentary evening?"

"This was supposed to be a lot of things."

"You're sure you're all right? That hotel has to cost a fortune."

"Sure does. I'm leaving first thing tomorrow morning."

"I didn't say you had to leave the place."

"I know Gus, but I don't know what I am doing there. Or here. I'm canceling every other david and I'm going to live in a cave."

"Well, if you're gonna be lost, might as well be lost for cheap."

"It's not about the money, I didn't pick this place for the money. I picked it because I wanted to be worth it for everybody."

"You're always worth it, Letty."

"Who isn't worth it when they're free?"

"Oy, you're too much."

"I am not too much!"

"What is this?! It's no to everything I say! You need money? No. So this was going to be complimentary? No. You staying? No. You're too much, woman."

"You think I'm too much?"

"Jesus, Letty!"

"Honestly, Gus, am I too much? You can tell me."

"And now you drop the no! For a joke? Ho boy, Letty. Letty Letty Letty."

"…I'm too much. Oh God, I am too much, Gus. I really am."

"You're not too much, Bubala. Come on. You're not an idiot and you're especially not whoever it was that answered that door. Give yourself a break, Letty, you're a hurtin' cowgirl is what you are."

"I'm too much."

"To who are you too much? Those fakakta Huxtable morons? All right, well, for them, you're too much. For me, you're not too much. I'd marry you this second."

"You don't want to marry me, Gus."

"OK I don't."

"You really want to marry me?"

"You're right. You're too much"

"You love me?"

"What am I going to do with you?"

"Be serious, are you honestly saying that you love me?"

"No, I'm not. I love the crap out of you but no, I don't love you. I don't love anyone Letty. I'm past that part of my life."

"You are such a liar."

"Who?"

"You! Past the love part, what a liar! No one is past the love part – you're such a liar!"

"Listen, do I love people? Sure, I love my kids. I could not talk with them for the rest of my life and I would love them. So I want to leave them as much as I possibly can and that's pretty much what I have left in life. And spending time well. I'm looking for good company and more to leave the kids, Letty. Which one do you think you are, toots?"

They'd been walking for about an hour and had made it back to Letty's hotel. Or across the street from the bench for po boys, whichever landmark you prefer demarcate the start of the walkabout.

"Gus?"

"Yes, Letty?"

"I have an idea."

"Do you?"

"I do."

"You want to go upstairs and try this again?"

Letty and Gus went up to Letty's hotel room while she laid out her whouse plan. She explained about having a whouse that took the best parts of the Huxtable and combined them with something more natural, something less overt. Way too many businesses compensate for not grokking their customers' needs with gaudy décor and kitchy tech. Bad boob jobs and apps instead of authentic, attractive people. Letty wanted to build something that was both less special and more special than The Huxtable. A place that people, not only men, but people could come to a couple of times a week if they wanted. They could hangout and if sex happened great, sex happened because sex is a part of life, a great part of life, but not the whole thing. Letty said it was like what Gus had said – life is about good company. Letty wanted a whouse where good company led where it led.

And Letty wanted it to be a franchise. Like Starbucks.

Gus said hmmm.

"Hmmm?" Letty asked.

"Hmmm," Gus said.

Then Letty said every whouse she'd been to or worked at had different positive qualities but always the same downfall – they all tried to build a sex castle.

"I have never sold sex and never felt at home in a castle," Letty said. "However, I have sold connection to human beings in delightful spaces. Sex is a part of a certain connection that men in particular have been starved of so I'm not saying that sex is unimportant. But you can't focus on the sex. When men are forced to focus on the sex they are being like cancer patients focusing on the headache. It's bad medicine to focus on the headache. Treat the disease and you get rid of the headache but you make them healthy for their whole lives. You build a place that feels relaxing but not like spa serenity overload. And you give great women the chance to create great connections."

Letty was sitting at the simplest desk in the very expensive place she'd used to give anal to Wall Street rich guy and put on too much eyeshadow. Gus was on one of the couches.

"Hm," Gus said.

"Do you understand what I'm saying?" Letty asked.

"Probably not but let me ask you a question," Gus said to Letty in the grotesquely golden suite. "What do you think this thing would cost to open?"

\*\*\*

The Deal That February Made

It hurts to be let go. It's shocking, even if you've seen it coming. You look around at all of the people who weren't let go and you catalogue their many inadequacies because they're the ones who suck not you. Them. Not you.

Then you realize it doesn't matter who sucks because you have to figure out what the Hell you're going to do for the rest of the afternoon. And tomorrow. And in seventeen years from now. Being let go is a miserable, practical process. No matter if you are laid off or fired.

Letty was laid off.

She was addressed with misguided sympathy and given an intimate sendoff. It hurt, it definitely hurt, and I'd never go telling Letty all about how it could have been worse.

Now,

It could have been worse. Because Letty may have been laid off, but February?

February was fired.

Jalopy and Mama and I came to her door at four in the morning. Mama was the foreman, I was supposed to keep things as calm as possible, and Jalopy's job was always the same.

First we took the hinges off the door. Didn't knock, didn't try to see if it was unlocked - when you're going to war you take total control then you ask for their assistance in your not having to murder them. Jalopy braced the door with about as much effort as it takes a normal human to hold a plain framed poster. He removed it from its slot and leaned it against the wall. We did not have to speak as we entered.

Oscar the Puppy's head popped up from the pillow his stomach and thigh made. He was sleepy and happy to see us but he was quiet because February was still asleep. He unwound himself and put his hinie in the air and stretched his back. Then he bounded up to the tippiest bit of the bed for one of us to pick him up. Mama hobbled over to get him. She waved us on.

Jalopy went to the opposing side of the Bed to the one I did. Once he'd made it into place I rustled her and said, February.

February.

Then she sniffed in and bolted the opposite direction of my voice without ever opening her eyes. She smashed into Jalopy and he held her and I said it was OK.

It's OK, February, I said.

Then I said that she could finally leave the Huxtable and that nothing was going to happen to her. We only wanted her to let everyone else be and we would take her anywhere she wanted to go. I told her she was finally free.

February's eyes were wide and Jalopy's hands were on her shoulders. Mama cradled Oscar who was staring at February. He wasn't barking but it was the only time I'd ever seen him look scared or in any way unhappy.

You're free now, I told her.

February looked over the room. She saw where Hildengarder was, where I was, the door. She saw how scared her sweet little doggie was.

Did you hear me, February? I said. You're free now.

I want to talk with Mama, she said.

No, I said, it's time to go, February.

You let me talk with Mama or I will scream and you will have to kill me to stop. You will have to kill me.

Mama said it was all right and she told me and Jalopy to wait outside. So we did and they whispered for a few minutes.

Then Mama came out and waved us back into February's room. February was stuffing a bag with her things and Mama stood with Oscar still in her arms. Jalopy and I came back in then Mama held Oscar out to February. February shook her head and continued going about gathering her things. She did not look up for the remainder of our visit.

Mama nodded then handed Oscar to Jalopy. Poor guy. It always comes to Jalopy.

Oscar barely covered one of Jalopy's paws.

Jalopy wrapped his fingers around Oscar who wasn't barking, wasn't scared any more either because February was no longer scared. He was nothing but a good puppy. Jalopy made sure to cover Oscar's whole head because it's easier for things with eyes to die with their eyes closed.

Then Jalopy squeezed and snapped and it was over because you really are that close to death all the time you are alive. All the time. Mama told us to deposit the body directly into the dumpster so Petunia would never see it.

Then February picked up her bag of things and walked out the hole where her door used to be. Survival upon her yet again.

*\*\*\**

The deal was simple, so long as Letty didn't prefer to marry Gus. Letty would be operations because she had lots of ideas and experience while Gus would be the money because he had lots of money. Letty said she did not want him to flat give her anything. This was an investment, she said.

Gus said this was not an investment, this was a loan. Or a wedding present, he said, her choice. She would have control of all aspects of the business, either way. Likewise, he said it was up to her if she wanted a white wedding. Either way, he definitely did not want a black funeral.

"Color, dawling. Color!" he said.

"Gus..."

"Oh honey, I get it. You don't want to be beholden to anyone. You think there's more to this than money. I've got veins like London plumbing, you'd have to deal with me for maybe fifteen years. Ten? Who knows it could be tomorrow. What's a decade in a lifetime? You're 40, 45 I would not be so uncouth as to ask exactly how old you'll be when I die, but I'm gone, you carry on with the pool boy along the way as long as you keep it discreet. You want kids? I'm snipped but you could adopt orphans, I don't care. Color at the funeral, that's all I ask. This is the deal you want, Letty. Not a loan. White or no white, up to you, but no black at my funeral – you really want to build a business? A business can fail. A marriage with an old rich guy can't. I'll be gentle with the pre-nup. Ha! You want love? You don't want love. You want a weak pre-nup is what you want."

Letty smiled.

"What a face. I tell you, Letty. The face alone is worth it."

They worked out the specifics of the deal. Gus would put up $2,000,000 and then asked Letty when she thought she could pay that back. She said in a year, no problem. He said how about half of it in a year? Letty said OK, one million dollars in one year. Gus said,

"One point one, honey, this is a loan. The rest the year after. I'm also retaining 100% equity until the first payment at which point I drop to 75, when you fully pay me off, I'll drop to 50% ownership. Not that any of this matters because it's not like you can take me to court for a brothel. But I want to be clear with you. Once you pay me off, we'll be full partners."

"We're partners now," Letty said.

"We're co-incentivized, yes. We're partners, no. I'm your banker until you pay me off, then we're partners."

"I see."

I hope you do, he said then he told her it wasn't up to him but that she should pay herself a fair wage too. If this goes south, he said, and most new businesses go south, then just about the only thing the banker does not have a claim over are fair wages.

"Now," he said. "None of this is going to matter because none of this can go to court. But I want this to be as legitimate as possible for you, Letty."

She said she appreciated that then asked what a fair wage was and he asked what she'd made at The Huxtable. She asked if more than fair was an acceptable answer.

"Letty, you're sure you understand that you've got a year to make that payment or that's it? It costs a lot to get a business up, you've got rent, political protection, marketing, laundering -"

"- healthcare."

"Oy Letty…" he shook his head. "…what a face."

Then Gus told her that he had a number of properties both in the area and not in the area that could work. Letty said that she'd love to see them but that she had some specific design ideas she wanted to try. He said that was up to her and that most of his buildings would provide some sort of renovation credit depending on the terms of the lease she signed and you're the one who wanted a loan so you better believe you'd have a lease, he said. Letty said she understood what she'd signed up for then told Gus she'd probably buy something, she knew that it normally didn't make financial sense to buy property but that rates were so low that it actually did make financial sense for the time being. What with rates. Gus told Letty she could do whatever she wanted but from a borrower's standpoint, which made more life sense: to create more collateral or less collateral? She said she'd look into it but Letty knew she was going to buy a place because she'd always known she was going to own her own place someday. And Letty was in a someday-is-this-day kind of mood.

Gus shook his head and said this was a tricky balance because he was trying to give Letty the real experience and she was over-leveraging herself which is the disease of dreamers and the dream of bankers. Don't get carried away by the beginning of things, Gus said. It's twitterpating to begin things and it's slaughter to finish. Pay yourself well, keep overhead low, and don't get a place any bigger than 6,000 square feet. Even that big is too big – brothel would have to be a front for a hedge fund to make any money. Don't be a dope, honey.

Letty asked what exactly was he going to do if she were a dope? Take her to court? Then she smiled because she felt like she was reminding him that the river of illegitimate business runs both ways. We're equals she felt herself saying.

Gus laughed.

Then he said he'd love to stay the night but his back was a nightmare from the walk. He said that the only thing he absolutely demanded as her personal banker and mentor was that he got to be the first customer. She said she could do that and they hugged and shook hands and he told her she'd have the money as soon as her laundering system was up.

***

Courage comes in moments,
Courage comes in bursts.
Courage leaves you things to do,
Courage is the worst.

\*\*\*

Letty and a real estate agent who hadn't sold a property in a year shuttled about Baton Rouge in a large luxury sedan the agent parked on the curb outside his refinanced hovel every night. Other than on street sweeping days.

Letty told the real estate agent that she was looking for a place to have a small market for fruits and vegetables. The agent said it was very important to eat organic.

Letty had decided to stick in Baton Rouge because she had a clientele that was used to New Orleans so she didn't think it would be too big a deal to transition them an hour and a half Northwest. She wouldn't be able to keep all of them but at least that gave her a place to start. She also decided to stick in Baton Rouge because she needed to get going. She had a loan, after all.

They checked out a warehouse at the edge of the safe place of town. She could see it working as a factory or hideout, not a whouse. Then they checked out an old dentist's office which could be leased or purchased which the agent said was a good option for a new business to have. Letty had no idea how the agent who had glued a pad of paper with his picture on it to the dashboard and who was surviving on savings could have possibly thought this a potential location for a boutique fruit and vegetable market. It was inside of an office building. On the second floor.

"You know what I'd love to see?" Letty asked.

The agent asked if the answer was curb appeal.

"A place that feels like home," Letty said.

The agent nodded and said curb appeal. Then the agent took Letty to a pocket of Baton Rouge called Spanish Town.

Tucked in between the Freeway and Downtown Baton Rouge was a sleepy segment of thick, bayou canopy hanged over house after house after house. This place was called Spanish Town. A historic district of 49 acres total, Spanish Town was a sleepy town but had beads in trees year round. Most roads were too thin for cars to go in either direction at once but there was no need to legally define any road a one way – people didn't need the Law telling them how to work it out with their neighbors in Spanish Town, Louisiana.

Oh, the moment when a woman first finds her home. And Grump & Granny's Bed & Breakfast on 8th Street in Spanish Town was home the moment it said hello to Letty.

Big front yard flush with herbs and bramble and almost overgrown, right on the edge of being something wild. Three wooden steps up a porch underneath a Juliet balcony. An exterior of pale blue slats and chipped black trim ran up two or three stories, you couldn't quite tell how big the Bed & Breakfast was with the trees framing it. But Letty felt confident in saying that this was a property with an honest to goodness attic. White-ish picket fence and a Foreclosure sign.

"It needs some work but it's cheap considering its bones," the agent said and opened the thigh high gate for his client.

Letty ran her fingers through some reedy brush and floated up the porch stairs to the front door which was locked. She strafed to a nearby window and cupped her hands around her face to look in. Between the sun and the dust, Letty couldn't see much but the haze. She knew that the B & B had nine bedrooms, one of which was a master with its own bath. Both the second and third floors had two additional bathrooms and there was a toilet with a sink on the first floor. A workable kitchen and a huge living room. It was 6,200 square feet. But that included the attic because the previous owner had insulated the attic and stuck a bed up there so said it was livable space. Letty asked if the attic was more than 200 square feet. The agent said probably and that he'd go get his tape measure if she absolutely needed him to right this instant. Letty said yes please then she said no never mind it didn't matter. She said she was wondering if the place was less than 6,000 square feet but that frankly, she didn't give a damn.

\*\*\*

First thing you do when you wake up in your new house is nothing.

You lay there and you baste.

You think things in duplicate like *This'll work; this'll work* and *Just a little longer; just a little longer*. Eventually, the sun gets too strong through the edges of the blinds you don't mind but won't keep because no one buys a house to keep the blinds. You say to yourself that it's time.

It's time.

Oh yes,

Letty bought the B & B and put it under the name of the corporation that the launderer made her create. She paid $962,000 for the whouse knowing that it needed a lot of renovations. She set an on-paper budget of $175,000 for the renovation and an in-brain budget of $235,000 and an Oh-Please-Not-Anymore-Than $299,000 budget.

For the next three months, Letty suffered the satisfaction of nesting. She compared tints of umber and splurged on flooring. She wished things were made in America and wrote check after check after check. She chose Netflix over decorating she'd swore she'd do the day before. She went back and forth over backsplashes and discovered infestations.

Letty lost as much sleep to excitement as she did to panic – she would stay up all night, squealing in her mind that she was really doing it! And she would stay up all night asking herself what the Hell did she think she was doing?

When she wasn't fielding the fourth Goddamned call from the electrician that day, Letty was steeped in hiring for her whouse that wasn't close to being finished. Daddy had always been like that too. Maybe that's what an entrepreneur is, someone so restless that everyone around them is forced to catch up. Themselves included.

Letty started with security because you shouldn't hire women until you have a way to protect them. Letty interviewed five former members of the LSU football team, five of whom had spent time in prison. This is standard practice because security for whouses and cooking in kitchens are asylums in the economy for released people. This is because prison makes you check certain boxes on applications for employment and provide certain answers in interviews. Or you can lie. As it is, honest ex-cons have re-entry issues. And honest ex-cons are terrific employees – they are disciplined, grateful, and usually a little stupid. They're perfect for most jobs.

FeDonathan, Cam, Banjo, Griff, and Steve who called himself Big Beer. Those were the five applicants that made it through to the interview. Letty had received a stack of a hundred applications from Jalopy whom she contacted through Gus who didn't say it was for Letty. Jalopy knew a lot of honest ex-cons looking for a job.

Each man weighed more than double Letty's weight, save for Banjo who had more that muscular, stabby, look. He was a trim 205, not counting tattoos. After three interviews held in public places, Letty put Cam and Banjo in the no pile, and FeDonathan in the maybe pile but only because she didn't like having one pile. Griff was a no-show. He'd been jailed because he'd skipped parole when he'd had a drink at a bar. The drink was a Diet Coke but that didn't matter because Griff was not supposed to be anywhere like a bar as a condition of his parole. The judge had told Griff that he was trusting him not to screw up again.

Thursday was Big Beer's day. Big Beer had printed his resume out at the Library and he had written the resume also at the Library with the help of the librarian who ended up typing it herself to speed up the process. Big Beer did not have a phone so could not directly contact Letty which he wanted to do to tell her she could call him Big Beer or Steve, whichever she preferred. Big Beer lived in a nightmare place they used to call halfway houses. He saw his daughter, April, under court supervision one day a month. He brought his daughter a new packet of beads for her hair every visit. His fingers were too thick a variety of kielbasa to braid a five-year old's hair, but he could sit and giggle with her while she did it.

April had stopped asking about things and she liked it when she saw her Dad.

April was living with her mother's grandparents because Big Beer had been released from a correctional facility after spending four and a half years as punishment for being in the room while his teammates had sex with a passed out co-ed. They called it a train which it was from one perspective. From another perspective, it was gang rape. Big Beer did not touch the girl but was in the room.

The quarterback took a video of the train and since no idiot is satisfied with but the one blunder, he peacocked it about the locker room. Big Beer was in the video then he was in prison. April was eleven days old. Big Beer got to check the sex offender box on applications too. Employers really didn't like that box.

Big Beer arrived at the coffee shop Letty had suggested instead of the whouse (because now the bloody basement might have black mold) 45 minutes early but he didn't step inside. The librarian had told him to be there fifteen minutes early because fifteen minutes early broadcast punctuality, courteousness, and awareness of the unspoken rules of employment seeking like using the word utilize whenever possible. So he sat at the bus stop where he'd exited. Big Beer filled the bench himself. Closer to seven feet tall than six, Big Beer clocked in at 385 pounds, down from the 430 he'd been the day he got locked up. He had a couple of tattoos, both on the upper portion of his right arm: one that read April and the other was a fleur de lys that everyone on the offensive line before homecoming or some other especially meaningful college football game.

Letty arrived and was relieved because Big Beer was the first one to have been on time, much less early (and also because the guy called and told her it wasn't black mold. He didn't know what it was but it wasn't black mold, so they were good.)

Letty approached Big Beer and extended her hand.

"Hello there, you must be Steve."

Big Beer spared the chair his glacier and rose to give Letty a handshake. Her hand was gnome sized in his.

"Steve r' Big Beer ma'am, 'chever yuh' prefer tuh' ewdulleyes."

His hand was trembling. Steve or Big Beer was either nervous or detoxing.

"Poligize fuh da shakes ma'am, jes that I's very excited to be under consideration for the position."

Big Beer had rehearsed the phrase "under consideration for the position" so his thumb of a tongue flicked the cascade of syllables correctly for once. Big Beer didn't like to talk because he knew he sounded dumb. He knew he was dumb too but not as dumb as he sounded. Big Beer was wearing what had to be one of the ten biggest grey suits ever put on Earth. It was the same suit he had worn to declare his intentions to attend LSU during his senior year of high school. They had televised the event because sports news networks could sell ads for showing Big Beer put on a particular college's hat. He handed Letty his resume which had not only been organized into four sections – education, experience, interests, special skills – but had a personal statement:

> *My personal goal is to protect people who need protecting especially people who other people don't think deserve it.*

Letty loved Big Beer. She offered him the job and told him that it'd be at least a few weeks before they could move in because the whouse was still a construction zone. Big Beer said that was fine. Letty said he would get rent for free and that any night a client came, he would make $200 and it would all come through a W2 form and be official so if he had parole or anything like that, he would be good. Big Beer said nothing bad would happen to Letty ever again or any of the other girls either. Letty said they'd be getting to other girls eventually and that something would happen because it always does. Letty said that the most important thing was that Big Beer tried his hardest to make it right when it did. He said he would and stood up again to shake Letty's hand and formally accept the position. They discussed neither trains nor April.

***

Since protection means more than security, Letty also contacted a lawyer. The lawyer had represented nine police officers in a civilian murder case with racial overtones. Nine White beat cops had pre-empted a robbery of a convenience store to be committed by a pair of dropouts on drugs (marijuana.) One died of injuries sustained and the other was left in a persistent vegetative state where he became a ward of The State for two years until he expired of natural causes. The patrolmen were suspended with pay for nineteen months until the comatose kid and his dead friend were found guilty. These were boys who did drugs (marijuana,) the lawyer had said. These were not good boys, the lawyer had said. The policemen who had families were reinstated other than one who received a medical retirement because he was too traumatized to work now that he had killed someone. This equipped the lawyer with a stock of grateful badges and a $200,000 retainer. The trial and the retirements cost $5.3 million of taxpayer money not including the amortized value of the courthouse.

Four months in: Letty had spent $1,354,760. The whouse was about 1.1 after the renovations, the lawyer who was worth it because lawyers are always worth it was 200, then there was 50 on setting up the launderer, and Letty had spent a collective $1,120 on a motel when she needed it, her food which was cup o noodles, her water which was tap, her phone which was old, and her entertainment which no longer existed. She had no car, some because she didn't want to spend the money and some because she hated cars.

Letty took no parties until her whouse was ready. She promised that the next time she had sex, it would be on her terms which meant her property. Now, she would reach out in order to keep up the relationships. - she wasn't so drunk on destiny that she forgot about what she was going to need once the whouse was open. She'd text and they'd try to be funny or send a dick pic and ask her schedule and she'd apologize and say Wait.

Wait until you see what's coming.

Most men did not want to wait.

Letty lost a lot of parties but more than that, Letty lost almost all of her davids saying no to the people who wanted to pay her right then and there. Fifth Law of Thermodynamics: A man wanting sex with a certain woman at a certain time will prioritize the time over the woman.

Wait, Letty would text.

It's worth it, she'd text. You won't believe what is coming.

Gus would check in and tell her it didn't matter to him because he was nothing but her banker but that she absolutely had to stop telling hungry people to wait for soufflé when there's whipped cream right there. Take the parties, he would say. Then Letty would say things like her brand mattered and that she was training her clientele and other slogans she came across online when she wasn't sleeping. He'd say it was up to her. He'd say he was nothing but the banker.

Letty kept a list of the men who had stopped reaching out. Letty would think about how spectacular her whouse was going to be and how they would never get to see it. Then Letty would think about how supremely delicious it would be to have the men who hadn't waited out when her spectacular whouse was finished so she could rub their snouts in how wrong they'd been to ever doubt Letty. She'd given them everything always and asked to wait once. Once.

This was the gig for the first few months. Fifty decisions she'd never thought she'd have to make every day, a list of the people who had done her dirty and schemes to punish them and/or get them back.

Eventually, fewer and fewer laborers were in Letty's way when she tried to go to the bathroom in the morning. The crown molding was installed and there was still plenty to be done, there is always plenty to be done, but so far as anyone who was not inside of Letty's maniac homeowner's mind was concerned, the whouse was ready.

So Letty told Big Beer he could move in.

\*\*\*

The Baton Rouge Bed & Breakfast

Four or so months after being sloughed off by the Huxtable, Letty welcomed her very first employee to her very own whouse.

She was waiting for him at the curb when he walked up. Big Beer had come from the nearest bus stop which was a couple of blocks away. He had a frumpy gym bag of all the things he owned in the world which were less than a week's worth of clothes and fourteen packets of beads he had purchased in bulk because there was a bulk discount. The bag was teeny tiny hanging beside him.

Letty welcomed Beer and he put down his bag to bow his head and shake her hand with both of his hands. She said Thank YOU and said she wanted to show him around.

She started with the sign. Turquoise and balsamic purple tiles in a mosaic reading "The Baton Rouge Bed & Breakfast" on a cross section of a petrified Malaysian tree. Big Beer had rehearsed the very genteel things he was going to say to Letty but he couldn't stop himself from whispering Whoa when he saw how classy the sign was.

Next was the porch. It was champagne colored mostly but the trim was now a deep maple syrup brown. Whole thing was enclosed in mesh which kept the bugs out but not the evening. Matching wicker rocking chairs and a swinging bench, all that maple brown. This time Jalopy whispered Damn.

Welcome home, Letty said and opened the door. The door was now red.

Inside The Baton Rouge Bed & Breakfast was a place to live a life. Reclaimed woods, raw but softened by creamy linens and cushions and pops of sheer turquoise tinged glass throughout the whouse too. No leather or jazzy vibe because Letty was done with that. This was a whouse where life would not be forced to announce sex. Organic antique, that's what Pinterest kept saying that Letty was doing. Big Beer was quiet because he was trying not to say anything else dumb and country and also because he was guessing which parts of the whouse his daughter would like best.

Letty showed Big Beer the bedrooms and the kitchen, the little table meant for breakfast and the big one meant for dinner. She showed him her bedroom which wasn't the biggest nor the nicest and she showed him his which was the only one downstairs. She said he could pick a different one if he wanted to and he said no, he should be at the bottom. She said all right then and that there was food in the kitchen and she'd leave him to it. Then she said to try and get a good night's sleep because tomorrow was going to be a big day. OK, Big Beer said.

Big day tomorrow, Beer, Letty said. The girls are coming tomorrow.

***

God bless the boss who monetizes their problems.

Letty could interview some women, even sleep with them. But women don't have sex with women like they do with men. Letty knew this. For that matter, women don't interview with women like they do with men. Women to women are sanctuaries or competitors.

So the Baton Rouge Bed & Breakfast opted to crowdsource.

Letty had four davids left. What had been an almanac had disintegrated into a blog post. There was Harry who was 61 and something like an investor, some sort of financial this or that. There was Jeremy who was 48 and had won the Powerball lottery. There was Abdullah, a 24-year old ex-pat prince of the royal Yemeni family. And there was Jose, a 52-year old member of the Major League baseball Hall of Fame. In reality, Letty undoubtedly could have contacted all of those davids who had told her they didn't want to wait and I'm sure they would have jumped right back on the Letty train. Anyone really – men tend to be open to hot women looking for sex. But that's not how Letty saw it, at least not for this first week. This first week needed to be the people who had stuck it out with her. The people who believed in her.

So Letty contacted the men who hadn't left and she told them that she was ready. They said great and said they were excited to see what Letty had in store for them. She told them that she didn't want to spoil the surprise but that for $18,000 they would get a full week stay, food, and parties with six different women fighting for the best jobs in the history of the sex business.

What about you, Letty? They asked.

If at the end of this week, you still have anything left, then I'll take care of you, Letty said. And you are always welcome to come back.

They all agreed. This meant that Letty had not hired a single woman yet, hadn't even officially opened, and she'd already done seventy-two grand in revenue. Not half bad for a brand new business owner, huh?

Men. Check.

Now onto women.

Letty was enamored of the idea of finding someone unsullied. Someone she could cultivate into noble prostitution not backseat blow jobs and alley pumps. That prostitute had somehow become a dirty word was as if astronaut became a slur. Real prostitution is powerful. Real prostitution is positive. Help humanity and yourself, she wanted to scream to the world, have sex for a living.

So Letty activated the internet and put up an ad on the LSU job board because is there any better place to go prostitute hiring than a university?

"MAKE A DIFFERENCE! We are a small team of individuals working to make our local community better. We balance the need to make money with the importance of making real social impact. Click for more information."

Within eight hours of posting, Letty had received 100 inquiries. She held a complimentary informational session at a local Greek deli which she rented out from the owner, Emilio. Emilio had a hairy chest, an open collar, and a penchant for gold chains which rested on his breast like a just-used hose in a well-watered lawn. His pasta salad was delicious because he used whole leaves of basil and fresh aioli. That was how his Nonna did it.

93 people showed up to the informational session, some due to Letty's passionate ad, some due to the pasta salad. About a third of the attendees were male because Letty had decided against including a Ladies Only clause. The right young woman for Letty would not be looking for a girl's only gig. The right young woman would not want to be charity.

Which brings us to Zoey.

Inside the mass of university sweaters and socially conscious sneaker brands was a t-shirt. Dyed black hair and a nose ring, not stud, ring like the one Ferdinand the Bull had. Zoey had big brown eyes and intricate tattoos covering her body which was covered by the t-shirt. The t-shirt was a big Peace sign. Zoey was from Portland, Oregon. In general, you can identify a Portland girl because she'll love strip clubs and independent book stores equally. Provided the dancers can actually dance.

The pasta salad had been served an hour prior so the collegiate mass was breaking up. The last clump of students exited Emilio's Delicatessen while Letty and Zoey talked. Letty had not yet said what the job to save humanity was but she and Zoey were engrossing each other. Letty apologized for the unorthodox recruitment system and said that in her experience, when people can't prepare for what they think you want, you see who they really are.

Zoey said that made sense but that Letty should know that Zoey had come for a good look at Greek chest hair. She laughed and said that a job helping humanity was extra now so far as Zoey was concerned. Helping humanity might even be unnecessary with man boob mane like that on the loose. Job done.

Zoey was short and had a pixie haircut. She was more curvaceous than you'd expect of a small lady, especially when she got naked. She wore t-shirts which usually pointed to Peace and Love but always masked her bust. Zoey was clever but not mean. That her hips hid in her height, her breasts hid in t-shirts, and her heart hid in her wit made it tough not to fall in love with Zoey.

Letty gathered her purpose and started in on prostitution. As you'd expect, Zoey had considered the idea before. For any males still with us, understand that most women have thought about having sex for money because most women have been asked to have sex in exchange for money. Yes, darling, women get propositioned without ever asking for it. And rape can make you pregnant. Fun fact.

"How do you stay safe? How do you do it when they're like gross dudes? How much does someone pay for you, Letty?"

Letty described her experience in the business. She said it was the best decision she'd ever made in her life. That it provided her adventure and a chance to help people.

"And money too?" Zoey asked.

You can make money in anything if you love it, Letty said. She explained about Big Beer and the lawyer, that they were as protected as it could get in any business. And that Zoey could leave whenever she wanted for whatever reason.

Zoey said maybe.

Letty said it would only be four nights of Zoey's life. Then they would talk. If it wasn't for Zoey, that was fine. Really, Letty said, it was fine. Then she asked Zoey if she was interested.

Zoey said maybe.

Letty said she understood then asked if Zoey were looking back on this in 50 years, would she be more upset if she went for it or if she stayed the same course she was on? The same course she could go back to in four days. Keeping in mind that she will be safe and no one but her ever has to know.

Zoey said maybe.

Letty asked where else would Zoey get $3,000 in cash just to see if she wanted a job?

Zoey said OK.

***

Zoey was the rainbow so Letty understood she was taking a swing at something special there. Every other woman she brought in was a more practical candidate.

Letty came across a horde of possibilities when she went online because the number of prostitutes on the internet is as mind boggling as the number of everything else on the internet. Craigslist, Backpage, online dating sites, legal whouses outside of

Vegas with their own websites, Brunettes, Asians, big boobs and planks – there is a continent of sex for sale on the internet.

Letty would call potential candidates and these women would pick up in the exaggerated voices they'd been corseted into, husky or girly, the caricatures bad pimps gerrymandered of women. As if no one had ever been attracted to a woman apart from the sexpot mom next door or a Japanese schoolgirl before. Letty would call and all she wanted to do was to scrub the hooker off of them. She wanted to tell them that this call was the opportunity they didn't realize they'd been working towards all along. A salary, safety, the space to make the sex that made sense to them, and using their actual voice to make actual people happy.

But Letty knew she was already reaching with Zoey. Letty needed professionals. Now they also needed to be women who had not yet lost themselves entirely to the mutations created by jewel toothed backhanders who don't get people. Of which she found and flew out five.

*** 

Four men of means, five experienced women and a Zoey. This is how hiring went.

The women were to arrive at the Baton Rouge Bed & Breakfast for a welcome dinner on Thursday night. One local and five out of towners. Letty paid each of them a stipend and put them up at the enormously expensive hotel she had abandoned after receiving a two-million-dollar loan or wedding proposal from Gus. Different candidates required different paychecks for participation. Zoey was the lowest at three grand. A woman named Rikki was the most at fourteen five. A woman named Pearl was between the two.

Pearl had taken the red eye in from her native Atlantic City because she'd had a party the night before. After settling into the hotel, she headed over to Spanish Town. Not to go inside the B & B but to walk around the neighborhood. Scope the scene.

So many houses, she thought. Hard to believe they have a whouse in all this. Goes to show you that you never really know.

Pearl had lived in Atlantic City for half her life. She didn't much like it but she'd stayed in Jersey because her son deserved to finish high school where he'd started. She didn't want him to lose her friends. Peter, the son who had friends, was graduating in the Spring then headed to Villanova to study mechanical engineering. She didn't understand how Peter popped out of a seventeen-year old. Mechanical engineering! Her son! There's nothing quite like having a kid as a teenager then parenting teenagers when you're in your 30s. That was you, you think.

And you had a kid.

Pearl had arrived another pair of double D's with big blue peepers to Atlantic City. She had felt ravishing walking the floors of those behemoth casinos. Parties of people screaming at craps tables and tourists snapping on disposable cameras. She could do five thousand bucks a week without any hustle. Then Macau ate Atlantic City. The internet ate Atlantic City. Super storms ate Atlantic City. Now it was rough for Pearl to cobble together five hundred. Now Pearl had to exist on stairclimber machines and say no to any food that tasted remotely good in order to maintain what remained of her figure. Not improve. Oh no. Life was about mitigating decay at this stage for Pearl. At least until her son was launched. Then she'd come up for air and see where she was at.

Candidate Pearl was in Baton Rouge but Candidate Sandy and Dandy was stuck on a layover in Denver. Both birth names, Sandy and Dandy were flying in from Montreal and to be considered as a single candidate rather than two. They only ever worked as a team and only ever went places as a tandem. This had been their way since they'd met in fifth grade. Letty contacted Dandy who explained their partnership. Letty thought it could work to have a double, if only to break up the week for the men. They assured her that they cost what one woman cost and delivered what ten women delivered.

The frontrunner was Candidate Rikki. Half Black, half Filipino, Rikki was becoming a major player in Iowa where there were no major players. That she could make davids in Iowa was enough to attract the attention of any number of destination whouses, the Huxtable included. Daddy had auditioned Rikki, even offered her a Bed. But Rikki didn't like the idea of living underground, nor did she like the idea of living in a busy city. She was an Iowan, she said,

We like persons but not people.

Rikki agreed to come for the audition after Letty spent a good deal of cellular data showing Rikki how Baton Rouge was quaint and how the Baton Rouge Bed and Breakfast was above ground. Ultimately, it was Rikki's Mom who convinced her to go.

"Think of it as a paid vacation, Rikki," she said.

"But it's not a vacation, Mom. I'll have four parties in six nights, five if I have to audition with the owner. It'll be work."

"But the owner's a girl, honey, so that one doesn't count."

"I guess…"

"And that's four chances to make a david of your own. Planes fly to Iowa too, y'know."

How could Letty say no to that! Not only was Rikki's Mother tolerant of her daughter's career, she was a cheerleader. To be supported – not abided or silently served at family dinners, but actually supported – that was the kind of cornerstone that Letty was excited to bring aboard. Plus, Rikki was transcendently sexy and Daddy couldn't get her.

Pearl, Zoey, Sandy and Dandy, Rikki, then last, and very much least, Scratch. Scratch had been at it for fifty something years. Everyone her age was dead or doing novelty pornography (porn porn porn – everything in sex went to porn with the internet.) Scratch was there to try out administration. She would keep the ladies in line as only a matron could and see if she liked playing Mama. She could also give the men a night off from sex, unless they wanted it.

Letty hosted her ladies for dinner where she explained how it would work. Each woman would audition with four men over the next week. They were expected to spend a full night with each male who had each been a david of Letty's so were safe. You'll hear hokey whouses refer to a full night with a prostitute as the Girlfriend Experience (GFE.) You will never hear a whouse of stature mention a GFE for the same reason Ferrari does not note its fine power turn signals.

Letty was sitting at the head of the dinner table. The table was made of a kind of petrified beech so looked like an artsy slab of driftwood and was overflowing with boxes of Chinese takeout. Letty wanted the dinner with her candidates to feel informal but also professional like co-workers working together after the office had closed. That's why Letty went with too much takeout.

Letty welcomed everyone then said that the Baton Rouge Bed & Breakfast was going to be a premium whouse so target rates would be right there with standards like the Sturdy Goose and the Huxtable. There would be salaries at the B & B also. Then she answered a few questions about timing and said under absolutely no circumstances were the women to accept tips.

"A tip says we either didn't charge enough or we don't pay you enough. Neither of which will be true."

She said they were welcome to stay as long as they wanted that night but that there was a shuttle waiting to take them back to the hotel outside. Then she thanked them again for participating and to enjoy dinner and Louisiana and that was it.

Pearl rocketed to Letty to thank her for the opportunity and Letty asked her about the flight, which had been a turbulent time trapped in a tube six miles in the sky.

"Fine, easy," Pearl said. Pearl poo-pooed with her hand and complimented Letty on something or other.

While Pearl went at Letty after the spiel, Rikki went outside for a cigarette and ten frantic texts on the porch. Letty didn't know Rikki was a smoker. Scratch moseyed over to Rikki. Everyone knew Scratch was a smoker.

"Now how's an old broad supposed to compete with you?" Scratch asked.

Rikki said thank you and she didn't know but thank you. Then she said that didn't normally smoke but that this was the first time she'd ever been South of Kansas City. Rikki said her mother would kill her on the spot to see her smoking.

Inside, Zoey was going hard on egg rolls. She hadn't eaten anything that day because she was a college student and had gameplanned around the complimentary dinner. Big Beer was amazed by Zoey, this rampaging badger. She looked up with eggplant entrails dangling from her lips to see Beer staring at her. Zoey laughed without a speck of shame upon her.

Letty liked Rikki's credentials.

Letty liked Pearl's professionalism.

Letty couldn't help herself but to like Zoey.

She had Scratch to manage the girls and she had a threesome to break the week up.

To the davids they went.

\*\*\*

The following are the comments regarding Scratch that Letty received on the forms she issued her davids. The men loved the forms because it is pleasing to give your feedback into well formatted feedback forms.

**Harry (61-year old Investment Guy):** *Waste of a night on one hand, although it's nice to have a night off on the other hand. Scratch is a woman who is not attractive to me which I made clear to be up front about. I thought it only fair in case she had certain expectations (I'm sure the girls talk too.) So we had a fabulous dinner which I am happy to provide, talked for a while, then went to a movie. Turns out we had similar taste in film oddly enough, wouldn't expect a woman with her background to have as sophisticated a palate for movies as she copped to. Selma, we saw. Very powerful film, she felt otherwise which surprised me. I didn't see how someone could sit through that story and not feel affected, perhaps she was disappointed that I had told her I was not open to sex. Perhaps that was insensitive of me but I thought we were both too old to play games. Perhaps a woman is a woman after all.*

**Abdullah (24-year old Yemeni Prince):** *Jose said a lot about Scratch so I was stoked. And I've never been with anything as old as her before, so I was down. She thought I was too much of a kid. I know she did. She kept her clothes on mostly but I saw her stomach and arm skin wings. Dem grammy flaps! I came and she needs to know I am a man. Just because you're old doesn't mean I'm not a man.*

**Jeremy (48-year old Dude Who Won the Lottery)** *I'm confused, is Scratch going to be Mama here? I follow that, she seems like it, obviously a very experienced woman too. As much as I like her, she's not someone who I would call attractive anymore. I'm sure she was something in her day and we had incredible conversations. But she isn't someone I would seek out for sex. Maybe this was a favor to her or you brought in for other reasons, I understand that. Like I said, a matronly lady. Very interesting and I'd be happy to have a cup of coffee with her. But from a sexual standpoint? She's a great lady but, well, I will say that you've got to be tall to play basketball. Don't give us too much credit here, Letty, is what I'm trying to say.*

**Jose (52-year old Hall of Fame Baseball Player):** *Very very smart, very very real. We grow up same way, both on our own, no parents. Both have kids that leave us, others that don't. We both spend our lives in business no good for families. But we good people. Very very attracted to her soul. More great sex, maybe not Rikki but different. More emotions. We talk about to see each other again. She say you wouldn't mind.*

***

Scratch had been born Cynthia spelled Sinthia for her career years. She had three kids after four births by eighteen years of age. One was her son and brother too.

Cynthia was fourteen when she first gave birth. The baby was very handicapped. Then Cynthia's father died of Cynthia's mother murdering him and herself. Cynthia's first son also died on the family farm. Although unlike his father and grandfather, Cynthia's mother didn't kill him. Winter did. Eighteen-month old's with spines outside of their bodies aren't meant for weather.

By sixteen she had taken a man whose biological makeup would not overlap with hers. Thus their mingling would not produce shaky babies. She made three new humans with the new guy.

The new guy and Cynthia couldn't marry because the new guy was still married to his old wife. They'd been separated for many years but could not afford the formal divorce. Because he had never reproduced with his estranged wife, Scratch who was Cynthia not Sinthia yet, did not consider her and his situation to be complicated. She thought of divorce as an errand he had to take care of that he couldn't yet, some day he would, and keep on trucking.

Truck on they did, right until Cynthia's nineteenth year of life. At which point, the new guy went back to his old-but-not-ex-wife. He said Cynthia had become controlling and didn't pay attention to him either. The oldest of their babies was about to turn three when her Dad left and she never saw him again because none of the babies ever saw the new guy again. Cynthia sold the farm which held mixed emotional resonance with her due to her having lived there her entire life which included some incest and murder and wonderful cups of cocoa while it snowed like God Almighty's falling dandruff outside. That's what her dad had called snow, God's dandruff. He had said this because Cynthia had dandruff as a child and was called Cynthia Blizzard at school for it. Worse than loving her father, Cynthia liked him. The mom had been the monster of the household.

Cynthia became Sinthia because somehow names mean something to people when they start taking parties. Before long, Sinthia had established a stable stream of davids. The kids grew up in a middle class house. She told them she was a therapist. This worked until the oldest one became angry at her mother after suffering through another round of catcalls from classmates (rumors of the sexual nature of Sinthia's profession was cul de sac scuttlebutt) and called an organization called Child Protective Services (CPS). The oldest one didn't think anything would happen to her mother. Though she screamed a lot at her mother for lying to her, the oldest one believed her mother to, in fact, be a therapist. The oldest one called CPS to make herself like the kids at school. The oldest one wanted to be an accuser too.

"You can do better," CPS said as they took her children and offered Sinthia a great deal of support should she make an appointment.

The system swallowed the family. Even if she had been able to find a legal stream of income with no high school diploma, Sinthia would have needed at least two years of uninterrupted victories in court proceedings to reassemble her brood. The oldest one's anger and confusion and genetic disposition spun into an identity unable to communicate with its mother. The other two checked in on holidays. Although the youngest one's interactions were more sporadic because he spent a fair amount of time in juvenile detention centers and then jail and then prison. The middle one did well for herself in merchant services.

\*\*\*

As much as Letty learned about the ladies, the recruitment process did more to illuminate her own business to her than she ever imagined. For example, after the first night, she learned she needed to soundproof every room. She learned this because at eleven o'clock, the Baton Rouge Bed & Breakfast metamorphosed into the Baton Rouge Bed & Breakfast Symphony of Coital Noises. Creaks, screams, some of the ladies were laying it on thick. The whouse rang with the clichés of intercourse save for the coiling and recoiling of springs because every mattress in the B & B was adjustable memory foam. Letty was horrified, she'd thought she'd blown the whole week. She came to her guests the next morning ready with her checkbook – why was she constantly trying to provide refunds when men were unhappy?

The davids didn't mind.

"Soft launch," Jeremy the lotto winner said over ham and waffles. Letty tried to apologize to each one of her davids but all they wanted to do was talk with each other about their previous evening's applicant and eat breakfast meats.

"Smoking pony are you a grunter!" Harry said to Jose. "Water buffalo. I thought you were gonna split her in two."

Abdullah was looking at his phone at the table.

"Who was that? Zoey? Was that Zoey?" Abdullah asked.

Harry shook his head and took a smug sip of the cappuccino for which he had settled after Letty had told him she'd forgotten to get the coffee brand he'd asked her to get. Letty would go get the instant coffee brand that Harry preferred after the morning council had adjourned.

"Wasn't Zoey," Harry said.

Jose sneered.

"El jefe had Zoey. It was…another."

Harry laughed to himself.

"El Jefe!" he said.

Abdullah focused on his phone.

"Good," he said.

Jose stood up from the table to wash his dish but Letty intercepted him. Letty had buried her face in kitchen chores because she was trying to be invisible and listen. Maybe it was that she had the whouse to channel her observations into or maybe it was that none of the men were thinking about sleeping with her, but Letty was listening like she'd never listened before. She was learning incredible things every time another david said something.

Jose sat back down.

"Jeremy had Rikki," Harry said. "Zoey had me and the Piano Keys had the night off."

"I banged Pearl," Abdullah said to his phone.

"I like Pearl," Jeremy said.

"She was cool," Abdullah said.

Jose had nowhere to go. He piped up, defensively but also very much a man speaking amongst his buddies.

"It was Scratch! Yes, OK, Scratch."

"There now! Nothing to be ashamed of, Jose," Harry said and chewed food. "So Scratch is a screamer."

Abdullah laughed. Jeremy smiled and left and Jose said

"I don't know, man. Never been with nobody old before but her. Damn. She start talking and she a woman, you know? Full woman. Not like these little girls. Didn't go out. Ordered dinner here, man – I do salad. Didn't get no meat and so what? She old, she don't care if I eat salad. So we talking like I talk with a man, you know. Talking like I talk with an equal. We take out pictures of our grandkids. I look at her pictures then I look at how she look at my pictures and I don't know man. I kiss her. Then she took it, man. Took it and took it. Dio de dios se encanta!"

"Jose!" Harry said. "You're my age, you'll kill yourself doing that to a woman!"

Harry was both nine years older than Jose and not a world renowned baseball player but at the drop of an accomplishment, men defend the image of athletes they never actually were. Jose shrugged and went up to his room.

Letty walked to the local market to get the instant coffee brand that Harry wanted. She was excited because her whouse seemed to be working but she was more fascinated by what it was like to hear a group of men talking who weren't seeing her. Not jealous, not at all – no, it was engrossing to learn so much all at once about these people that she thought she'd known. Especially to frame the things she was learning as a business owner. Then Letty groaned because it was going to be expensive to soundproof the damned place.

Letty bought the coffee that Harry wanted which cost 3 times what the normal brand cost but that was all right, Letty thought. As she strolled back to the B & B, Letty made out a figure slumped on her porch steps. It didn't move and it wasn't a package.

Letty got closer.

It wasn't one figure but two. One was a lumpy black trash bag and the other was the shambles of a human being. Skinny arms wrapped around skinny legs, and knotty dry hair.

It was February.

***

Candidate two was Pearl who spent the week pulling her partner out of the whouse each night, going to expensive steak dinners in crowded locations. She dressed in sinuous black ditties and was sure to be on the arm of her david. Pearl knew how to look like the credential with which some men like to be seen. She hunted Letty down every morning to ask if Letty needed any help which Letty never did. Pearl sent a handwritten note when the week was over thanking Letty for the opportunity.

Here are Pearl's comments:

**Abdullah:** *Pearl is crazy! I mean, she got so horny that she was all like "I want to feel you." So yeah. SHE WANTED ME! So awesome. We also went to dinner.*

**Jose:** *Fake. Very fake. Not bad but fake. Dinner was OK.*

**Harry:** *Last girl of the week, back to life! First of all – attitude. Pearl has to be tired but she looks great and is very cheerful. Much appreciated. Classic look. Black cocktail dress and we had a fine steak dinner. Not exactly scintillating conversation, restaurant was too loud. I have to say I was on my game tonight. I counted five orgasms on her end.*

*But what happened with Sandy and Dandy???!!! That was a horror show.*

**Jeremy:** *I liked Pearl but I don't know how much she liked me honestly. We talked a lot about sex, seemed forced. Maybe she was nervous but we never really clicked. Looked great though. Takes great care of herself. Over buttered steak for dinner too.*

*** *

On the novelty side of the spectrum, Sandy and Dandy finally arrived Friday morning. Frayed but not frazzled from travel that took two days all told, they had interdependent looks. Both were pasty Canadians with excellent bone structure in their faces. Same height, 5'8". Dandy's hips were wider and Sandy's breasts were bigger. One was blonde with Cinderella length hair, this one was Sandy. And the other had a sharp crop of crow black bangs that came to a precise line midway down her forehead. This one was Dandy.

The six women candidates said they appreciated that they had a night off during the week and the four men said it was smart to schedule a double. A double broke up the week well. But the men also said that Sandy and Dandy were a lot to take on a date.

Then there was the incident.

Three things before we get to the davids' comments on Sandy and Dandy. 1, Sandy and Dandy were not hired so don't worry about trying to track which was which – I doubt that they know themselves. 2, after an easy start to his life in whouse security, Big Beer had to do some work with Sandy and Dandy. 3, to answer your question before you know to ask it, no, Letty did not know what Sandy and Dandy were planning. And when Letty found out what they'd done, she offered to refund Jeremy's admission. But he said absolutely not, that he wanted to support Letty and that this stuff happens (which it does, by the way, a whole lot more than most muggles think anyhow.)

To the forms:

**Jeremy:** *I don't know how to begin, but I know how to end. Exciting to have a double and I'd heard about what they can do from another guest, so I was prepped. For the price for the week to have five parties and one of them a double is a fantastic deal. Really incredible – I'd do this every year if you'd offer it. Even with what happened. So Sandy and Dandy delivered, they did. I don't remember ever orgasming that hard. Went to dinner and some drinks first but nothing special there. I guess it was kind of fun to be two girls one guy out in public. Then we come back and wow. Wow. The blonde one, after I finished in the condom (I can* *never finish in condoms,) asks if I want any more? Her tone has changed. I say I'm pretty beat plus I have a flight tomorrow, last night and all. She asks if it's OK if they take care of each other. So right off, that's kind of a weird question. Like, if you two want to do whatever you want to do, go do it on your own. I want to go to sleep. But fine, a show to end the show. So then, honest to God where do these people come from, she begins to massage the other one's stomach. Sandy, Dandy – who knows who the Hell each one is. Starts to ask if "baby has a tummy ache?" They don't connect other than that and the whole thing feels more like a medical rehearsal than sensual role playing. Whichever one has the black hair is lying on her back on the rug. She poops. She poops all over the rug. The blonde starts encouraging her, "good girl, that's a good girl." More poop. Complete logs – I'm not joking. I cannot believe what it is going on. I'm stunned so I start to tell them to stop. Oh my god, stop. Please. But I might as well have been on Jupiter because these two don't hear me at all. And I'm not going to touch them. I should have thrown something but I didn't want to hurt one and end up with that situation. I scream for security, Beer shows up and so does Harry. Harry looks like he's going to vomit. But god bless Big Beer, you got a good one there Letty. He takes off his jacket, rolls up his sleeves then folds up the rug and carries them out like they were fried fish in a big soft taco. The whole week I couldn't believe the value, I guess I had this coming to balance it all out. They didn't do this to the other guys did they? I almost don't want to ask. Harry said he'd never seen anything like it. But the Middle Eastern kid describes them like they're goddesses. Is this something that guys actually like? I mean I know the answer is yes. But is this something you do, Letty?*

**Abdullah:** *Best night of my life. One licked my butthole and jacked me off while I was doing the other one. Then we did a steamer and smeared it all over her pretty face.*

**Jose:** *Don't trust them. They bored doing threesome. Don't trust girls bored in threesome.*

**Harry:** *Smart to do a menage a trois, broke up the week nicely. They seemed more interested in each other than me though, even when they did this trick. One tossed my salad while the other one pumped me out and slapped it on. But they felt like they were having sex with each other through me which would have been emasculating to most other men (I'm trying to look out for your well-being, Letty.) Obviously I am able to fulfill any sexual request a woman might ask, you know that firsthand. Fun for what it is, but I wouldn't do it again. More a story than anything else.*

\*\*\*

Letty got February into her room then asked how she'd gotten there. Thank God it was daytime so none of the davids were around to see.

February recounted her path as if it were happening to someone else.

"She is tired. The driver tells her to get out. She calls him on the phone. He doesn't answer. The driver yells at her. She calls him again. He is sad because he misses her so he doesn't answer. She misses him too. The driver is very angry. She picks her things up to set them down beside her in a booth in a restaurant she walks to.

Is it all right if she brings the dog in with her? He's only a puppy and he's very sweet. What dog? The booth has cushions. She would like a menu. She does have money. She would like a menu. Banana pancakes please. Syrup is good. She goes to sleep for a while. He calls her and tells her where Letty is. She should buy a hat."

February had a pristine baby blue cotton cloche hat with a bow and a downbrim. The rest of her was mudcaked and sweatstained. Her face was scabby and her fingernails full of dried blood. She weighed 92 pounds, down from 120 when she was thin at the Huxtable.

Letty told February the hat was very pretty. Then Letty told her to stay right there because she was going to bring February a snack. Letty left. February stood a few steps past Letty's room's door. Her trashbag of things rested on the floor beside her and she continued to hold it. Letty came back with a cartridge of yogurt.

"I'll trade you," Letty said and reached for the trashbag.

"All right," February said and her grip disintegrated. Letty moved the bag a foot in her direction. Then she handed February the yogurt.

February held the yogurt.

February watched Letty take the bag and go to the other side of the room.

Letty wanted to respect February's privacy but several tears had opened up in the black plastic trash bag. She saw a scuffed heel of a very expensive shoe and piles of fabric. When Letty set the bag down, the weight shifted and it made a clang that Letty knew to be a dog bowl. She turned to see February standing in the same place. February held the yogurt.

Letty came back to February and mixed the blueberry preservatives at the bottom of the yogurt. She did not take the yogurt from February's hand. February watched the yogurt turn purple.

"Blueberry OK, February? I have other flavors."

February nodded.

"Give it a try, February."

February did not look away from Letty nor did she reach for the yogurt.

"Go on then."

February went for the spoon submerged in the yogurt and see-saw leaning against the edge of the plastic cup. Her fingers did not respond to her arm so she ended up knocking the spoon out onto the floor.

"Oopsie daisies, I'll get it, February."

Letty picked up the spoon and held it up for February to take back. February lifted her arm which was twiggy like a cockroach antenna. She took the spoon, scraped yogurt from the skim of the cup and set it in her mouth. Letty watched her swallow then checked the hallway to be sure that the path to the bathroom was clear. It was.

"Now what do you say to a bath?"

Letty herded February toward the bathroom.

"How about it?"

February did not have the strength to prevent Letty from pulling her into the bathroom. She did not have the strength to help either.

"We'll go slow."

February floated along. They made it into the bathroom and Letty reclaimed the yogurt and turned on the faucet. She told February that February could finish the yogurt in the bath.

"Let's help you take these off first."

Letty revealed February.

Her ribs were xylophones, bruised and her skin was so very dry. She had a six pack stomach by default. Dried blood all over but the oldest darkest bit was some running from her vagina until it tapered away around her knees. Standing at rest, her arms did not touch her chest nor did her thighs touch each other. Spiderlike, Letty took February's hand and supported her into the warm tub. The bathwater darkened like the yogurt had.

Letty gave February the cartridge and wrung water from a washcloth onto the nape of her neck. Water sloshed back into itself, sliding off of the scapula and spine.

"Would you stay here with me tonight?" Letty asked. "Would you like to stay here with me, February? How does that sound?"

February held the yogurt in both hands.

"Would you be willing to stay here, February?"

Letty started to swab the body that housed February. It did not react then it started to shiver. Letty turned on the hot water again and rubbed February's body's arms.

"What do you say, February??"

"Y–y–you can havvvve m–m–my davids."

Her teeth were chattering.

"Thank you February, that's very kind of you. Would you like to stay?"

"You can have my davids."

"I heard that, thank you. There are some davids here now but why don't you stay with me tonight and we can talk about the other stuff tomorrow?"

February started to sob instead of eat yogurt. "I'm not always this," she said.

"I know, February. Hey. Hey I know that. I know that, OK?"

Letty took the yogurt from her so she could wipe her nose.

"I'm n-n-not this."

February cried so Letty wiped her eyes.

"You let it get away from you, didn't you, February? Did it get away from you?"

February vibrated so Letty rubbed her back.

"That's OK, February. You can sleep here. Do you want to sleep here tonight? How about you sleep here tonight?"

February sniveled and nodded.

"Great! I'll get a room ready for you – you're going to love it!"

"I love you, Letty."

"I love you too, February."

"I love you so much, Letty."

***

Hire. Young. Talent.

Those are the three words in the holy stone tablet of the religion of recruitment. Hire young talent. If this is the story of building a business, then that is the lesson. That is always the lesson. Hire young talent.

So,

Zoey.

Zoey showed at 6:20 for a 7:00 PM party. She was wearing a scarlet red lace teddy underneath a trench coat and had glopped on as much makeup as would stick to her face. Zoey texted Letty from the B & B porch. She was there. What was she supposed to do now?

Letty excused herself from a conversation with Harry about the value of 401k's to employers. She walked out into the muggy to find Zoey sitting on a step.

Zoey told Letty she was ready then asked if she looked ready. Letty said she looked ready if she felt ready.

"Do you feel comfortable?" Letty asked.

Of course she didn't feel comfortable! She was a mime wearing lingerie underneath a coat in Louisiana heat, Zoey said.

"Here then."

Letty was taller than Zoey, but they were close enough in the waist that a few outfits would be all right. Letty took her up to her room, wiped the geisha from her face and put her in a blue dress that stretched tauter around Zoey's chassis than Letty's.

"Would a little wine help?" Letty asked.

"You know what I really want?"

"What?"

"Grilled cheese," Zoey laughed.

"You should tell that to Jeremy," Letty said.

"Who?" Zoey asked.

Letty did not respond with words.

"Oh," Zoey said then Letty removed the last bit of the make up from Zoey's face.

"But I thought he pays for me to make him happy," Zoey said. "Isn't that the point? Or have I been misled?"

Letty escorted Zoey to Jeremy's room then introduced the two. It was 6:55. Letty received a text from Zoey five hours later. It read:

TOTALLY MISLED

**Harry:** *It comes down to Zoey or Rikki. I'll be interested to talk with everyone. Zoey is extraordinary. Electric personality, sassy, vibrant – I would say that she doesn't seem entirely at ease with her own body yet though. What a cutie! What a bright light! I'm glad that I was able to show her about herself because I don't think she understood what an orgasm could really feel like. But I got her rolling – these old bones have it in them yet! Great girl, not much else to say. You've got quite a decision ahead of you, Letty. Remember that a competitive 401(k) package can make you a much more desirable employment destination.*

**Abdullah** *Honestly I thought about giving her low marks across the board so I could claim her for my own. LMAO!! I found Zoey extremely good looking. Either her or Rikki is the most beautiful. Good conversation, super smart. The problem was that once we started to have sex, she got her period. She said it was very embarrassing but I think she might have done it on purpose because she didn't like how I was. I'll get better for her and she won't have to do that again. So cool. I want her.*

**Jose:** *Good girl. Young, I can't talk enough English to keep up with her like she want. She good girl, try to be nice but she a talker. We try to go dance and I teach her salsa, but she laughing always. It's OK. Good sex, very very wet.*

**Jeremy** *First night! And if Zoey is any indication, what a week do I have ahead of me! Beautiful girl, very smart too. It was great. She's a local so she took me around town and we got grilled cheese sandwiches (tell her "melty belty" I know she remembers!) I didn't think she was like amazingly beautiful at the beginning of the night but by the end...she's infectious. A natural in bed too!!! No awkward transitions, didn't get over erotic or too business like. It felt like we were people who liked each other having sex.*

\*\*\*

Finally, comes the powerhouse.

**Harry:** *I spent ten minutes trying to start Rikki's review. This was the best sex I have ever had in my life. I hope that doesn't offend you to hear, Letty. Rikki is so beautiful, so sexy, I don't know what fruits got thrown into the blender to make the smoothie that color but I love it. Don't even want to know because the mystery is romantic. Rikki has a special womanhood. I have to give it to you Letty, I was concerned after spending the night with Scratch. I thought you had taken this whole thing too far and that you'd be better off running a solo operation – nothing wrong with being a freelancer. And then I had Rikki (or perhaps I should say, Rikki had me!) A fine young woman, somewhat unexceptional personality despite her look. Had dinner at a crabshack. She'd* never had crab claws before! Can you imagine what life must be like in Iowa? But who am I to talk? Life is life wherever it is! Anywho, when we came back she began with a subpar oral sex warm up, I must call it what it was. She was intimidated. Now normally I don't do this the first time but knowing she was with you, I trusted her. So I performed cunnilingus. She was in Heaven. From that point on, I brought her to new places. And to her credit, she took me to places close to the ones I was taking her.

**Abdullah:** I feel exhausted. Conversation was whatever, she's nice but we didn't talk all that hard. Then we did coke and had sex. She'd never done coke before and really hadn't because she was like crazy excited to see how good coke felt. Magic vadge. I haven't had the other one yet but the chick with the nose ring and Rikki are the two prettiest. The blonde one is hot too but she's kinda beat too. Damn.

**Jose:** This the one to pick.

**Jeremy** One for the record books. Easily one of the most beautiful women I have ever seen much less been with and right up there in terms of sex itself as well. Maybe not you, Letty, but I'm not sure you're human. Rikki is incredible. What struck me was her pussy. Perfect. Her pussy is Georgia O'Keefe perfect. I don't know what else to tell you. Tight, yes, but here's the really weird part – it was warm. Noticeably warmer than the rest of her body. It makes you feel like an animal. Fun girl, not all that too bright but fun. Asked if I had any coke which I don't do so I didn't have. And either she's the best fake orgasmer the Lord has ever put on Earth or that woman had the time of her life last night. I don't want to be the

*guy who thinks that, but I almost can't help myself. She made me*
*feel so valuable.*

\*\*\*

And that was what the men said.

Part 3: The John

Are you scared, February? I used to ask her that because that was our thing. I'd ask her, are you scared, February? And she'd say

"Yes but I'm other things too."

That girl dissolved into whouses. Then she'd reemerge with a new dog for a few weeks. Woodwork or whacky with a puppy, those were February's settings.

Her first few nights at the Baton Rouge Bed & Breakfast, February slept in Letty's room because the hiring davids were still there and Letty didn't want to expose February to anyone but Letty.

February's very first night she spent with itchy bones beside Letty who stayed up telling February all about her new whouse and Gus and the emotions Letty was finally letting herself feel. Like pride because Letty was really trying to do what she'd always wanted. Like fear because Letty was really trying to do what she'd always wanted. Letty said this all to February instead of being quiet beside someone who was shivering and sweating and getting up every half hour to run to the bathroom for a new emergency. Morning swelled up and Letty had either run out of things to say or the energy to say them, but she hadn't gone to sleep. She had not abandoned February. February's teeth and joints clattered and she told Letty that she would leave as soon as she could. Letty said February didn't have to go anywhere but that Letty had a whouse to take care of. Letty said that she or Big Beer would be checking on her all day.

Eventually, February leveled out and the men left the Baton Rouge Bed & Breakfast. Letty asked February to stay to be the whouse girl. February said she would and she would do it for free. Letty said February had two jobs: to be the whouse girl and to gain weight. February said all right and got her own room and painted constellations on her ceiling. Hairy star swirls, more from the impressionist school of cosmology than the looking up one. But accurately scaled – the stars were as far apart in inches on her ceiling as they were in light years in the void.

When the final hires were made official and the girls moved in, February was up to 104 pounds. February thought she was good, there aren't even that many radio stations higher than 104. But Letty said she had to get bigger. No, not fat, Letty said and February laughed because Letty was the best. We take care of each other, February said. Letty said no. We take care of the whouse and the whouse takes care of us, Letty said. Then February smiled and said all right because Letty was weird about the whouse. But that's OK, February thought. We all have our thing.

***

He Makes Dominion of His Purchases

It had been seven weeks and Gus hadn't seen anything yet. Not the redone exterior, not who Letty hired – nothing. In fact, the only thing that Gus knew was that Letty had five and a half months to make a one point one-million-dollar payment.

Gus had brought daffodils.

Big Beer was a totem pole on the porch. Scratch had instructed him to stay that way. Of the six applicants to the Baton Rouge Bed & Breakfast, Letty hired three. First, she hired Scratch to be Mama.

During the pre-party meeting, Scratch told Big Beer not to help Gus with his bags, not to say hello, not to do anything but be big and Black. Letty said Beer should help Gus with his bags. Scratch wasn't having it.

"Honey, you got to let a man be a man on his way up into a whouse. Plus, he gon want to see that mean ole security o ours. Beer, you ain't to do nothin but stare straight 'head."

"Shuddn I say hallo?"

"You may nod, young man. You may nod and that is all. Until I tell yuh to halp him."

"If'n da man gon need halp, shuddn I halp straight off?"

"Yeah, Scratch, I'm with Beer here. Just help the guy, he's our guest."

Scratch threw her head back and forth and wiped her hands along the same path in the air.

"No no no! Honey, yuh ain't ever tuh show yuh can think uh nothin on yer own. Old rich White man ain't tuh see you think uh nothin but being mean. And you, ma'am, you best learn to let yo Mama be yo Mama."

Scratch was a great hire. She had that mix of nasty and nurse you're looking for out of a Mama. And she was great at disagreeing. To me, that's about the most important trait you hire for when you're talking about a general manager type position – someone who knows how to disagree with the owner.

So it was that Big Beer did not move as Gus approached the B & B porch. Also, Scratch was sitting on the rocking chair.

"Stinking humidity," Gus said.

"…" Beer said.

Scratch stood up from a rocking chair to open the porch door.

"There he is!" Scratch said.

"Oh please no. I don't know who he is, but he can't be this old thing."

Scratch Mama swatted Big Beer's chest. She had agreed to take the job so long as she got a good salary and a skeleton key. She could make anything work with a skeleton key and a good salary.

"Go on now, yuh ox. Halp the man."

"Yes'm."

Gus stopped Big Beer.

"I can't use him when I'm inside so I better not out here either. Gimme a minute to get the ole natural lubrication going."

"Iddn't it the truth?" Scratch propped the door open. Gus arrived at the trio of plank steps pathing up to the porch proper.

"Can you imagine if I wasn't on glucosamine?"

"Glue – what's a mean?" Scratch bent in to breezily kiss Gus on the cheek. She had never in her life met the man. She also knew what glucosamine was. And CoQ 10. Gus returned peck.

"Glucosamine. Takes a lot to keep going at my age."

"Oh honey, I remember your age and it wuddn't nothin I don't wish fo now. So you remember to tell me about that glue uh yours before yuh leave."

Gus looked up at Beer before crossing the porch threshold. Beer had fixed his eyes forward. Gus folded towards Scratch, away from Beer.

"Yow!" Gus said.

"Ah yes, Steve. Goes by Big Beer. Lovely man once yuh get tuh know him."

"No-ho thank you!"

Gus again looked up at Beer then shook his head. Big Beer, who had spent the morning talking through the differences in handsome princes who would buy aquamarine and handsome princes who would buy sapphire with his six-year old daughter who was going through a blue gem wedding ring phase. Big Beer, who was planning to use his first few paywads on buying the most indestructible minivan on the market. Big Beer, who did not look if Scratch told him not to look.

"This way."

Scratch charted the route to the red front door. She opened the door and Gus walked into the Baton Rouge Bed & Breakfast.

"Love it!"

He plopped down his satchel sized bag of clothes and toiletries and surveyed the interior. February, barefoot in a muted baby blue dress and her cloche downbrim hat stood at the staircase rail. She curtsied. Scratch waited a moment for February to remember the second half of her instructions then reminded her by coughing in her direction. February remembered and scurried to Gus's bag.

"Now who is this?" Gus asked.

"Dis here Ms. February. She from Da Huxtable."

February stopped moving when Mama said her name. February stared at the floor waiting for them to finish talking about her like a first grader meeting her teacher. She swayed too.

"Ah, stealing from Daddy already – that's my girl! That is my girl. Where is the business chickadee?"

"Letty is but a bell ring away."

"Then I would say we should ring that bell."

"No tour, no getting settled – right at her?"

"Right at her! Ring that bell!"

"Right at her we go. Man aftuh m'own heart."

Scratch waddled to a string a few steps from the staircase. The string stretched up to the second floor where it was attached to a bell. Scratch looked up the staircase and Gus took a step towards her to peak. Scratch shewed him back.

"Now now, yuh made it dis far, don't ruin it now!"

Gus backed up and held his hands up like a gun were pointed at him. A good Mama can yell at you, make you grin, and keep you horny all at once.

"All right all right!" Gus said.

Scratch sniffed loudly and watched Gus assume his previous position. He stopped and she waved her hands for him to take another step back. He rolled his head as much as his old neck would allow and took another step back. Gus stared at Scratch.

"Am I good now?"

Scratch said she hoped not and pulled the string.

\*\*\*

The Baton Rouge Bed & Breakfast echoed with the prairie home companion kind of dingaling makes us know to wash our hands because pancakes are ready. Big Beer rotated inside. February stayed stood where she was, the weight of the bag pulling her shoulders down and in. Gus smiled at February who could barely breath she so much did not want to screw this up for Letty. She scrunched the old leather grips in her hand and looked up from underneath her bashful. God, she didn't want to screw this up. Please don't let her screw this up.

"Sir, da Baton Rouge Bed & Breakfast is proud tuh offer yuh three jewels this evening."

"Whoa, if I wanted Jews, I'd go to synagogue."

A familiar voice broke the upstairs silence.

"Gus!"

"OK OK!"

Gus again held up his hands like he was submitting to a robbery. He bowed his head to Scratch who cleared her throat.

"Let me the pleasure of introducing you to Zoey."

Hire #2, Zoey.

Letty and Scratch had spent the past few weeks making Zoey more Zoey. Making sharper sprays of Zoey's hair, taking it to total black, having her start masturbating. When they told Zoey that the men loved her but she didn't seem to be comfortable with her body, she got suddenly shy in a way that didn't seem to add up. Scratch asked her how long it took her to orgasm when she masturbated. Zoey looked to Letty then to the floor and said that she didn't do...that. How and why the world is filled with women who do not please themselves is an astonishingly overlooked problem of humanity. Especially because the solution is simple:

Start doing...that.

Gus saw a Zoey in a black bikini getup, no fancy side clips or flares of metal. String style but not such dental floss that her anatomy would absorb it. Zoey was wearing a handkerchief tight bikini. She looked at ease and had on shockred lipstick and mascara. Her skin was milky other than where it was tattooed. Cobalt blue homages to wartime lady employment efforts on her upper arms and an orange elvish script that read, when translated, *I do not kill with my gun; he who kills with his gun has forgotten the face of his father. I kill with my heart.* A pooch of a stomach too, not chunky or skinny fat. A pooch. Zoey was become delectable.

She exuded a kind of feline friendliness from the foot of the staircase. She was pleasant but not cloying like the neighbor who brings you brownies and a bible group schedule when they see the moving van. Letty was paying Zoey $120,000 a year. Zoey dropped out of college.

Scratch continued ringmastering.

"Next pleasure on my part would be introducing yuh to the Baton Rouge Bed & Breakfast's own Pearl."

As much as Zoey had been sculpted between the david week and Gus's visit, Pearl was the same Pearl. The third hire, Pearl was big bright eyes and big balloon boobs in a white negligee. Pearl wasn't much of a david lady, though she did make repeat customers out of a younger meathead kind of man. In thrust, Pearl did her damage with johns. She flashed a megawatt come hither straight at Gus and descended the staircase with her abs flexed and good side facing out.

Gus loved what he was seeing: a classic blonde bombshell, a spicy raven who couldn't have been more than twenty, a saucy Mama who bantered, a really big really scary really Black dude and

"Of course, our third girl don't need no introduction. Least'f all from me."

Letty.

I wish I'd been there. I've talked to Gus about that very moment and he goes to roses. He talks about how humbled he was to watch Letty come down those stairs. She wore a pine green dress, exposed shoulders and calves but not something anyone secular would call scandalous. Satin with a brown raw leather belt lolling around her hips. A weathered copper bracelet around one wrist. And confidence. The kind of confidence that comes from knowing you are wearing the exact perfect thing for the exact place you're at.

Yes, the whouse was in order.

Letty arrived at the foot of the staircase and assumed her slot in the lineup as if she were nothing but another lady. She stood for a second without greeting their visitor. Gus was agog. Then Letty laughed and the room exhaled. Letty gave Gus a huge hug.

"So what do you think?!"

She turned back to the lineup.

"What do I think? How's a guy supposed to think in all of this?"

Pearl laughed because she knew to get into the action or get out of the way. Zoey looked at Scratch. Scratch winked then wedged her way in between Letty and Gus.

"Well sir, the Baton Rouge is happy yer happy. May I send yer bags to yer room?"

"Shore!"

February was too much on it this time. She started to run up the staircase then thought better of it, stopped, turned back and curtsied again. Then she hurried her way upstairs. Scratch smiled. Pearl smiled. Gus called after February.

"Why don't you wait for me there? Letty and I will be up in a minute."

Scratch didn't drop her smile but she watched Letty curdle to hear Gus call for February. Scratch also watched February's feet hiccup to hear her name from a man's mouth.

***

Before she'd been hired, Scratch knew February would be a problem for Letty. So on the day that Scratch signed on, she asked Letty what February's party rate was going to be.

"She's not taking parties," Letty said. "Are you kidding me, Scratch? She can't take parties."

"So when she leaving?"

"She's not leaving either – February is the whouse girl."

"So what's her rate?"

"I told you, Scratch. February is not taking parties, February is the whouse girl."

"She gotta have a rate then."

"Scratch!"

"Listen, Letty, you never put nothing out at a garage sale ain't for sale. Even the seat you sitting on has a tag."

"She's not taking parties right now, Scratch. We can readdress the situation in a few months."

It's hard to watch young people you like make simple, fixable mistakes. You know they'll be all right but if they'd only listen to you they could be so much better than all right. They could lap everyone else on the track. But then you remember that you didn't listen, that's how you learned, so maybe that's how everybody has to learn. Scratch cleared her throat and said

"Rikki."

"Rikki, right, I want to make an offer to her as soon as we can," Letty said.

"Well now hold on. Rikki a great girl, we know that. But she setting out to find out about the world. She lived boarded up, ain't never seen a boarded up trick before, but there she is. That girl been protected her whole damn life. You see her with them cigarettes?"

"I did. I didn't know she smoked."

"Cuz she don't! That's what I'm sayin. Girl like that goes through a lotta changes when she break out. Might go well for her, might not. If'n we trying to build some girls who'll last a few years, then I don't want Rikki."

"Scratch, she could be the best in the country."

"Well that ain't no good thing so far as I see it."

"How is that not a good thing?"

"Because this B & B got no need for the best in the country."

"I'm kind of thinking it does."

"Then you ain't thinkin."

"You're a strong, odd woman, Scratch."

"I'm yo mama, honey! It's yo decision in the end but when I see something, I ain't just seeing the thing, I seeing two o yer whole lives worth o experience. Like with this Rikki the best business – I know you all impressed but I ain't seeing it that way. Even if she is the best, don't make no difference. See, a new restaurant has gotta have a hunnid dollar dish. One. New whouse's the same way. A man gotta know which thing the most expensive thing at a new restaurant. Whether he get it or not, man gotta see the big number dish. You our lobster, Letty. Until we got us a name, then men gonna truss the name and buy whatever they got the taste fo. Until then, they buy on the money they got. We get us you for the spender, Zoey who some kinda whouse special dish, and Pearl's the chicken."

"Pearl took everybody to steak."

"And it weren't no good! I talk with Jose all bout it – Pearl taking them men to the spot men go to be seen eating a steak alongside boobs in a black dress. Smart girl, that Pearl. She good chicken."

"Jose liked you."

"Jose so dumb he like the right gorilla if'n it don't bite for blood."

"I don't know, Scratch…"

"We got you for rich fellas been at it forever, we got Zoey for adventurous types, and we got Pearl for any guy what needs something to eat. Ain't got no spot for Rikki. Even if we did, she ain't gonna be cheap."

"No one is going to be cheap here, Scratch."

"Mama."

"Mama – no one is going to be cheap."

"Then Rikki gonna be a whole lot more not cheap than any o da others."

"We can afford it."

"What about that whole loan paym –"

"We can afford it."

"Well, let me tell you like this. There more to a cost than money, specially to the owner. You gonna be spending you a lot of time doing things – you awready seen that from buying dis place, yeah?"

"This is true."

"And I'll tell you what, you want to keep on that February then you better expect to be spending some time on that whouse girl o yers. You know you will. Zoey gonna need some teaching too. Then there this Rikki girl smoking cigarettes and getting into coke."

"Oh, come on Scratch, it's the first time she's ever traveled and she got into having fun for a second. It was in the flow of the party so that's fine."

"No it is not fine! First of all, there already plenty of illegal in a whouse without needing no drugs in it – seen too many good whouses go down to drugs that they had no use fo either. Second off, it's exactly what I's telling you – she so green that she getting bent up in whatever wind blows by."

"That might be true."

"Might be true, it is true! And fine, she daggone good and all but if'n you spending time with the one then where you getting the time the other one gonna need? I ain't gonna be able to do it- girl don't hear her Mama that way. She need other girls like her. You know that."

"You really think it's either Rikki or February?"

"No, I think it's neither. But I know you ain't a lady to let go of nobody."

"Oh boy."

"You know what I'm saying?"

"Oh yes. Yes, I do. And I do not know what to do about it."

Scratch frowned while Letty puffed out her lower lip and stared at nothing. Then Scratch sucked up a bunch of air and said

"Keep the whouse girl. Drop the looker. Get on with it."

So The Baton Rouge Bed & Breakfast did not hire Rikki. It did hire Zoey and Pearl, and February was retained as the whouse girl and only the whouse girl. Scratch was Mama Then Gus came to town.

\*\*\*

Gus had sex with Letty for the first time in a long time that night. And Pearl too. He did not have sex with Scratch who laughed and declined the invitation. Nor did he more than neck with February who Letty signaled leave the room while Gus groaned. He didn't mind. Letty explained February's situation and Gus commended Letty. He said morality in hiring is the only real morality. He also said to be careful who sees February because a man comes to a whouse to turn off certain parts of his person. Then he said he felt like a putz for asking February to participate. Letty said it was fine. He said he was a putz. She said it was fine. He still had an erection. Viagra.

Neither did Gus have sex with Zoey because a caravan of black SUV's picked her up from the B & B an hour after he arrived. He had made a deal with Abdullah for three months of Zoey's in-field private services in exchange for $140,000. Zoey was taken to the airport. Abdullah knew to go to Gus because February told him. February admitted this when Letty came out of Gus's room and asked where Zoey was. February was patient while Letty berated her.

We're a team, Letty said then looked up at the ceiling of artsy accurate astronomy. February wrapped her arms harder around her legs which were folded up to her chest.

Zoey is going to be all right, February said.

I know but that's not it, February.

And it's good you have that money.

That's not it.

Don't we need to make a lot of money or you lose the whouse?

Yeah but February, we're a team.

We're the best team.

So why aren't you telling me about stuff like this?

Because we're a team.

They talked for a while longer before Letty left February to go at Gus who actually knew what he was doing.

"This is what you do to the woman you say you want to marry?!"

Gus had been married four times to women between 22 and 38 years of age, and once to a 19-year old but he was 21 then. Gus had spent many years as a husband so knew not to make a sex joke to Letty even though they had been having sex all of an hour earlier which is exactly what he wanted to do to the woman he said he wanted to marry. In fact, he was still in the bed [he had paid for] and he was still naked other than the white undershirt he never took off in another person's presence. Letty had put on a sweater, sweat pants and skewered her hair up in chopsticks too.

Letty gave it to Gus. She went on about trust. She went on about respect. He listened, every thirtieth word or so he would say I'm sorry. Then there was a break and he would apologize again and explain that he was only trying to take care of her and of course he wanted to marry her. That he was afraid she wouldn't see the smart decision was to marry him because of the same reason he wanted to marry her.

She said it wasn't so easy a decision and that was her point and was he even listening to her and he was supposed to be the banker not the owner. The banker.

He said easy was different than simple and asked how else she expected to make that much of what she needed to make in a whole year in one night?

"It's fine."

"Letty…"

"Pearl's pretty, isn't she?"

"Letty, making money means making money. I'm trying to show you how to make a hard decision. Did I overstep my bounds? Probably. But you know I'm doing it to help you."

"Which helps you."

"Which helps us."

Gus ducked his brow level to find eye contact. He confiscated her hands into his and held them like he was praying. Letty left them limp.

"You said you wanted to be an investment, Bubala. That was you, not me." Gus said. "You said investment, I said wife."

"You said loan."

"Even worse! Loan gets a couple million and has to pay it back – wife is a bottomless pit. You're a wonderful person, Letty. My favorite. But let's be honest here, not a great business decision, no? Woman who chooses business over marriage? Not smart business."

He was being kind and she looked down and he still had an erection from the Viagra. A smile snuck across Letty's face then she yanked her hands from him and wrapped her arms around herself.

"I get it, Gus."

He leaned back against the headboard and made an I'm-listening-now-and-what-you're-saying-is-very-serious face. A smart husband does that once he gets through the heat of the initial assault. First, she vents. Second, you explain yourself and make her laugh a little. Not a lot. No big laughs yet. Third, you provide the affirmation for a coming back together.

"I get it," Letty said. Gus nodded.

"You have to make money. Of course I get it," Letty said. Gus nodded.

"What? Do you think I don't get what money is?!" Letty said.

Fourth thing a smart husband does, and this is the one that gets a ton of talented husbands who haven't quite figured it out yet, is nothing. Women will try to get you back into the fight. Do not click the pop-up. Do not click the link no matter how brightly it flashes. Gus really was an expert husband. His third wife had told him that.

"Of course not. I'm sorry," Gus said.

"I get it, Gus."

"I know that. I'm sorry."

She shook her head then looked away. He licked his tongue across the sheath of his front teeth without opening his mouth.

"Then why do you make the deal without me, Gus?"

"Huh?"

"If you really think I get it, Gus, then why do you go around me to make the deal for Zoey?"

Final phase of a productive fight with a woman: make it about you and how she's actually the one hurting you.

"Honestly, honey, I was surprising you! This is wonderful news! Go around? What are you tawking about!"

"Go around me, Gus. You didn't think I'd make the deal. You didn't think I'd let her go."

"Letty. I'm joking before with the wife this and that, but come on, if I didn't think you'd make that deal, then do you think I'd be in business with you?"

"Then tell me!"

"Oh for Chrissakes!"

He started to throw off his covers to put on pants and storm out himself. His penis boinged like a kicked door jam.

"No, now Gus…"

Letty went to him before he made it out of bed. He tightened at her approach but surrendered at her touch. She put the covers back over him, taking care to lift the fabric up and over the manhood. Letty massaged his shoulders. Gus dropped his head.

"I know you want to surprise me," she said. "And it's great. It is. It's great that Zoey panned out. It's great that Abdullah wanted her. It's great that you got the money for me."

"For us!"

"For us, you're right. I'm sorry."

"Well…" Gus's eyes were closed because he was demonstrating his effort to take in the olive branch that was her massage rather than allow himself to get angry at her previous, womanly hysteria. "…did you like the daffodils?"

"You know I did."

"See, you don't tell me things either."

"It's great that you got the money. But it's like you said, Gus, we're in business. A hundred grand isn't flowers."

"Flowers at our wedding if you wanted, I tellya that much. She's going to be fine, Letty. I know you worry."

"Well I care about her."

"I know you do."

He reached backwards and found her hamstring. He caressed it. She let leak a murmur so as to demonstrate his stimulation was stimulating.

"You made about a hundred and forty thousand dollars in the last twenty seconds, Letty."

"What a day."

"What a day. Little bit o this, little bit o that – and we got us a business."

"<sub>Letty</sub>?"

February had walked in. She clutched her broom like a kid who can't swim holds the ladder in the pool.

"Letty?"

"Yes February?" Letty continued to rub Gus's shoulders.

"…"

"What is it February?"

February scratched her neck below her ear. Gus exhaled, unapologetically tentpoling

"Pay me $629. For working. Yes."

Letty's lips piqued. She closed her eyes to match Gus's.

"OK," she said. February dashed off. Gus kept his eyes closed and said

"What a good Daddy you are, honey."

\*\*\*

You think about doing something meaningful for a long time
before actually doing it.

What happens is
The bottom falls out of a different thing
Some random thing you'd found yourself in and never considered
to be who you were so much as this thing you were doing.
And you start the big thing.
You finally start.

It's fun at first
because it's joyful to begin things.
It's bubblegum and Sunday sunshine to see these pieces you've
had in your head finally become real.
I can do this, you think.
Why did I wait?

Then
The challenges mount.
Things you hadn't known you hadn't known.
You wince to see what you thought was fine the day before.
You get more jealous and you laugh less.
You consider other options.
Maybe you jet.

And

people

at dinner parties

tell you

how proud

they are

of you

because

it is the trying.

That's what matters,

The trying,

They say.


And you give up.


Unless you're trapped.


If you've managed to trap yourself in doing the big thing,

The thing you've protected in your inaction for all these years,

You grind.


You grind and you grind and you grind.

Because beginning is easy,

Beginning is twitterpating,


But to finish?


To finish is a cold siege.


\*\*\*


February told Letty she looked tired. Letty said it was fine and that she was a little tired but that it was fine.

They were falling behind.

It had been another three months after Gus's visit and they'd done about two hundred thousand dollars in profit. Which made it ten months since Letty had made the deal with Gus and about four hundred of revenue which was about two hundred in profit. They had settled into about 60k in profit per month which had them pegged for 330,000ish at the one-year marker plus the buck fifty or so they had left of the loan which would be about 500, a. k. a. less than half of what they needed. And who knew what costs were going to end up because the Bed & Breakfast itself continually needed work. Something with the roof then a window breaks then a politician needs a bribe. New regulations required new laundering gymnastics. How was it this expensive to run a business? The revenue was fine – the B & B was doing well over a hundred grand every single month in revenue. It was these costs. All of these costs. February told Letty that Gus should count the whouse as worth something too.

What am I going to do, Letty said to February, sell the place so I can own the place?

Well aren't you paying back the loan with some of the money from the loan?

Now, the B & B had only been open for eleven weeks by then so it wasn't as though the meteor had struck and the dinosaurs were all dead. And what was Gus going to do? Sue her? Take the whouse? It was making a profit. The Baton Rouge Bed & Breakfast was a profitable business. People were eating, they were making a nice profit, paying for four salaries and $629 and no, February was not going to take parties, Scratch, so stop asking. We'd have to pay her more too, you know so there's that.

"Letty, you could charge that girl and she'd figure out how to stay near you."

Letty and Scratch were sitting on the porch, enjoying the late afternoon before the night brought whatever circus it would. February was lingering in the margins, sweeping.

"Maybe we hire Rikki after all."

"Cokey Hot Crotch? Oh Letty, I aweady put in a call to her mother. Rikki done moved to France and got herself married."

"How long did she know the guy?!"

Scratch dragged a full inch off of her cigarette in one suck. She spoke with smoke and sass and wisdom pouring from her mouth.

"I am neither answering that nor knowing the answer. You have got to stop worrying about the rash decisions idiot women make."

"How's Beer doing?"

"Beer's fine, Letty. Everybody's fine."

"You're so good, Scratch."

"I'm good?"

"Yeah, you're so good at this."

"At what? At not letting full grown adults starve or telling you that you're being ridiculous again?"

"You think I'm being ridiculous?"

Scratch flicked her cigarette free of ash. She took another drag instead of answering straight away. Scratch had learned to allow Letty time to simmer in silence anytime she asked a self-defeating question like it were productive.

"If you're asking me, honey, the ridiculous part is paying what you got to pay when you got to pay it. Any business body would call this place well off and I'll tell you it's a dirty kind of bank make you pay more than half back in a year."

"It was my idea."

"I'm sure it was."

"Listen, Gus is whatever Gus is but it was my idea to set the schedule like we did."

"Then why don't we do another week long things for 4 or 5 guys, look to make another long deal with one of em. Bring in a few girls. Look at, you did a bundle doing the david week and then twice that with Zoey. That's a helluva interesting business, if you ask me."

Letty agreed that it was an idea then said she wanted to see how it went with Zoey. Scratch asked what happened if they didn't make the loan. Letty said she'd work that out with Gus.

"Call him and ask," Scratch said.

Letty said she should.

"Then do it. Here." Scratch stood up to grab Letty's phone and brandish it at her. "Call him," Scratch said. "Enough of this."

"I'll do it another time."

"Do it right now."

"No, Scratch, I'm not thinking about it."

"Yes ya are! Yuh thinkin bout it so much yuh don't even know what it's like to think bout nothing else. Yuh done got too used to feeling like some old man got something over yuh and now yuh don't know what other kinda thinkin even feel like."

"Scratch, some old man does have something over me."

"He ain't got everything on yuh though."

"HE HAS EVERYTHING OVER ME!" Letty bazooka stomped to standing and glared at Scratch. February dropped her room and ran over to Letty. Letty shook her head and sat down when Scratch did not look away. "He has everything."

"Call him," Scratch said and did not sit.

"Oh my God, Scratch!" Letty cackled from her seat and February hugged her across her body.

"Honey, what have yuh got to lose?"

"I don't want him to know we're short. How about that?"

"Then ask him what happens if you pay more than the amount set too. Tell him yer figgering yer options."

That shut Letty up. February was still holding her.

"Fine."

Letty brushed off February, sneered at Scratch, pressed Gus in her phone. Letty had the conversation right then and there. She didn't stand up to make it private or pace for her brain, she stayed sat and sneering.

Conversation started off chipper which is always funny to see when someone is as pissed off as Letty was going in. Pleasant and energetic. Gus must have asked how Letty was doing because Letty described how she was doing. She asked him how he was doing then listened for a while. Then Letty said Thank you, that's sweet to hear.

"Gus I have a couple of questions just to make sure we're on the same page." Letty repositioned in her chair for the first time since the call started. "Yes, yes, incredible how quickly! We'll have to go back for a po boy there! Yes. Anyhow, wanted to ask your thoughts on payment. Because the year could go a couple of different ways for us from here so I wanted to know what would happen if the Baton Rouge pays more than the 1.1. Or less."

Letty had stopped scowling at Scratch. Letty's face now betrayed no interiority. Letty was a professional person on a professional call. Scratch was sitting back down, allowing her body the time it required to sit without breaking.

"Yes yes, I follow," Letty said. "No I know. I know. Absolutely, let's figure out schedules and then we'll have you out again. Of course you don't pay! You're our papa. OK, uh huh, buh bye."

Letty clicked the phone and set it down on the table. Gus and February respected Letty's silence. She collected herself then spoke.

"Gus was very nice. He, uh. He said that he'd be happy to take any early payment without interest on the early payment part. So we could pay the whole thing off at 2.1 instead of 2.2."

"That's good."

"It is. Gus is a good guy."

"And then if we don't pay?"

"Well there are a few scales there, he said. If we're close, within 10% he said, then he'd just roll over the extra. He said if we're 15 or 20 percent off that we'd roll over and also have to look at him sending in a manager or someone to help the place get on track."

"Ah."

Letty scratched her ear.

"What are we tracking at right now, Mama?"

"Honey it's three months out – tracking don't do a thing yet."

"What are we tracking at, Scratch?"

"It don't matter."

"Oh I'm quite sure it does."

"We'd need to pick it up."

"What are the numbers?"

Once again, Letty and Scratch locked. Only this time it was Scratch who looked away.

"540. 535 to be safe."

Letty picked up her phone and pressed its screen a few times. A tight pursed line bifurcated her face where her mouth normally was. February marched off to her room. Scratch lit another cigarette.

Letty set down the phone.

"We're at 48.636%."

"And did Good Guy Gus say what happened at 48 whatever percent?"

"Nope." Letty said. "He did mention anything less than 70 would be liquidation though."

"It was what?"

"Seventy percent was liquidation. We're not going to hit fifty. Seventy was so bad it wasn't worth it to him. We're not even going to hit fifty."

"He ain't nothing but a greedy old fool shutting down a business making money. He turn around – he jes scaring us."

"No he isn't Scratch. He said he'd forgive the debt and that I could keep all the money we made. Said that too. He said he'd be sorry to see it go but that the risk exposure wasn't worth it to him. Which I understand. That's why he said he'd have to liquidate the property."

"He called it property?"

"He called it property. Other than when he called it collateral."

***

Zoey never did come back to the B & B. About a week before she was to return, Gus emailed Letty to tell her that Abdullah had issued a buyout offer of $220,000.

"But it's a negotiating culture," he added.

Letty told Gus that she wanted to talk with Zoey. Gus told her that Zoey was a big girl then asked if the Baton Rouge Bed & Breakfast was on track to make its payment. Letty said she either spoke with Zoey alone or there would be no deal.

***

Zoey met Letty at an outdoor bistro. Letty stood and hugged her protégé when she arrived. Then Letty turned and went to do the same with Abdullah who politely refused to do anything but shake her hand. He smiled and bowed and said he'd leave the girls to be girls. It would do his Zoey well to be with Letty, he said. Then he dadkissed Zoey on the forehead and asked if she'd be all right without him. Zoey nodded then held his fingers in her hands until the distance he made from walking away lifted them up and out. Zoey said she was blessed and that Abu was buying her mother a house.

Abu?

Oh, right. Abdullah.

Are you all right? Letty asked. Are you all right?

How much was I? Zoey answered. He won't tell me. Was I more than a million? Was I?

Zoey, are you all right? You can tell me if you're not. I'll help you. Has he made you do anything you didn't want to? It's all right if he did, you can tell me. I can help you.

Was I more than a million?

They talked a circle for a while. Eventually, Letty told Zoey that yes, she'd been more than a million. Zoey said that was good because that meant Letty met the first payment. Letty said Yup.

As Zoey walked away with Abdullah, Letty saw Zoey lean into him and whisper Thank you. Abdullah did not respond.

Letty let Gus lead the negotiations for Zoey. He got $220,400 for Zoey's buyout from Abdullah. This brought Zoey to a nice round $360,400. You have to respect the tenacity of negotiations that would result in such a number.

As for Pearl, Letty saw her about as often as she saw Zoey. Pearl made her quota converting johns so she did most of her work prowling hotel lobbies and convention centers.

Pearl was a good employee. If Scratch said Pearl needed to be at 25 parties in a month, she was at 25 parties. If Scratch said 31, then it was 31. Letty asked Scratch what would happen if she said 2,000. Scratch said

Two thousand tired men.

Pearl was at the gym in the late morning, skyping with her son in the afternoon, and hunting for johns at night. Pearl didn't hang out at the Baton Rouge and took most of her parties off premises. She only ever called for Beer a few times and only once did he have to do anything other than pick her up but she was back at it after less than a week. Doctor said to take a month but Pearl knew Letty was stressed so said she was good to go after six days.

The Baton Rouge Bed & Breakfast was mostly empty. Plenty of people lived there: Pearl, Scratch, February, Big Beer, and Letty all lived there. But Scratch lived a little life, Big Beer watched TV and made sure he was scary whenever Letty had a party, Pearl was Pearl and February was February. The Baton Rouge Bed & Breakfast was a bunch of people who occasionally passed each other in the hallway. This was what Letty had created.

\*\*\*

Desolation Row

The calendar had collapsed. There was one month left and The B & B had $487,313 of free cash. Letty could write Gus a check for $487,313. Letty didn't think of it as her money either. Of course, Letty didn't. That money would be split evenly between everybody who had worked for it. Which was some solace to Letty – at least no one was in trouble.

Trouble or no, a cloud had settled over the Baton Rouge Bed & Breakfast. Letty took parties and so did Pearl, Beer was scary and Scratch was wise. No one was unprofessional. No one was happy. Everyone endured the day.

Letty stood up from her morning cup of coffee she had around one every afternoon at the breakfast nook table. She was back to going to sleep at sunrise because she was back to the drunk, late night parties she knew were sad skits compared to the conscientious, normal hour parties she knew everyone would prefer if only they'd treat sex as sex should be treated. Didn't matter now. Letty didn't have the mana to fight for eight o clockers left in her.

The television was on in the other room because Big Beer was asleep. Big Beer had stopped sleeping in his room for the most part. He'd flip on the television and stay on the sofa and Letty would jostle him awake after her one o'clock coffee. That was the routine. Although April was coming over later that afternoon, that was new. Before business opened, Big Beer's daughter was finally going to see where her pops lived and worked. Beer liked that April would meet Letty too.

Letty put her mug into the sink, shook Beer's foot and went upstairs. She stopped at February's door en route to hers. Another month had passed so Letty had exactly six hundred and twenty-nine dollars cash to give her whouse girl. Letty knocked. February called out.

"Busy."

"February it's me, I have your pay."

"BUSY!"

"Take the money, February."

February rustled in her room. Dogs or cash, Letty thought. That's how you get February to leave her room.

February opened her door. Letty held out the money.

"Here. Good job, February."

"Don't need it."

Letty sucked her lips into her mouth, blinked, then said Okee dokee and went to take a bath. February closed the door.

***

"T'ain't a thang that's bad, yuh know I ain't saying that. It's uh, well…"

"I get it, Beer, nothing about work."

His neck unclutched.

"Thank you, Ms. Letty. It's a thang for the courts, don't want her t' say nothing that might end up a prollem. Not fo me or you."

"She's six, Beer. Why would I talk about anything but ponies with a six-year old?"

Big Beer's daughter wore pigtails with plastic beads at its knuckles and told Letty she was pretty. Letty said April was pretty too. They talked about April's favorite cartoons and Letty said she had liked other cartoons when she was young then showed them to April on YouTube. April said they looked weird and Letty said they did now to her too. Then Letty said, No, I do not have a boyfriend. Do you? April squealed like a stuck balloon and covered her eyes.

Nooooooooooooo!

April split her fingers apart and peekabooed a sliver of vision like February made of her doors. She squealed again to see that Letty was still smiling at her. April assured Letty that she was in $2^{nd}$ grade and $2^{nd}$ graders aren't silly like first graders. $2^{nd}$ graders know that boys are stupid.

But your Dad is a boy, Letty said.

No he isn't, April said and she handed Letty a purple bellflower she'd picked from the overhang beside her. They had met on the porch of the Baton Rouge Bed & Breakfast, but April wanted to play in the front garden. It was her first go at seeing where her dad lived. Beer had spent six months working on April's grandparents to allow her to visit without supervision. They found the B & B suitable when they inspected it. Charming even.

For me? Letty asked.

April crumpled her index finger into her mouth.

Thank you, April! I'll bring you a present next time. Would you like to see me again, April?

She whispered yes.

Well I want to see you too!

April hugged up at Letty. The adult knelt over and gave the child a body to hold. Big Beer watched from a window. He felt like a father. It was the first time in a long time that Letty hadn't been thinking about how to make more money or how to spend less money. It was the first time Letty hadn't been counting her shortcomings or wishing ill upon the people who had [correctly] doubted her. She wasn't thinking about how tired she'd be at the end of a party or why oh why had she not married the old fart and called it a day. Letty was having fun with a little girl.

And lo, a word came upon Letty.

A special word. The abracadabra that had not crossed her lips nor mind in far too long.

Timothy.

Letty had forgotten the timothy.

***

Letty assembled the team with four weeks left and said that the Baton Rouge would be accountable for two things from now on: being cash flow positive because they were a business and servicing two timothies because life is more than business. Letty told everyone that in all likelihood, this would be their last month and she understood if people wanted to leave now or start making preparations. She said she was sorry and that everyone would be getting a share of the profits and sale of the whouse. Beer asked if he could stay if he paid rent.

Letty said it wasn't up to her but if it was up to her, no, Beer could never ever pay rent because it would always be a part of his job. Then Letty said that they had at least a month left and then there'd be a delay in selling the place so it was a while until anything happened. She told Big Beer that April was a beautiful girl and always welcome but that Letty would like it if April spent the night on Mondays. Letty said that would be best. The Baton Rouge Bed & Breakfast would close every Monday it had left in it and they would all be expected to be there for dinner which they would be doing together. Beer said he'd ask April's grandparents. Letty asked Pearl if she had any questions about what was going on. Pearl thought for a moment. Her son was on his way in college and she'd come out of this with some good money. Nope, no questions Pearl said.

"Actually," Pearl said and pulled up a picture on her phone. February went upstairs to her room.

"This guy," Pearl said.

"Who is he?" Letty asked.

"Says his name is Fred. Says he's a dentist, but who knows. He does hate his wife but doesn't want to deal with a divorce."

"And you think he could be a timothy?"

"I don't know, how much do dentists make?"

"Dentists do pretty well, Pearl. And it's about more than money– a timothy is someone who needs sex, deserves sex, and can't get sex."

"Letty, his wife is terrible."

Letty said she loved the thought and that they would talk more about it later. She would talk more with everyone about everything later. Then Letty apologized and said thank you and she had no idea what was going to happen but that everyone was going to be all right.

So let's do the best we can with what we've got left.

\*\*\*

The Baton Rouge Bed & Breakfast became a community. They took a reduced workload, still profitable on a monthly basis, but not on track to match its ludicrous loan. Letty didn't care. They took parties. April came on Mondays, everyone was there for dinner, and they satisfied a timothy. Didn't make their own quota which was two if you remember but hey, Letty thought, they got the one. One was something.

The story goes that Letty had grown a david from a john who was a dean at LSU. After a party, she asked him if he knew anyone who really deserved sex but couldn't afford it. He grumbled and coughed and asked if she would be the one doing it. She said no, which was probably a lie but she could feel the david knew someone and was being clingy. He said Well all right then, and described a widower adjunct faculty member who was about to have his class load cut.

"He teaches jazz appreciation. Black. Is that in the purview?"

Letty shined.

"I don't think so. We stay away from jazz at the Baton Rouge."

The timothy was in his seventies and spent the evening talking with Scratch, having sex with Pearl (Letty came upon her ripening as we say in the menstruation metaphor wing of the business,) and telling Big Beer about Louisiana when it was racist.

"Used to be White people go on and tell you what's what," the timothy said. He wore a maroon vest and black jeans and got dressed immediately after finishing. Big Beer wore the same suit he always wore. The timothy continued.

"Slap you right across the face if they felt it, right in the light of day. Not all of em, of course, but enough you knew it best to be careful in the street. Church was worse cause it get you killed. My Ma had us stop going after a few was burned down. She said the spirit would follow us so long as we followed the spirit. Course if you actually read the damned Bible you see it's all about slavery and people turned black cause they bad. Christians today in the business of cherrypicking the Christmas cards from the scripture. I tell you what young man, Jazz is the god a body needs. Because there ain't no god, certainly not one any human being knew about all them years back. Science might write the real Bible in the end, not yet, might though."

The timothy crossed his arms and asked if it would be all right if he told them about his wife. The whole B & B was lounging in the living room together. Scratch said it was his night.

"Her name was Margaret, Maggie until we found out she was pregnant," the timothy said. "Hard woman, made me let her take the girls to church. Whooped em too. I never liked it course that was the custom then. You hit your kids and you took em to church, that's what being Black was. Negro we was then. Colored too. So I got talked down. But I got real hot one morning over it. Oh lord, I can't ever remember being that hot. I happened to come across the youngest one getting out the tub and she all marked up across her behind. Slashes like she a wall by a bed in a jail. I don't know if I was planning on staying on the sofa for the next year but I went on up to Margaret and asked her which one of our daughters was to tend the cotton and which one was up for sale. Ha!"

He guffawed and Beer snickered. Letty liked how open the room felt. Like it was nothing but good people having a good night together. Letty also liked that she had something interesting to listen to while she tried to cope with cramps. The timothy continued.

"A racist is lazy, principally. I tell you that, for sure. Bored, scared – sometimes that too. But every single racist thought is a lazy thought. Maybe other things too, but every real racist sitting on their rear not thinking it through. Jus like Christians – it don't make sense that somebody dumb or smart cause of their skin. And it don't make sense there a god. Why? Because there a church? Thas the real reason. People think there gotta be a god they can't see cuz there certainly is a church they can. Same thing with race, Black folk gotta be bad cuz we the ones in jail and poor. Ain't got nothing to do with slavery, course. Cuz we fixed that. It ain't like the confederacy all vote one way today and the Union vote the other. But that's lazy people for you. People who ain't got the energy to think through the truth staring em in the face, I should say. Cuz a man who run a marathon and don't want to walk afterwards ain't lazy, he tired. I bet that's why so many racists so daggone out of shape. Either way, I spent my life with this woman Margaret, Maggie when she liked me. Ha! Loved her some, got bored some too, cheated, raised daughters, damned great women. Damned great. I made the best of things – sure she did the same by me. But she didn't have the energy I did. Too lazy for a life without God. Maybe I took it out of her. Didn't mean to but that woman did so damned much – cooking, cleaning, the kids here and there – maybe she was doing the work and I was living the life. Maybe that's what was happening the whole way through. I never asked for it though, never meant to anyhow. I tell you I'm glad she went first. Glad I got to give her a partner at her death. Because the thing is in the giving. You all understand this – the thing is in the giving."

\*\*\*

Hiraeth

Paid his wage he hit the stage asking
*Whose john am I tonight?*
Mine! Cried a Blonde and
Mine! Cried a Black and
They swarmed and warmed his body.
Then he spent his wad on a sexy broad
And exited empty of pocket.
Yes he spent his wad
On a sexy broad
And exited
Empty
Of pocket.

Became he a saver

Tamed his behavior

To lay her the days he may.

They'd meet on the street and she'd be very sweet asking

*Where are we off to my david?*

*Oh where are we off to my david?*


But things went awry and his money ran dry

So she stopped seeing him altogether.

Now on his own he sings to the road

And whoever has ears to hear him:

*Pity me, I'm a timothy*

*Yes pity me, I'm a timothy*

*Please pity me, I'm a timothy*

*But I wasn't*

*always*

*this way.*

\*\*\*

April arrived with a pink and purple overnight bag the last Monday of the month. Big Beer met her halfway up the walkway and waved to the car she'd exited. She waved too. The car drove away without needing to watch her walk inside.

Letty made spaghetti for dinner because April loved spaghetti and meatballs. Scratch made the meatballs which were veal and eggs and binder. Because veal and eggs are scrumptious, aren't they?

Since April was a more methodical than rambunctious girl, the Baton Rouge did not echo with a stampede or howls when she visited. No, April was quiet and slow in her investigation of the big place in which her daddy lived. Beer loved that his daughter was interested in things but he told her to check with Letty first. Letty told April to explore to her heart's content which was the exact reason why Letty had made the Baton Rouge a place to live rather than a sex palace. There was no dungeon that April could stumble into that would require explanations no one wanted to give. Big Beer added that April had to be in bed by 10. She whimpered. 11. Don't tell Nana.

It was Monday so no men would be coming to the B & B. Everyone was home and relaxing and digesting dinner. Big Beer insisted he clean up while April explored so he took over the sink. Scratch watched television while Pearl told her all about her son, Peter. Scratch more paid attention to the television than contributed to the conversation. Letty came out from the bathroom to see Big Beer thrust into the mountain of dishes that results from homemade spaghetti and meatballs for six people. She told him to go play with his daughter and that she would do that. He said he was fine and that she already did plenty. Letty said no, he said yes, and they danced that dance for a while. Then she said to leave them, that she was his boss, and that February would do them tomorrow. Scratch yapped from the living room that it was smart to get them done before they dried because dried food is ten times the work Beer said he could do right then and there and daggone it wouldya jes lettim halp? Letty said this was treason and she knew to the bottom of her being that her next whouse would get it right. Letty saw the mistakes she'd made and they were big mistakes, but they were discrete. Letty's problems were not systemic, at least not as she saw them, she wasn't in a position where she was having to say things like Wow, everyone hates me, or Wow, we never turned a profit. She'd borrowed more than she'd needed so her goals got a little loose. The Baton Rouge Bed & Breakfast was a profitable business staring at liquidation because of an impossible loan. Letty would do better next time.

Letty said she was going to get February to do the dishes and that Beer better not be here when she came back.

Letty went upstairs and knocked on February's door. The knob spun, the hinge flexed, and February slithered through the breach. She shut the door behind her, went downstairs and did the dishes without Letty ever having to ask. Letty never needed to ask anything of February. All Letty had to do was need and February would take care of it.

***

Gus called five days before the deadline. They hadn't spoken since they'd spoken about the consequences of Letty being a loan rather than a wife.

Gus was terse and meandering and deferential in a self-congratulatory way during the call. He told Letty that she had done her part and that a lot of it obviously had to do with his negotiations for Zoey and that he'd be rolling over the shortfall as per their previous agreement.

Um.

Letty asked Gus if he'd seen the financials. He said he had, yes, very impressive and the check had cleared and they'd be in touch soon regarding payment schedule for the remaining principal.

Um.

Gus said Good start, now the real work begins and hung up, actually hung up, because he was on a land line.

Letty set down her phone then trickled through the B & B to find Scratch. Letty said the weirdest thing had happened. Letty said she just got off of the phone with Gus who was saying that they made it. That the B & B had made the payment. She asked aloud how Gus could think that. How could Gus be taken by such an obvious error?

Mama confirmed that the financials were correct.

"How is that possible?" Letty asked.

"I run a good whouse, you girls look good, and them men are rich."

Letty told Scratch that she couldn't lie to Gus. That she understood the change was scary but that Letty would figure it out and she'd keep everyone safe. Scratch said she wasn't lying to Gus and she'd been a whole lot less than safe for a whole lot more life than she'd spent with Letty and it'd worked out just fine.

"You can't lie to Gus."

"I ain't lying to Gus!"

"Then why is he calling me like he received the payment?"

"Was he sore?"

"Yes! He was, Scratch. As a matter of fact."

"Men get so pissed off when all you chicks they trying to marry pay back the debts they made you think you wanted. Make em feel like they don't got nothing over you no more. Like you beating their game. Make men real sore when pretty girls pay em back."

"Or maybe he's unhappy that we are lying to him."

"We are not lying to him, I swear to you, Letty, we are not lying to Gus."

"So you're lying to me?"

"Now I know you ain't here in this room with me cause ain't no Letty I ever met go saying snot like that."

"Did Gus receive a loan payment?"

"Yes."

"In what amount?"

Scratch closed one eye and flexed the other.

"One million twenty-two thousand and forty-eight dollars."

Letty was shocked. Her face went limp then it went taut because her stomach opened so her mouth closed and her eyes did too. Was she going to vomit? Oh God don't let her vomit. Letty took the kind of breath that involves swallowing.

"How?" Letty said with one hand around her stomach and the other in a fist, safeguarding her mouth.

"I run a good whouse, you girls look good, and them men are rich."

"No – Scratch -" Letty started to get excited again but collected herself before getting pukey. Her fist went to her chin and mouth and she swallowed again and set her skull in an easy position on her neck. Scratch smiled.

"How could we possibly have done that, Scratch? And if we could do that, why wouldn't you tell me before you did it?"

"It's a bunch of things, Letty. First off, we had our best month ever this month. So you was right to do that free stuff – big month. I talk with the money guy too and tole him about where we were at so he gave us a free month too. We had a bigger chunk left of that first loan left too. Plus, I had a little bit saved up."

"Scratch…" Letty's nausea stopped and she gazed at this aging cranky lady so much softer than she ever let on. Scratch pointed her bare tree branch of a finger at Letty.

"Now that's a loan too! I's taking back off the top too jes like any other smart old asshole getting young things to do business. But I ain't no fool – this place making money. Only gonna make mo money too. Don't take a genius to give yuh a loan Letty."

"Scr –"

"So now you know why I ain't say nothing to you because you about to tell me that I shouldn'ta put none o my money into you.

Course that's cuz you too young and dumb to know you a good bet, Letty. You think I's doing you a favor and all I's doing is being old and greedy and seeing some pretty young dummy in need."

"Thank you."

Tears welled in Letty's eyes. Has Letty cried in our story yet? I don't think she has, has she? Well, either way, Mama hasn't and you better believe Mama won't. Scratch frowned and swatted at a fly that didn't exist and turned to walk away.

"So we made it. Course the truth is that you made it. The truth is you did a whole bunch more than any female I ever met in this business. So thereya go. And don't thank me, stop thanking everybody! I's taking interest off you just like that old turd did."

By then, Scratch was hobbling up the staircase saying most of what she said to the whouse so she wouldn't have to look at Letty who had sprung a leak. How was Scratch Letty's employee? How had that happened? How did Letty have any employees? Really, how the Hell had all of this happened? To Letty, Scratch felt like this guru come down from the mountain that lived there and for some reason put up with Letty. Then there was February and February was whatever February was and Letty couldn't let her come apart. February wasn't her employee though. Zoey was on an adventure and as much as Letty worried about her, Zoey would be all right. Again, not her employee. Big Beer was more her little brother than her head of security. Even Pearl who kept Letty at the clinical definition of professional distance felt more like a roommate than an employee.

Eventually Letty went to sleep. Eventually, everybody was asleep. Big Beer, Letty, Pearl, February and April because it was a Monday. The Baton Rouge Bed & Breakfast was tucked in. Until April crept out of her room, down the hall, and did what she'd been doing for almost a month by then:

April did her part to help her Dad.

\*\*\*

This is the story of a business.

First, there was Scratch. Scratch who had not lied to Gus but had certainly lied to Letty. Scratch who had seen April up late the Monday before. Late like an hour that was the night to a raver but the morning to a baker. Scratch who knew something was amuck about a month earlier when a set of lighting equipment and a camera arrived at the whouse. The receipt said they were for February. The receipt said $629.00.

Mama delivered the delivery to the whouse girl who scuttled a Gollum to claim it. Mama said whoa and told February to be careful with that and that she was only allowed to use it in her room. February hurgled agreement.

Then money started pouring into the system. Money that Scratch could not source. Not at first, anyhow.

Then there was February. February who, to her credit, had obeyed the commands to keep the camera in her room.

Finally, there was April. April who did not speak.

So it's 3 AM and Mama has laid a trap. Like the kid, she'd waited for the whouse to dwindle into the creaks of sleeping wood. She'd posted in a pool of shadows and waited.

Then came April.

April leaned against her door until it opened, managing every noise it might make. The groan of its board, the squeak of its hinge. Mama watched her walk down the hall, not tiptoe, no, the child had learned that her mass stirred not thump nor moan in the floor.

April could walk. So,

She walked.

Walked right down the hall in her flouncy purple dress and into another room that had, in Mama's experience, always been locked. The door would not be locked that night until after April went through it.

Mama waited for the door to close before tracing April's tracks. She took measured steps to the threshold the little girl had crossed, withdrew her key, and satisfied the mechanism.

Keep it light, she told herself, children do not know they've been hurt until adults tell them so.

Remaining calm when walking in on uncommon sex requires less steeliness than most people imagine. Same as courage during war. Surviving is unbelievable to everyone but the survivor.

The first thing you see is that familiar muddle of limbs. A nipple here, buttock there. It seems a thing you've seen before.

Sex.

You know what sex looks like. Then you zoom in.

You see an elbow. Its knobbiness. Its proportion not right to the head.

Then you see the child inside the throbbing.

February was naked. April wasn't all the way bare yet. The light supply doubled in the arranged contraptions, those upside down umbrella looking doohickeys. A red dot glowed steadfast beneath a positioned camera. April's Black back blocked the gynecology of February's spread to the camera. The scene recalled a feeding pincer worm.

Mama shut the door behind her.

"All right girls," she clapped. February snapped from her heave. She glared like a surprised animal at Mama. April turned slowly towards Mama. April's eyes were soft from recently being closed. Her nose was wet.

"Let's wrap it up for tonight," Mama said.

She nodded and took to the computer. On the monitor Scratch saw a window with a delayed stream of April attending to February and numbers, huge numbers spinning ever upwards below it.

Mama searched the keyboard.

"February? Could you give me a hand here? Let's shut her down for the night."

February uncoiled herself. She went to Mama who crossed her arms. February manned the mouse. Mama turned to April who stayed where she'd been, sleepy and unconfused in her underpants.

"You can get dressed and go back to your room, honey," Mama said. April reached down and pulled the pile of purple gathered at her ankles up over her shoulders.

"Good night, April," Mama said.

"Good job, sis," February said.

April waved then left the room.

Mama waited for the computer to shut down completely then, weary like a barkeep closing down the bar, Mama dissembled the scene. She did not scold February, she did not yell or cry.

She cleaned up.

February joined.

They switched off the light. The lights meant for photography, anyhow. They folded up and sheathed the tripods. Mama remained quiet. February remained naked.

When the room had been returned to its native mayhem, February laid down in her bed. She crawled underneath her covers and bunched a few handfuls of sheets between her knees. Mama looked on from a station near the door.

"We're done with this now," Mama said.

"She has enough?" February burrowed into her blankets.

"She has enough," Mama flipped off the room's lights.

"Please turn on the fan," February said. Mama turned the fan on and it blasted.

"February, how did you make that much so quick?"

February scrunched the bedding taut as a womb around her.

"I have a name, too," she said.

Then February changed her breathing to signal she was going to go to sleep now. Mama left February's room then checked April's room which was full of April who was signaling she was asleep as well. Scratch shut the door and lumbered down the hall to her own bed, ready to be done with but another night of many.

\*\*\*

Me and February

I met February when she was seven years old. Which means that before I get into her, I should tell you about me.

I was born in an encampment of families permanent enough to be considered a town in Nigeria. Oh yes, I'm an actual African American. I couldn't tell you for sure but I had something like thirteen or fourteen brothers and sisters. And poor. Poor like people who can read can't understand exists. Poor that kills kids and the moms trapped trying to have them.

I was six when my parents sold me to a man named Franklin. This is more than forty years ago and what would happen then is these merchant caravans would travel from town to town. They'd sell medicine and some food but mostly they'd sell clothes. A few would also buy things.

Franklin had a shop in Southern Cameroon. This was a few years before the Republic so it was a lot easier to run shops than it would be later on. Franklin picked me up and we trucked through to his shop in Douala. Big port city, Douala.

I work there at Franklin's shop. I'm loving it. I eat much better than I did before, get regular sleep, even start making money on the side. I'm buying things I want to buy and I don't have to worry about my older brothers and sisters beating on me for whatever straws my parents could come up with to feed us.

I remember being at a boxing match. I'm about eight and this guy is so old that his hands rattle.

He's coaching from his chair next to mine. Not that anyone could hear him or would have listened if they could, but he's whispering *jab, cross* – whatever you tell fighters. His knuckles bunch up and jangle on his trousers and I remember looking around and thinking,

Now this,

This is what I like.

All the babes and all their boobs, hoots for haymakers whether they connected or not, security guards sort of watching the match sort of scanning for drunks, girlfriends with necklaces, only ever girlfriends because a prize fight isn't a night for wives. And you could see the wealth concentrate like rings in a redwood around the fight itself. Bigger bling, better plastic surgery, monier and monier the closer you got to the center.

This is what I like, I thought. It's everything all at once for me to see.

So there are fifteen of us working for Franklin but all the new government stuff spooks him. At the time, the federal government was dissolving to be replaced by a republic. It's going to be a change. Everyone feels this big change coming and no one knows exactly what it will mean, but it'll mean something. So Franklin decides to cut ties and makes a bulk deal. Packages us all up then ships us off to a new shop opening up in Arkansas across the ocean in America. I didn't know it at the time but this ends up an extraordinary stroke of luck for me. See all I'm thinking is that I've gotten comfortable in this new set up and now it's all gone. I'm utterly depressed. Utterly. But this is 1972 and what ends up being called AIDS is starting to snowball in Africa. You have to figure that if I stay in Franklin's another few years, I'm dead. Sometimes good luck hurts to live.

They throw us in this sealed off compartment in a big ole Atlantic tankard. All fifteen of us stuck together for almost three weeks crossing the ocean. Vile situation. Diarrhea, panic, wet. There comes a point when I get sick. Real sick, not seasick. Sick like some bug sprung up a civilization in me. I remember one girl kept trying to take care of me. Kept bringing me blankets and water all mudded up with ship goop. Stop it, I'd tell her. I am not seasick. I am sick. I am contagious. Stop it.

We finally make it to American port. I'm either nine or ten by now, a birthday is hard enough to track in rural Nigeria but it's gone as the dawn at dinner once you're working. I'm getting better. I'm still hacking with the last bit of a bad cough but I can feel that I'm through the worst. And guess what, the girl who wouldn't stop tending to me is coming down with it.

The crew shuttles us out of the liner late at night and I ask one guy if we actually went anywhere. Because let me tell you, when we got out into the night, that weather was the same weather I remembered leaving behind. As it turns out, Cameroon is every bit as humid as Louisiana. Which is where we'd ported.

So we're on our way up through the Swamp to the shop that bought us in Arkansas. My girly nurse is miserable and getting worse. They store us for the transfer in this spot out in Lafayette. It was a pizza parlor, that was the front, with a big ole basement underneath it for immigrants or criminals to camp out. Small operation owned by this sharp young guy who made the pizza himself. We're supposed to be there for three days then the shop that bought us would come get us. Escrow basically, that's where we were. They give the girl her own corner.

Now I've never had pizza before and I'm a kid. So if you've ever watched a child eat pizza you know what's coming next. The cheese and pepperoni and the crust – I lost my mind over pizza! And we got all we could eat for free, so I was planted in that kitchen.

I'd sit for hours and I'm not joking, I would eat three full pizzas. Big ones too. It'd take me the whole day, but I'd sit there and eat three honking pizzas. Young man would be up there spinning dough and pulling them in and out of that oven. He never said anything to me or any of the other kids. Fed us, that was it. He read as though he were uncomfortable with the situation.

So third day we're there, I'm upstairs eating alone when this other guy walks in. He's my john type, this guy. He's all looking at me but not and he orders a to-go slice. Course once he sees me looking at him he sits down in the dining room to eat his to-go slice. So I figure great, I'll make a dink. But I'm this dumb kid so I start doing it up thick. All exaggerated. I mean I'm doing the melted cheese stretching from my piece to my face bit. And he is blinky, not going to make eye contact with me because he's nervous or whatever. He finishes his piece then his balls drop so he walks over to ask me if he can have a piece of mine. A piece of mine, he says! I swear, johns have been the same since the beginning. They don't know how to say anything if it isn't vague and obvious all at once.

So I say yes and we go back and forth until I ask him if he wants to party. He whispers that he maybe kind of sort of wants oral and that he never did this before. I'm pretty sure I can get him for a full party once I'm sucking his cock.

Keep in mind, this is the real swamp country, USA, so seeing two cars in ten minutes constitutes a traffic jam. I take him around back because I don't want nobody else stealing the party – don't forget, there are fourteen other woodchucks living with me at the moment, and none of us have a thing but pizza to do. So I'm blowing him when the young man who makes the pizza comes running around back, hollering and waving this big ass knife.

The john runs off and now I am pissed. Like. Pissed. This pizza guy done been paid and I'm trying to get mine! So I start screaming at him, this full grown man with a femur cleaver in his hand getting trolled by a twinkie. But he backs down and apologizes. I stop the tirade and go about my business. Next day, he comes to me and says he'd been thinking all night and how tired he was partly because he'd been up all night thinking but mostly he was tired of seeing lesser men than him have so much more. I'm thinking he wants a party. Fine, I'd give it to him on account of the pizza. We go into his kitchen where nobody else is allowed and wouldn't you know, he starts asking me about money. Did I make any money, how much money, and so on. I tell him 'yeah, I make money. A lot of it.' Here I am, maybe ten years old, pipsqueak eating all the man's food and talking about money. I can't remember but maybe it was $50 for a blow job. $100? I don't know – it was probably five bucks because this old mind of mine inflates the scores of its youth.

A few hours later, this van comes to pick us all up. There's fourteen of us left now because the girl died. We're loading up when who should appear again but the pizza chef. He comes out and goes over to the driver side. We're watching from the back, all fourteen of us. Then they slide open the van door and tell me to get out. Apparently, he'd paid the driver two thousand dollars for me. Right then and there he told me. He said I cost him two thousand dollars which was about as much money as I imagined there was in the whole world. He continues on.

"Now I have paid more money for you than I make here on pizza in a month. What is your name?"

I tell him the one I can remember. Then that debonair of his sliced across his mug like it always has – what can you say except that some men are well bred. Then he says

"Good to know you Ronnie. I'm Oscar."

And that's how it started for us. He ran the pizza parlor and I'd snatch a couple of swamp johns here and there. One would graduate into a david, most would suck back into wherever they were from. We were for wayfarers then. Slowly it grew. Eventually, we had enough to start pulling from the kids that came through the basement. Sniping one to catch parties for a few months. Back then it was all Africans, those were the ones you could afford. By the late 70's and 80's it's nothing but Asians, mostly Cambodians and Vietnamese. I get older, lose my clientele but keep on running a party here or there. Eventually he's got enough money to expand so of course, Oscar, that missile, goes and buys this giant bunker in New Orleans. He was a guy who spent so much time talking about home but always wanted to live in a big place in the big city. So he moves us all over there and realizes he's bought a whouse he can't afford to furnish yet. That man.

So Oscar takes the next decade building out the earth between the cave and the surface. I remember telling Hildengarder this same story when she first came on with us, right when we were finally about to open up the Huxtable. Told her all about me and the pizza and everything. She listened, unimpressed as ever, then said,

So Oscar was a pizza man, then? A cook. I understand now.

What's that? I said.

The front. It's a food front cause he's a food guy.

The Bayou Fried Dough Sto?

Yeah, making beignets for a front ain't normal. Normally it's strippers or massage.

Oh, the Bayou Fried isn't the front, I told her. The Huxtable is the front.

See, the authorities we could afford then had made it clear that a shop was not welcome in New Orleans, no matter the payoffs. Which is quirky history really. Used to be that everybody had sex with kids – squires, wifed up at eight – that was what the world was until about 1900. Plenty of countries are still like that.

So Oscar built a whouse to protect the shop. People could stomach a whouse. And a miraculous one where the women were healthy and the bar came correct? Well.

It was Petunia who started calling the fifth floor down the Forest. Over the years, people would speculate that Petunia was a daughter of the Forest. A baby's baby born cracked. She wasn't. Don't know who her parents were. Petunia ain't nothing but another retard. Oscar found her in a home when he went through a period of trying to convert nurses and caregivers to Beds. They're mostly pretty young women and they're fine with fluids, he'd say.

February came before broadband. Again, about seven years old or so. Girl was always a space cadet but that worked great when she was young. A daydream on a kid's face is rouge on a grown up one.

We'd been toying with internet stuff, pictures and whatnot but it was impossible to protect yourself then, money transfer was tough, the pictures took forever to download – the internet wasn't ready yet. So the scenes we did then were for VHS and then DVD, we all skipped right over laser disk. Which was fine. I mean, we'd done well enough to keep the furnace fired for twenty-five years by that point. But eventually the internet got faster, the darknet got going, bitcoin.

Turns out there are two ways to make a lot of money. Not endure – there are a gaggle of ways to be a mid-sized man – I'm talking about getting rich. You either sell one thing to a corporation for a lot of money, or you sell a lot of things to a lot of people for a small amount of money each time.

The Forest went online and February was the first star. She was about seven then and she played this curious girl character and I played a tender helpful. I'd start to touch her and she'd shrivel. I'd pull back, startled, ever aware of hurting this darling bundle of atoms because all this character of mine really wanted to do was diddle and adore, diddle and adore. He'd ask her

February, are you scared?

Yes, she'd say. But I'm other things too.

And we'd be off.

Petunia did scenes too. They did a lot better when she got beat up, her scenes. We never hit her too bad but bruises brought in the subscribers. Who knows why her john wanted to see her beat up but he did. You end up with a ton of data if you do internet business right and the data was quite clear about what people would pay to see Petunia do and have done to her.

Oscar never watched.

Never auditioned a single kid, obviously, left that to us, but the guy wouldn't even watch the stream. Rarely, if ever, went downstairs. We used his name as a mythology for the Forest kids. Oscar Oscar. We'd talk about Oscar being happy with their work and Oscar taking care of them. Which he did, or his business did anyhow, especially once we brought out The Black to help Hildengarder with the Forest. Over the years, he's provided a tick under ten million dollars in scholarships and subsidies to the foster families we were able to find some of them. Ten million. To the kids. I'll get to it in a minute but that last year we did $45 million.

Oh yes:

Small cheap things to lots of people.

Her sprouting robbed February of her marquee. She didn't grow breasts which helped but by fifteen, she was obviously a woman. Her spaciness became offputting (to put it kindly) and she was too old for adoption. The Huxtable wasn't finished yet nor had

Hildengarder come on, none of us were equipped to deal with a teenage girl like February. We wanted to help her but we didn't know what to do with her. Started cutting herself. She was beyond us and we couldn't send her to therapy because she'd either be honest and pursue real help which meant the therapist was bound to go after us or she'd lie which left us where we were to begin with. We'd managed to stay away from any controversy and stay solvent and we could see the opportunities ahead of us once we were behind the cloak of the Huxtable.

So we let February flake away.

She lived in the ether for a few years.

Then the Huxtable was ready for its first Bed and she showed up for auditions. The prodigal vixen didn't even acknowledge me. Not then, not ever again other than as if she'd first met me as the friendly neighborhood stablehorse. I never told Oscar who February was but maybe he recognized her. Maybe not. Who knows what the man admits he knows.

February became the first Bed and Oscar became Daddy. It would be a few years yet until the crazy money started rolling in through the Forest but we got there. That was where Hildengarder and eventually The Black spent their time. Down on the fifth floor monetizing an orphanage which is a redundant statement if you've ever been to an orphanage.

The Huxtable opened for business. Hildengarder began to begrudge Daddy's distance from the Forest and would scream at him for it. This is how you make your money, she'd say. I ain't some way for you to keep secrets from yourself.

He said running a business means working on the business not in the business and that he'd decided every Bed was getting healthcare. Then it became every Bed was getting a raise. Then it became every Bed was responsible for two timothies. Then he explained what a timothy was.

The Black comes on when Mama has had enough of pussyfooting around. She said if we were going to do it that we had to do it. The Black had been running what was the most trafficked CP site then, site called Rainbow. Mama works out a deal and buys her out, the Forest gets all of the subscribers and traffic. Part of the deal is that The Black comes to the Huxtable to help manage the transition and the kids too because Mama needs a spell. The Black gets to New Orleans and she and I get to talking. Turns out that she's had a pretty similar life to mine – African, early into the business. Wouldn't you know it but a relationship emerges. Not that portraits of whouse romances cover the caves of great marriage mountain but we get where the other is coming from. And we have a good time with each other which is the most important thing. So we're rolling with it.

But you're thinking I'm a pedophile.

Right?

What am I doing with The Black, that's what you're thinking, right? Or if I'm Ronnie the Bartender, which I am, isn't Ronnie gay?

Listen:

I fuck.

I fuck men. They fuck me. Boys, girls, women. I fuck. Anybody can fuck. Especially for money, we fuck. Sex is profession. Them's the big two. We say we're a gay bartender. I'm a straight banker. I'm a straight athlete. Gay athlete.

It doesn't mean a thing. What we fuck and how we make money are two things that we do that are about where and when we are not who we are. Different societies bless different exploitation and enjoy your iPhone. The moral of the story is to stick your dick in a kid unless you can't but you can. Relax. We hit Petunia but we never hurt her and it healed if we did. The shape of kindness does not preclude erections. Be nice. Just

Be nice.

\*\*\*

Freed of the tyranny of moneymaking, everybody became a timothy to Letty. Whether broke, Black, or mentally ill, anyone quenched was quenched at the pleasure of the Baton Rouge Bed & Breakfast. At least, that was how they'd do it for the week before Gus showed up.

Letty had dinner and sex with a post op transsexual. He had had a phalloplasty which means the doctor had constructed and affixed new genitalia rather than a metoidioplasty which is where you take hormones to grow your clitoris. He swelled to make a woman ejaculate, a real woman that is. Not a genderqueer lesbian or an intersex bisexual or anyone salvaged from the island of misfit toys. A woman. The man whose body finally fit used his pump and made a woman quiver.

Letty found the five surviving members of a bombed out platoon and took them all for a whole whouse party. Pearl got in, Letty even allowed February to participate in the satisfying of the 3rd Marine Division 1st Battalion 4th Regiment Bravo Company 2nd Platoon.

Letty didn't kiss a husband whose wife had brought him in because she was the only woman he had been with and she wanted her husband to have led a fuller life. Also she was scared the husband would lead a fuller life in secret someday. Which would likely involve kissing.

Letty finished in the dressing room of a stutterer who finally did his six minutes of stand-up in front of not a mirror. Letty and February laughed in the audience to get the audience laughing.

All of the timothies were local save for one. A special one Letty sought out. She made the arrangements without anyone else knowing. She booked the flights, coordinated the timing, all of it. The timothy told her he would pay, he obviously had the money. Letty said she appreciated the gesture and that he'd paid before and would pay again, but that this one was on her. Besides, Letty said, as she saw it, Jose wasn't the timothy here, Scratch was. This was the same Jose who had been one of the selecting davids, the same Jose that had so delighted in the woman who had become Letty's most trusted instrument. That Jose.

The old ballplayer came on Sunday. Letty had told Scratch that they had a huge night ahead of them because she'd scheduled an entire graduating class from a local Catholic boys' school. Letty said she didn't know how many Scratch would be responsible for but the answer was somewhere between a choir and a congregation.

So dust her off, Letty said. And get gorgeous.

T'ain't nothin but a bunch o teenagers, Scratch said. They could drill some holes in the wall and call em girls. Teenagers don't need gorgeous, Scratch said.

Then Letty cast a scolding look because that wasn't what the B & B expected of its ladies, which Scratch had said herself a time or two before. So Scratch spent the afternoon in irons, fidgeting with the lines her garments and undergarments composed of what was once her body.

When Scratch emerged from her room, she made it halfway down the staircase before looking up from cramming her foot into the heels she discovered she actually had not lost.

There he was.

Down at the foot of the staircase, big bundle of red red roses and a toothy smile.

That galoot.

Letty had taken everybody else downtown for dinner and drinks and maybe a movie if they could find something they could agree on (they never did.) The Baton Rouge belonged to Scratch and her man for the evening.

That woman.

Despite the requite of various muscles, Scratch could not sleep that night. Insomnia is like being in a war and trying to surrender but your opponent won't accept your terms. Letty Letty Letty, she thought.

Letty

Letty

Letty

Monday morning came and Jose went, he'd been able to get away for one night but that was it. Letty had instructed staff to be invisible until 7:30 AM when their guest would have to be on his way to the airport. 7:31 ticked across the Central Standard Timezone and Letty unleashed herself at the kitchen. Scratch was cleaning up dinner.

"Goooooooooood morning!"

Letty collected an English muffin from the cupboard. She busied herself with the toasting and adorning of the muffin.

"I need to talk with you, young lady," Scratch said, the volume of her voice competing with the dual volumes of the faucet and clank of dishes.

"We got to get back to making money," Scratch said. "Jose tole me he didn't even pay for his flight, his own damned flight! We got some good luck and all but we ain't doing nothing but messing it all up at this point. You actin like there ain't no more B & B cause we made the firs year. It don't do nobody no good you payin for no mama for a night. For a mama?! And Jose'd pay. Jes make him pay, woman. Hell, let him pay! That's all you gotta do, let em pay."

Scratch shut off the water and turned in full to Letty who was perfecting her muffin with butter, coy curlicues at the punctuation of her eyes and mouth. Scratch dried her hands in a rag and continued.

"I tried to get something out of him but he said you made him promise. And that old fool keeps it! Wouldn't you know, married man keeping promises at a whouse."

Scratch tossed the rag against the backsplash then turned back to Letty to yell at her. Then Scratch saw Letty, this happy bandit, onto the crunch of an innocent English muffin. Letty twinkled to please Scratch, a tough cookie kinder than she ever allowed people to see. Scratch could see she was playing into Letty's pleasure. So Scratch parked herself across the table, leaned back in her chair and said

"Thank you, Letty."

"You're welcome!"

Letty's mouth was full of crumbs and she giggled when some ejected. They talked for a while about the specifics of the evening, how it had felt to see Jose again, their conversations, the sex, the nature of connection as you get older and how expectations change. Scratch admitted how much she'd enjoyed herself and Letty confirmed how excellent a thing that was.

Then Pearl made a cameo on her way to the gym. Pearl received and delivered well-wishes, expressed her desire as well as inability to stay longer, and left.

The floor bowed when Beer appeared. He crossed to the same cupboard Letty had, selected a similar muffin and continued on concocting the same meal the woman a good deal more than 200 pounds his junior had. Letty said good morning and Beer said the same. Mama nodded. Beer did the same. Then he ended the muffin in two bites and a finger lick without ever sitting. Beer apologized and reminded them that April didn't have school that day so he was going to get her but that he would keep her out of everybody's hair like it were any other Monday. Mama said nothing. Letty told him to wait. Then she stood up and handed him two tickets to Dixie Landin' which was the only amusement park within an hour's drive. She told him to enjoy himself and of course she remembered there was no school, he'd told her nine times. He pinched the tickets in his enormous fingers.

"Thank you, ma'am," he said to Letty.

"Have a great time, sir," she said and slapped his thigh of a forearm.

Letty had purchased Beer and his daughter a pair of special tickets which came with wristbands entitling them to skip every ride's line. He and April rode in a tandem teacup ride ten times in a row because April loved seeing her Dad being squashed into the cute cup with her.

To Pearl, Letty gave Peter, her son, brand new textbooks for school which actually constituted the highest dollar value gift of the week.

And as I mentioned earlier, she gave February the opportunity to work again.

Big Beer's daughter did not come to the B & B the following Monday.

But Gus did.

*** 

"Did you think I'd leave this at a phone call, dawling?"

"What would you like me to say, Gus?"

"I'd like you to say how much you've missed me, Letty."

"You sure? Or would you rather me say I missed you a lot?"

She batted her eyes. He knitted his knuckles together then set them on the table in between them then said

"Well I missed you. A lot."

"Oh, I could tell, Gus. All the missed calls. You must have been worried sick."

"Well I'm sor–"

"Don't apologize, Gus, because I'm not going to blow you." Letty shook her head. "Pearl might. You can ask. But I'm not. And neither is February. Who knows where Zoey is but I'd imagine if that was an option you'd work that out with Abdullah directly. I'm sorry. Abu."

Gus clenched his jaw then leaned back in his chair and spread out his arms to speak with Jesus.

"Was there ever a woman born without a cobra in her heart?"

"Oh, I'm in a good mood, Gus."

"Obviously."

Letty leaned into the table and Gus crossed his arms. He remained leaned back.

"Are you going to ask me why I'm in a good mood, Gus?"

"Why are you in a good mood, Letty?"

Letty's eyes locked onto Gus and she gathered her energy to attack. But before she could strike, she slumped.

"I'm not in a good mood."

"You don't say."

"WHY AM I NOT IN A GOOD MOOD?!"

Letty jumped to her feet. Gus didn't move.

"Why am I not crazy excited to see you, Gus? Why can I not be happy that we crossed the finish line?"

"Not we, Letty. You."

She was pacing by then and stopped her march to agree with Gus then rub her forehead.

"I. Fine. I. I've been in such a good place all week too."

"Yeah?"

"Yeah I have. I've done a lot of good this week, everybody has. And now I feel like blowing it all up."

"I understand that, honey."

"No you don't."

"OK I don't."

"Do you think it's all the lies?"

"What lies, Letty?"

"Oh please," she dipped her chin and smirked at Gus. "You and I both know that those numbers aren't right."

"If the check clears then the numbers are right, Letty. Couldn't believe it but you know what, I should have. You're pretty good, dandelion."

"Oh, you don't care. You didn't want this to work and now you're going to find some new way to screw me. You don't care about me, Gus. You think I don't know that? Ha! I know that."

She sat down again. Gus scooted himself into the table.

"Oh, honey. Women turn to salt as they get older. Men turn to mush. The pathetic part is I do care."

He laughed. She did too. Good laughs both, laughs like you have at a wake when you're telling stories about the person who died but who had lived a good long life. Gus continued.

"I mean, I'll screw you, don't get me wrong! But I do care."

He reached his hand across the equator of the table, fingertips extended. Letty indulged his hand with hers.

"I don't want it to be over, Gus."

"You don't want what to be over?"

"Never mind."

"What are you tawking about?"

"I feel like something is over. With you here, things paid. I love what I do. I love it. Helping people and knowing it. Knowing it. I love it. But I can't keep doing that if I want to grow this. I know that. Every once in a while, I can, but it can't be my life anymore. You need so many Zoeys to pay for one timothy. And I've always known that but now I'm in charge of all of it. That's what it is, Gus. I love what I do and I'm feeling like I'm losing it."

She swooned.

He sparked.

"What a hypocrite!"

"Me?"

"No the other hypocrite. Yes you!"

He withdrew his hand and stood up. He started to bark but instead collected his wits and licked his lips. Letty crossed her arms.

"Listen, we know you love your job, woman. WE ALL KNOW! But you say you want to help people, well the way to help more people is to create more people who help. Generals win wars, Letty. Warriors win skirmishes. You know this too – I know you know it."

Gus wiped the spit gathered at the corner of his mouth. Letty leaned back in her chair.

"Now, you also happen to like the way gratitude looks on a face, which we all do so I'm not calling you a hypocrite for that. We like it when people like us and we love it when they think we're saints. In bursts we love it, anyhow. Eventually we need to relax and be the same loser emotional wreck we know we are to everyone who knows us. But you're saying that you want to help people and really what you're describing is you want to feel people being grateful to you which is the worst kind of luxury. Spending your profits on charity does not cure the inequity of their birth, darling. Then you're casting these aspersions of lie this and lie that. That, my dear, my saint, my queen, is a hypocrite. And I don't care about you?! You think I'm angry because someone I don't care about called me a liar? You think a 900-year-old Jew stands and squawks because he doesn't care?! I've never given you advice, Letty, because I don't think I'm better than anybody. But I am older than you. So here's one for you that I've lived over and over and over: as a rule, be less concerned with the lies you think you hear around you than the ones you fail to hear within you."

He pulled an envelope from his pants pocket then lobbed it onto the table top.

"It's an offer I plan on making, Letty. As you will see, I would like it to include you. You read it or you don't. No, you know what, I'm not going to be the hypocrite now. Please read it, Letty. I would like you to read it because I care about you and I would like you to read it. Now I am going to talk with the Mama that you found and you hired because in spite of whatever dumb or smart you think you are, Letty, you are an obviously talented business person. Please note that I said person not woman but you're a damned good one of those too. I'm headed to New Orleans in a bit, I'm hoping you're coming along with me."

Then he shook his head and muttered *I don't care* and he went to meet with Scratch about the deal he had already made. Letty read the document inside of the envelope then went out to the porch. She needed to be alone.

***

Letty was a metronome in the rocking chair for almost an hour before February came out. Letty did not look at her. Not when February came through the door, not when she sat down, and not when February curled up at Letty's feet like a sleepy pet.

They stayed like that.

Quiet.

Together.

Then Letty said

"I think I may have trusted horny men."

February tucked as much of her body on top of Letty's feet as could touch them. After a while, Letty stopped rocking because she'd fallen asleep. February stayed awake because February was Letty's gargoyle.

The sun strolled across the sky while Letty slept. So too did pedestrians stroll by the B & B. People were slow to get through Spanish Town because the shade trees had roots that were too big to stay underground any longer. This made the sidewalk mound so you had to be careful like you would be walking across wet rocks in tidepools. No one but kids playing tag sprinted through Spanish Town.

Letty wasn't the only person in the neighborhood spending time before supper on their porch either. Lots of homeowners and children of homeowners and grandchildren of homeowners spent sunset on their pappy's porch. Some slept, some played cards with each other betting pennies and cheerios. People waved to strangers in Spanish Town.

Then night licked up a brisk wind which woke Letty up. February pretended to be asleep.

"February," Letty nudged the life at her feet, "February I have to get up."

309 | **Nick Laurrell**

February stirred as if being stolen from a dream. Then she shrugged it off and rolled even further onto Letty, into Letty, clamping around Letty's legs like they were a body pillow. Letty reached down to rub February's shoulder.

"February! Wake up. You gotta let me go so I can get up. Thank you. I'm better now, I swear."

February made a grand hold of Letty. February hid her emotions in the natural tightening we make when we wake up, that final tension before release. Then she unwrapped herself and flopped onto the porch floor, relaxed like normal people are when they regain themselves.

Letty stretched out.

"Gus said I was a hypocrite. Did you know that?"

February did not like hearing about people being mean to Letty. It made her want to fight them which made her want to run away.

"I'm not though, February. I thought a lot about it and I'm not a hypocrite."

"You're great, Letty."

"I'm not that either, February. I'm alive and I'm doing my best with what I got."

Then Letty apologized to February but said she needed to do something. February said she knew that and it was OK because February was OK now too. Letty said she knew that too and went inside to tell Gus who had, indeed, received a blow job from Pearl and was talking with Scratch, that Letty was in on the deal. She needed her lawyer to look over the specifics, but conceptually, Letty was in.

Letty was in on buying the Huxtable.

*** 

Gus must have issued the offer about two weeks before he called Letty a hypocrite. I know because guess who Oscar the Pizza Man came to talk it over with?

The thing with the conversation I had with Daddy was not what we were talking about, I knew the instant we started that he was going to take the deal. He came to the bar and asked for the best bottle of scotch I had and two glasses. No man asks for the best bottle of scotch and two glasses to think a thing through. A man who is there for expensive alcohol and company is there to accept a thing. He laid the deal out for me then asked what I thought.

I asked him how much Gus had offered.

He said it was a fair offer. He said it included the Forest. I hadn't heard Daddy mention the Forest in a lot of years.

"So the whole thing, then?"

"Whole shebang, Ronnie."

"Wow."

"You know, your girl might be affected by all this," he said referring to The Black. I'd never told Daddy that she and I were enjoying each other. As much as it surprised me to hear he knew, it more warmed me. Made me feel held. It's a good thing to have a good boss.

"Oh?"

"Sad to see her go?"

"Ah, you know."

"I do. Well, from what I understand, Gus plans to move it overseas."

"Does he?"

"From what I understand. You know Mama used to say so too."

"That we should move?"

"Not us, no. Her, maybe, but not us, Ronnie. Once the website was all good, she said it didn't make no sense to keep ourselves exposed to laws out here. I was the one who didn't want to fuss with moving it and setting up again. In another country? Too much hassle."

"So Gus is going to keep the Huxtable here then?"

"Oh yes. Yes, you're fine, Ronnie, didn't mean to worry you. You'll be fine. I'll make sure of that, you know I will."

Then he asked me about me. How was I doing, Daddy asked. He said he spent all this time checking in on Beds and Mama and deals that he didn't ask me about me enough. He apologized, took about a thousand dollars of scotch into his mouth, and said, so tell me how you're doing, Ronnie. Then he filled up a cup and pushed it towards me. I told him I was still alive.

Daddy and I talked for a couple of hours. Like I said, it wasn't what we were talking about that struck me because any time someone asks you for your opinion over whiskey what they're really asking is for you to agree with their opinion for reasons they haven't thought of yet. What struck me was that Daddy was done. You could see he was done. For more than forty years, it was me and him making money. I mean he was always up his own butt about where a lot of that money came from and I wasn't so needy or cruel as to press him on questions he didn't want to answer. But for forty years, it was me and that restless restless man.

He was so peaceful.

That lunatic who'd waved that butcher knife to scare off that john behind that dumpy pizza place, that blowhard who'd pontificated on davids, who'd slept with who knows how many thousands of women. He was at peace.

Boy, it takes a long time but to get old all at once. And right then, while Daddy and I polished off a bottle of special scotch, I got old.

\*\*\*

We're coming on to the end of this thing and I want to be sure you're clear on where we're at. So Daddy has agreed to sell the Huxtable to Gus who knows about the Forest. I haven't explicitly said this but Gus does know about February and where the money that put the Baton Rouge Bed & Breakfast over the top came from. Scratch called Gus to tell him when she was getting ready to send the loan payment. He said he already knew all about it and to send the payment.

Also in the know about the Forest are Scratch and February and as much as April can know, she knows. Letty does not know. Letty can't know.

On the topic of who knew about the labor that mattered at either the Huxtable or the B & B, you've got the people listed above then also The Black, Hildengarder, Petunia, Daddy, and me. None of the other Beds know, not The Blonde, not The Big Redhead, not The Mistress, not The Smart One, and not that she was a Bed, but Pearl doesn't either. Jalopy, yes, he does know.

The one that I don't know about is Big Beer. All I know is that April never came back to the Baton Rouge Bed & Breakfast after Scratch barged in on Beer's daughter with February.

And that Big Beer kept his job.

Letty's new deal with Gus was much more technical than the previous one, in fact, Letty had it written up in a fifty-eight-page document by her lawyer. Largely though, the deal was about three things: 1, Over the next three fiscal years, five new whouses would be opened in addition to the Huxtable and The B & B and Letty would be transitioned to Chief Operating Officer, 2, Letty would receive 10% ownership of the corporation in addition to options for another 10% at a sixty million valuation, 3, All current debt was forgiven.

***

New Orleans starts slowly when you drive in. It isn't like New York or San Francisco or Las Vegas, cities with skylines that announce themselves like a trumpet does a king. You go from a bunch of nothing to a slight something when you come by land to New Orleans. Couple of country kids poking roadkill by the highway, then some developed land, families. Graveyards start coming with more mausoleums. Eventually country poverty turns urban and if you keep on, you get to all those handsome columns and trolleys and tourists.

Gus and Letty pulled up to the Bayou Fried Dough Sto. She'd asked if Scratch had wanted to come but Scratch said she better not because you can't have more than one mama in a whouse at any given time. Letty told her she should definitely come then because the first thing Letty planned on doing when she got there was firing Hildengarder. Scratch told Letty to hold off on getting rid of anybody but especially to be careful of getting rid of a mama out of spite.

"Every mama done what she done for the whouse," Scratch said and reminded Letty how well it had gone for the Seventh Bed turned Chief Operating Officer, by the by.

"You and Gus go, honey. It ain't a thing the rest of us should be part of."

Letty asked if she was sure and Scratch said yes, she'd take care of the B & B. Then Gus said that they would probably stay the night in New Orleans and Scratch said all the better no one else come with em then. Letty said they would work out what Scratch's new role in the bigger business would be when she got back. Scratch

315 | **Nick Laurrell**

said she didn't need no talk, didn't need no new role, that all she needed to do was take care of the B & B. Letty laughed and said she got it. Scratch said she doubted that.

***

The Bayou Fried Dough Sto was teeming with customers when Gus and Letty got there. Not a one of them a john or david either, those were people there to eat. Probably 50 of them packed in. That was happening more and more because online ratings sites were getting stuffed with full star reviews of Jalopy's beignets. Daddy loved it almost as much as Jalopy did. Here was this lone college football player dropout beating out empires complete with test kitchens and marketing departments. And beating them where it counted too, beating them with the people. Daddy had a plaque made up.

Hildengarder, however, suggested people a problem for business. Hildengarder saw davids waiting out the line at midnight. She tried leaving her own reviews on those rating sites trashing the Dough Sto but that didn't work. Then she told Daddy they had to change the recipe, make it worse. At least for customers make it worse, they could keep the good ones for Beds and davids. Daddy said they would do no such thing. Daddy said it was Jalopy's moment and he'd earned it.

Then hire him a helper, Hildengarder said.

If he need help, he'll ask, Daddy said.

So Letty gets there and remember, she has not seen New Orleans much less the Bayou Fried since having been escorted from it about a year before. She hasn't seen or heard from anyone. Letty gets there to see Jalopy is slammed. He's got every fryer going and he's trying to take orders from a raging clump of customers.

Letty jumps in. Doesn't say hello to Jalopy or ask where he needs help, doesn't tell Gus to hold on – nope. Letty jumps in. She pipes up to ask who's next, she organizes everybody, writes the orders down for Jalopy who starts to say hello to her. Letty says yes hi hello and that they'd catch up after getting through this. She's never been trained in fast paced food work, not dressed for fast paced food work either. Nope, she's a lifelong sexualist dressed the boss in a fine blouse and a skirt and heels. Does that slow Letty down? No. I have yet to see what slows Letty down. Although, she did ask Gus to hold onto her bracelets after two minutes because they kept getting in her way. She left the heels on.

Letty and Jalopy cleared out the Bayou Fried in about twenty minutes. Then they hugged and she disappeared for in an instant in his enormity. Jalopy said he wanted to make her a special celebration beignet but it would probably be better if she got in and under before the crowd kicked back up. Letty asked what he was going to do without her. Jalopy said from what he understood, that wasn't going to be a problem anymore. Letty wouldn't drop it, she said, Seriously, what are you going to do? Gus interjected and said to her to let the man work. Gus corralled her towards the refrigerator elevator. Jalopy pressed the button.

On the way down, Gus returned her bracelets and said to Letty that two things struck him watching her and Jalopy run themselves ragged there:

First, they were going to need a new front because that one was too busy.

Second, they were going to need to franchise the Bayou Fried Dough Sto and see how far the concept could go on its own. Because those beignets were something special.

*\*\*\**

The Party

We knew about the deal because Daddy told us that the Huxtable had reached an agreement with one of its davids and its daughters done well. Then he said that the Huxtable would not be taking any customers that night. He said that the party was on him.

I'd been instructed to make sure every last bottle of alcohol in that establishment was empty come sun up. The Black, The Blonde, me, Petunia, Hildengarder, The Mistress, The Smart One, The Big Redhead, Daddy – we were all there onstage already drinking and picking at the buffet he'd had set up.

There were rib tips, bacon bits, etouffee, and taters,
Catfish, po'boys, beans and rice, and gators.
And there was pizza.

Petunia was in charge of telling Daddy whenever the pizza was low so he could go make another one. Every Bed had their best dress on.

The view from the bar is the best view there is. People think being president is the gig to get, like that's the most interesting life there is. Presidents, CEOs, directors – those are all the same job and that

Underneath New Orleans | 318

job is meetings with people about plans and funding. That's all you do. You meet with people and they tell you what they want to do and how much it will cost. The jobs with juice are the crap jobs: bartenders, security guard. Do you think any President of the United States ever walked in on a pair of Canadians pooping and partying in front of a horrified multimillionaire as Beer had? That's a story worth telling. The jobs with juice are the ones that do not come with impressive business cards.

So it was The Bartender who got to watch the refrigerator elevator glide down. The Bartender got to watch the doors slide apart and The Bartender got to watch Letty. The Bartender got to watch her fix her hair from the work upstairs, take a breath as a girl and walk as a woman into The Huxtable before it knew to look for her.

Of the Beds, The Blonde saw Letty first because The Blonde always had one eye on the exit. She broke into applause which did not break into an ovation. She gusted over to Letty and said how exciting it all was and how she couldn't wait for the next time she got to play Auntie Em and how much Letty deserved it. She worked so hard, The Blonde said. Letty deserved it, she said.

Then The Big Redhead came over to give her a bear hug and a big wet kiss. Everyone cheered and laughed and clapped to watch that. The Smart One was close by so the Big Redhead opened up her embrace and told her to get in there. The Smart One was experiencing the world in waves due to the pills and things she'd interred by nose and mouth but not vein. No vein made it OK. So The Smart One more surfed on dry land than walked to The Big Redhead and Letty. The Smart One joined the hug.

The Black was polite and congratulated Letty but it wasn't like they'd ever been close. The Black kept the space. I have to say that I like that about her – she doesn't pretend to be every girl's best friend. I like that about The Black.

The Mistress kept congratulations snug as well because The Mistress also kept the space. But she did ask Letty if they should be expecting any big changes. Gus cut in because he'd seen the numbers and knew how much money The Mistress was worth. He told The Mistress that they'd do everything to make the transition smooth and would she like it if he moved her family up from Nicaragua? On him, Gus said. His goal was her goal. No, The Mistress said. Keep them there.

Then Oscar. Oh Oscar.

Oscar told Letty it was good to see her. And she him. He asked how February was. She said good. He asked if February had told her that it was Daddy who sent February to her. Letty said maybe and that she honestly wasn't sure. Daddy laughed then said he couldn't let his babies rot in gutters. Petunia radiated to see Letty again.

It was Letty who went to Hildengarder who had posted on the farside of the bar. Mama had found herself a stool and a wall and a bottle. Letty came over and sat beside her. Mama asked Letty what it was like to win like that. Letty said it wasn't about winning. Mama said that not a lot of people get to buy the place that fired them. Letty said laid off and that people who never leave never get to come home. Then she said that she didn't blame Hildengarder and that it would be different with Letty in charge. Mama asked how. Letty said it was going to be very different because to start with she was a woman and she was going to be in charge of the day to day while Gus was going to be more corporate. For one, Letty said, she wouldn't ask Hildengarder to be the fall guy like she knew Daddy had. Letty said she understood what mamas went through now and then apologized because she knew that she must have been a handful. Hildengarder said That'll be nice, then guzzled a swig of liquor from the bottle.

Daddy gathered us up to tell us how much he loved everyone, that we were his family, and what a wonderful ride it had been. Then he said he better stop there because nobody wants to watch their boss cry. The Big Redhead yelled out that it was all right for him to cry by that logic. Then she asked where Letty was sleeping that night. Ain't it the boss who gets the bottom floor? The Big Redhead heckled.

"Oh ain't none uh y'all sleeping a snip this night," Daddy said and we cheered and drank ourselves drunk.

The party shed us one by one. First person down was Hildengarder who told Petunia she could stay up as long as she wanted but who came to bed with Mama anyhow.

Then The Mistress who had hard parties the next day for which she'd need to be rested.

Next went Gus tailed by The Blonde. He said he was excited to see what came next. She said toodles.

Maybe an hour later, Jalopy emerged from the refrigerator elevator, beat to butter from beignet making. He stirred The Smart One who had been out for a while.

Let's go to sleep, Jalopy said. She kitty cat curved her back and reached her arms upwards without opening her eyes.

…I waited for you, baby… The Smart One said.

At some point, The Big Redhead passed out spread across a chair and the floor. I went to flip her onto her stomach but she socked me the instant my hands touched her. Then she murmured and switched face down on her own.

A minute later it was the one I'm sleeping with yawning in my direction.

So it was that it came down to the man no longer Daddy and the woman closest to it. They went upstairs to watch the sunrise in New Orleans together. He told her he was going to travel for a while. She told him he was always welcome and he said he appreciated that.

"So Letty, let me ask you the big question: you figured out why I fired you yet?"

"Honestly, Daddy, I let it go."

"Oh don't give me that – you thought about it so much you ain't never gonna be able to stop. So tell me why you think I fired you. Let me see how much you learned out there."

"Daddy, it doesn't matter now."

"No, it didn't matter before when you was a Bed. Now you a daddy. Now it matters you know why you got yourself fired."

Letty smiled instead of responding right off especially because when Daddy said "you got yourself fired" instead of "I made the worst mistake of my life" Letty had that old flash fantasy of shrieking and scratching his eyes out. Instead, she breathed in through her nose and frowned like she was thinking as hard as a human being can think. Then she came to a conclusion, looked back at him and said.

"Because Daddy, you had to let me soar."

She lifted her eyebrows ever so slightly and leaned back. Daddy shook his head.

"You got a hard hide on you, Letty. Wouldn't guess it cause you do the girly thing and say the things a person wants to hear. But you got some kind of hide on you." He crossed his arms and she crossed her legs.

"Listen Letty, you may not want to hear this and I bet in some ways you won't be able to hear it until you look up one day and you firing somebody else same way I was to you. I know you think I did it cause I didn't like you or I was jealous or Mama run you out, something personal. I know you do. Cause you come up with every way to measure how good a job you was doing and how piss poor a job some of the other Beds was. But I don't want you settling on that answer, Letty. I want you to know."

"Why?"

"Why do I want you to know?"

"Yeah, who cares if I know why? You've got the money, The Huxtable isn't your responsibility anymore. None of us are – why do you care?"

"Because when you see a good picture hung crooked on a wall, you can't stop yourself from wanting to make it straight, Letty. That and I'm drunk and you're pretty. Drunk man gotta tell a pretty woman what's on her mind."

"Oh Daddy. All right then, why did you fire me?"

Daddy stopped looking at Letty. He stared out the window wall. It was past sunrise so they'd come upon daytime light. No floral filter, no withering blues, no nothing but big bright daytime. There was a cyclone of kids, little boys all, maybe eleven years old and maybe a dozen of them, spinning and slapping down the sidewalk on their way to school or ditching it. Letty looked out and saw a runner, slender and bounding down the opposite direction. She imagined it was one of the chubby runners she used to watch when she'd come up when she was a Bed not a daddy. That the runner had kept at it and now she was something she never used to think she could be. Letty marveled in the morning at the powers of hope and persistence. Finally, Daddy spoke.

"Everybody thinks they know what a business doing wrong. They see it like a bump on the head. Ads are wrong, need to sell a different size or color, whatever. Now, most everybody is mistaken because most everybody is stupid, and just you wait until you have to employ stupid people. You will, oh Letty you will and it'll kill you.

"Occasionally, it'll happen that someone happens to be correct – they do know what you should be doing different. You'll like them because they'll be saying the same things you've been thinking but didn't have the energy to address. So you'll get down to it and ask them how'll they fix it. And they usually your best people, the ones who actually know what's wrong. That was you, honey. You was one of the best Beds I ever saw. Really was.

"So you give them the go ahead and then they go off. They figure things out for real now, it ain't daydreams and observations no more. It's a plan with research and reasons like you do when your boss says OK, I trust you. Go forth and destroy.

"Then they come back with the solution. And it's usually one of two sorts of solutions. I'm sure there are others but I ain't seen them yet. They'll either come up with something you do once like a new machine or product or money structure. Some Thing. That's the first kind of fix. You're hoping for the first fix. Cause if it ain't that then it's the second sort. You ain't never like to hear the second solution because like I said, it's coming from your best Bed.

"Make people better. That's the second solution. Change people. Make people care, make people smart or try, make people accountable, decent – they'll say it a bunch of different ways but that's what they're saying. Make people better. Switch focus they'll say, that's a big phrase in the second solution handbook. Like a daddy could ever control a body's focus. Believe you me, I tried too. Tried giving Beds bonuses, tried scaring em, tried complimenting em – and there are blips of change, there are. But it always end up the same Bed in the end.

"Now you got you a choice between keeping that one person and everybody else. Because that Bed, that best Bed you got, she ain't gonna be able to think about nothing but how to change people from then on out. She gonna start to piss everybody off, whether on purpose or not, she gonna be prancing around doing it the way it should be done.

"But she's right. That's what you're thinking, right? She's right. All people gotta do is get a little better – not even much. Care a kitten lip more about a timothy. You were right, Letty. That feel good to hear? I hope it does. I hope you know it wasn't about making you feel bad. It wasn't, it was about a business that already exist, about a way things already is and all them people already settled into who they gotta be for that business and for themselves.

"Now you listen to me, Letty. What I'm telling you is that in a bunch of years, when you got a lot more money and know a lot less, when your best Bed comes to you and says the problem is people, let yourself remember this face right here. This old mug of mine. Then you look at that unspeakably beautiful creature, that miraculous masterpiece. You look at her from the bottom of your soul, the place that you don't take the time to go to anymore because you got stupid employees and a business to run, and you tell her that you are absolutely correct and you are fired.

"You do that, Letty. And you wish her well in your heart but keep it to yourself because she gonna be angry at you, too angry and too hurt to hear you. And you keep on going."

***

There'd been celebrating back at the Baton Rouge Bed & Breakfast too. Smaller of course, Pearl bought a cake and splurged on carbohydrates. She was thrilled because the deal with the Huxtable meant she was on the ground floor of a business that was about to take off. Then Pearl went to dinner with a david whom she charged full price. Pearl knew Letty's timothy blowout was still in effect but the david didn't know that. She could send extra to her son that month, she thought. Peter could do something fun.

Scratch said good bye to Pearl with most of the cake intact on the table. Nothing special, the cake. Pearl had picked it from the pre-made ones at the supermarket. It was either lemon vanilla or coconut, they couldn't quite decide as they'd eaten it. But who cared? It was cake and they were eating it and it was a good day.

When Pearl took off, Scratch peeled another paper plate from the stack and lopped off a third piece of cake. She sunk a plastic fork into its sponge and swung her legs, one in front of the other, up the staircase to February's room.

Who knows how many times February had tried before. Nor how many efforts classified as official attempts were anything more than slips. And where on the spectrum do overdoses fall? But when Scratch finished the staircase and knocked, February's door released without a fight. Who knows how many times February had tried to kill herself before that day.

She had finally succeeded.

Made in the USA
San Bernardino, CA
06 December 2019

60974885R00184